EVERY MAN MUST DIE

Also by G.D. Flashman

Apache Dunes
2020 Colorado Independent Publishers Association EVVY Award Winner

Justice Is Pronounced: Just Us

What readers say about *Apache Dunes*

★ ★ ★ ★ ★ "A great read. You will feel as if you are watching the action REEL time!"

★ ★ ★ ★ ★ "Best read ever!!"

★ ★ ★ ★ ★ "Couldn't put it down."

★ ★ ★ ★ ★ "Extraordinary novel!"

★ ★ ★ ★ ★ "Superb Read"

★ ★ ★ ★ ★ "Tarantino meets Walter White"

★ ★ ★ ★ ★ "Warning: you can't put this one down"

★ ★ ★ ★ ★ "Great new read!"

EVERY MAN MUST DIE

G.D. FLASHMAN

ISBN 978-0-578-84111-3 (print)

Also available in ebook

Cover and book design by Sue Campbell Book Design
Cover images by Melan Jurga/depositphotos; Luna Maria/depositphotos

Contact the author: magcltd@aol.com

Dedicated to
Emma, Kate, Mary, and Gregory

In another time and place, Apache Dunes could have been a stop on the Silk Road between Europe and the Orient that facilitated the movement of commodities like tea, silk, spices, fabrics and ceramics, but this was the twenty-first century and the border between Arizona and Mexico. The commodities du jour were drugs and illegal immigrants. Violent cartels replaced traders who plied their wares with tact and diplomacy.

Sheriff, Tom Ward, was the nominal overseer of a fragile co-existence between various acronyms: DEA, FBI, ICE, etc. whose presence was mostly symbolic, and those who made their daily bread from smuggling, which was pretty much everyone else. No other industry existed in the desert. In the best of times it was a Live and Let Live kind of place. In the worst of times, such as the past four years, it morphed into Live and Let Die, where killing became a business of its own and business had been good.

The sheriff was uniquely qualified to be the arbiter of justice, when called to be. He and his best friend, Dylan, had been local heroes, leading their small high school to an improbable Arizona State Football Championship in their senior year. Both received full scholarships from Arizona State and seemed to have the world at their fingertips. However, Tom was more the proverbial grasshopper than ant and was drafted for the Vietnam war after losing his college deferment. Although Dylan was an exceptional student, as well as athlete, he dropped out of ASU to join his best friend in the Marines.

When they left "The Dunes" for college, they doubted they would ever return and why would they? However, after four years in Hell, and despite each attaining the rank of Captain, they were scarred emotionally and physically and sought refuge in the one place from which they couldn't wait to escape. A few years later, Dylan and his wife were killed in a head-on collision with a semi smuggling illegals with its lights off.

Tom and his wife adopted Dylan Jr. and would eventually take in a second child, Jake, who became the brother Dylan needed. Like Tom and "big" Dylan, they were inseparable.

It was inevitable that one of the hundreds of drug transactions that took place in the desert would end badly and, four years ago, a deal between the ruthless Garcia drug cartel and a Hispanic street gang from Chicago went horribly wrong. The desert was littered with dead bodies and over thirty million dollars of cartel funds disappeared.

Worse yet, Dylan, Jake, and two of their teenage friends became prime suspects in the case of the missing loot. The quest to find the money would eventually ensnare a host of disparate characters including the local Apache tribe; some bent federal agents; Las Vegas and Chicago mobsters; a burned-out Chicago gang-crimes detective and his violent protégé; a psychotic Mexican assassin; and three stunning, but very lost, souls who looked for love in all the wrong places.

When the dust finally settled, the Garcia cartel had been destroyed and its heir apparent, Carlos, escaped to L.A. with his ill-gotten fortune. Three compromised feds died violent deaths as did the Mexican hit man, one of the teenagers, a couple of mobsters, and two of the femme fatales.

The survivors, besides the sheriff, were Dylan, Jake, and their friend, Dusty, now "Livin' La Vida Loca" on the Costa Del Sol; the Chicago gang crimes detectives, both now persona non grata back home; the strangest of bedfellows, Las Vegas mobster Sonny Day and the beautiful, but troubled, Bobbie, the ultimate survivor; and the hapless and star-crossed, wannabe mobster, Petey.

As for the Apaches, it had been Groundhog Day, just one more recurring conflict, in a seemingly never-ending war to protect a godforsaken piece of desert from interlopers.

However, if there is one lesson that the sheriff learned in the jungles of Vietnam, it's that calm is merely a portent of a coming storm. When so much money is at stake, any vacuum will be filled quickly. It's a high-stakes whack-a-mole. The Garcias went down only to see the Sinaloa, Gulf, and Zeta cartels pop up to take their place. And, human nature is, well, human. It never changes. Power corrupts and absolute power corrupts, absolutely.

CHAPTER ONE

The Wolf

Los Angeles, Early 2016

Vito Rotelli must have been born under a good sign. Teflon, perhaps. Despite being destined to live a life outside the law it was the law that always seemed to come to his rescue and that process was about to repeat itself. Vito and the law were like the couple who couldn't maintain a stable relationship, but were never far away when one needed the other.

Vito's introduction to this symbiotic, if queer, relationship began in Little Rock, Arkansas in the 1980s. He was a young wise guy. A big fish in a small pond, until he made the acquaintance of the enigmatic pilot and smuggler, Barry Seal. Seal had moved his operation to a small town in Arkansas that was literally off the radar screen. By that time Seal's operation had grown exponentially to include guns and military hardware, as well as drugs, all destined for Latin and South America.

What was different is that Seal was now working for Uncle Sam. The CIA, the "Company," specifically. Busted for smuggling drugs from Colombia, he was given the option of continuing to do so for Uncle, with the revenues going to fund what became known as the Iran-Contra Affair, or he could do life plus in a maximum-security federal prison. Arkansas was the perfect venue for a black op that required a blind eye from the highest level of state government. Bill Clinton was Governor—enough said.

1

The only branch of "government" that hadn't been covered was the mob and that's where Vito Rotelli entered the picture. He provided muscle if it was ever needed and helped Seal move some of the money offshore. It's likely the Company knew, but it was like owning a bar—bartenders were going to steal. It only becomes a problem when the "slippage" is deemed too much. In this case, the money was, well—fuggetaboutit—they wore out the counting machines.

All of this was arranged and overseen by another enigmatic character, the Company's Mr. Wolf, a.k.a. "The Wolf." Rotelli was smart enough to read the writing on the wall when Iran-Contra and its Colombian cartel connection were exposed. All the government had to do was destroy all files and communications. The Colombians would take care of Seal and they did. It was merely a matter of time.

Rotelli had never personally interacted with either the Wolf or the Colombians, but he had access to the offshore funds and knew it was a good time to get out of Dodge and never look back. He was a made-man and L.A. was a relatively open town. It was a place where everything was for sale. He patiently built his own crew and bought his way into L.A.'s most lucrative business, the motion picture industry. His entrée was through the unions that controlled most aspects of production and distribution. Careful to keep a low profile, he bought the loyalty of others and installed his men in union leadership positions. By the time 2016 rolled around everyone who was anyone in "the trade" understood that Vito Rotelli controlled the unions in town.

But, like they say, "You can't make an omelet without breaking a few eggs." His ascent to power had created enemies—those jealous of his power. Someone more tactful and diplomatic might have been able to "build a golden bridge" for his rivals, but he possessed neither tact, nor diplomacy. His Achilles's heel was his outsized ego and its lust for even more power.

His most recent power grab involved trying to take over an obscure Indian reservation near the Arizona/Mexico border through a combination of bribery and force, if necessary. He believed the legal autonomy afforded reservations could shield the operation of a sophisticated meth facility from the prying eyes of the government. His macro plan was to add Arizona to his L.A./Hollywood territory. He was also hopeful that the recent mob conflict in Chicago might even put their Las Vegas satellite in play. If those plans came to pass, he would be boss of the largest mob-controlled domain in the country.

That plan, however, was in peril of collapsing when a tall, handsome, African American attorney with the Department of Justice paid an unannounced visit to Rotelli's personal counsel, J. Nelson Wood, at Wood's office in Beverly Hills. The former college football star, Dwight Hayes, had patiently waited for Wood to return to his office before entering.

Retaining Wood had been expensive, but was the best decision Rotelli had ever made. Wood affected the demeanor of a good old country boy from the Midwest who got his law degree from John Marshall in Chicago, but his combination of unmatched street smarts and a keen legal mind was the stuff of legends in the legal community. More than a few "scalps" from Harvard, Yale, Stanford, Georgetown and Duke Law schools hung from his belt.

The proof was in the pudding as, to date, Rotelli had avoided any serious legal problems. None, however, would rival the news that the DOJ messenger would deliver to Wood that day.

Law Office of J. Nelson Wood, Esq.

When his secretary handed Wood the DOJ agent's card, he had little option other than to see him. Hayes entered the plush office just off Rodeo Drive and introduced himself.

"What can I do for you Mr. Hayes?"

"I have a ninety-four-count indictment charging your client, Vito Rotelli, with a variety of crimes under the RICO Act."

Wood sat back in his chair as he pondered the news. He gestured for Hayes to take a seat.

"Do you have a warrant for his arrest?"

"Not yet."

Wood raised his eyebrows. "Why not?"

"There are some complex issues involved that are, frankly, above my pay grade. My job is to inform you that a special representative of the DOJ, who is empowered to engage in that dialogue, is arriving in town tonight and would like to meet with you and your client tomorrow morning if possible."

Wood appeared pensive before he replied, "I have two questions. Is there any chance that my client will be arrested tomorrow? And, will the meeting be on or off the record?"

"I assure you that no arrest warrant will be served tomorrow and we'll provide you with an affidavit that the meeting is entirely off the record."

"Another question, who all knows about this?"

"Due to the sensitive nature of the situation, it is strictly need to know basis and even I don't know the details. I would have hit the DOJ's expense account and treated us to a steak dinner at Musso and Frank otherwise."

"Well, I see no reason not to meet. What time and place?"

"How about ten at the West L.A. Federal Building on Wilshire? I'll meet you in the lobby and escort you to a conference room."

Wood was looking at Hayes' card. "Ten works, by the way, I started in the business as a sports agent. I remember you at USC. I always wondered why you didn't go pro."

Hayes smiled. "Believe it or not, my dream was to become a lawyer. I only played ball in college for the scholarship. Going pro was enticing and I had a lot of sleepless nights, but I knew I was one chop block away from walking with a cane for the rest of my life, when I was offered a scholarship to Stanford Law. It came down to my fear that, if I deferred Law School for several years, I might never pursue my real passion. By the way, for me, it's an honor to meet you. Even though we're on

4

opposite sides of the table, you're a legend in the courtroom."

"That's kind of you to say and maybe we can have that dinner someday after this business is over. I'd like that."

Hayes stood and extended his hand. "I would too. See you tomorrow at ten."

Wood called his client. Rotelli didn't take the news well, but Wood convinced him that he had no choice.

"Vito, if they wanted to arrest you and charge you, they would have done so."

"So what do they wanna talk about?"

"We'll find out tomorrow. My guess is they want something from you."

"What could they want from me?"

"Am I a fucking swami? We'll find out tomorrow. I'll pick you up at your home at nine."

West L.A. Federal Building

Wood and Rotelli arrived at the Federal Building fifteen minutes early. Hayes was waiting for them and escorted them upstairs to a conference room where another DOJ attorney, Franklin Diaz, was waiting. Wood didn't know Diaz, but guessed he had also played o-line somewhere in college. Between Hayes and Diaz there was well over 500 pounds of beef. Any idea of intimidation, that Rotelli may have entertained, was a non-starter.

Wood and Rotelli were seated on one side of the table and provided with water and an affidavit, regarding the meeting being off the record, as promised. It was clear that Hayes was the senior of the two DOJ lawyers.

Rotelli may have had the right to remain silent, but he didn't have the ability.

"I've seen this show before. One of you is the good cop and one of you is the bad cop. You need to get a new game."

Hayes' eyes bored into him. "Game? This isn't a fucking game and one of us isn't good and the other bad. We're both bad." He turned to Diaz. "May I speak for both of us?"

Diaz nodded.

"Since you want to dispense with pleasantries, so be it. We think you're a fucking pimp and if it was up to us, you'd be Italian pussy for a brother twice my size and three times as mean for the next thirty years. But, it isn't up to us, so we'll excuse ourselves, the person to whom it is up to will join you shortly. Mr. Wood, it was nice to meet you."

Wood had to suppress a smile as Rotelli appeared to be still in shock as they departed from the room. Very soon after, a dapper, sixty-ish gentleman entered the room and sat down opposite them. He exchanged business cards with Wood. His card simply read: Simon Wolf, Attorney at Law. He smiled at Wood. "Your reputation proceeds you Nelson."

"And yours, as well. Am I to assume you are the Wolf of legend?"

"One in the same. Shall we get started?"

Wood nodded.

Wolf looked at Rotelli. "Mr. Rotelli, you're a very lucky man."

Rotelli sneered. "What? It could have been a two-hundred-count indictment?"

Wolf laughed. "We have a complicated situation here. I don't know if there are any rumors going around, but within twelve to eighteen months there is going to be a bombshell that will rock this town, and the movie industry. It can't be suppressed, only delayed, and it will involve some of the biggest players, maybe the biggest, in the trade. When this situation came to light, there was genuine concern whether the industry would be able to survive a double whammy, so to speak. The general consensus is that it can't. Now, I don't need to tell you how important this industry and its key players are to the current administration and the expected incoming administration, which has enough baggage of its own to deal with."

Wood raised his hand. "Question. You said 'When this situation came to light.' How did it come to light and how many people know about it?"

Wolf collected his thoughts before replying. "The charges came from, someone who it could be construed, has a vested interest in your client's demise. As of this day, it is confined to a small group of attorneys. Team players at the DOJ."

Wood and Rotelli made eye contact.

"Are you at liberty to identify that person?"

Wolf smiled. "You know I'm not. I can tell you that several of the claims were properly vetted and they would hold up in a court of law."

Wolf took a legal pad out of his brief case and a bold marker. He proceeded to print a capital T and a capital P at the top of the page. He looked directly at Wood when doing so. "Our top priority, capital T and capital P, is finding a reasonable solution to this problem."

Rotelli was completely oblivious, but Wood got the message and nodded slightly to Wolf. God bless professional courtesy.

"FYI: I have heard some rumors about the industry, but this town survives on rumors. It may sound self-serving, but I, too, have concerns whether the industry can survive a two-pronged attack."

Wolf smiled. "I agree."

They could have been speaking Greek for the look of confusion on Rotelli's face. Wood leaned forward. "What can we do to help the … uh … government?"

Wolf smiled again. "Well, as fate would have it, there happens to be a couple of synergies that might go a long way to override the benefits to be gained from prosecuting this case. But the claimant is a problem."

Rotelli looked like a fan at a tennis match, switching his focus back and forth between the attorneys.

Wood took a sip of water and appeared lost in thought before he replied. "Maybe the problem will disappear. What are these synergies you allude to?"

"We understand that your client has certain relationships that can facilitate someone wishing to cross the Mexican border to Arizona."

"I believe he knows of people who assist immigrants."

"It so happens there is someone who may require some assistance, very discreet assistance, but it has to happen tomorrow night."

"That shouldn't be a problem."

"Good. I didn't expect it would be. Here is the name of the hotel in Mexico and the room number. He'll be expecting contact."

"Anything else?"

Wolf reached into his brief case and withdrew several pages of what appeared to be condensed architectural drawings. He passed them across the table.

"It is our understanding that your client may be involved in a construction project on an Indian reservation in the Arizona/Mexico border area. Some friends are interested in building facilities that can house immigrants for indefinite periods of time."

Wood laughed. "Indefinite—like election time?"

Wolf smiled. "I'm glad we're on the same side."

In the limo on the way home, Wood seemed deep in thought, while Rotelli remained confused.

"Okay, Woody, I give up. What the fuck was that all about?"

Wood turned to him, "What that was all about was how to save your ass from spending the rest of your life being someone's bitch in a federal prison. It's actually pretty simple. You have three things you have to do. The person who filed the complaint has to disappear, you have to help get someone across the border, and then create a space for an illegal immigrant refuge on the reservation."

"How can I make someone disappear, when I don't know who it is?"

"He told you."

"I must have fallen asleep during your lovefest, because I didn't fucking hear him tell us who it was."

"He didn't tell us, per se, but he told us."

"I don't have a fucking clue what you just said."

"Remember when he said he couldn't tell us who it was?"

"I'm getting a fucking headache."

Wood laughed. "He couldn't say it, but he wrote it."

Rotelli was now completely dumbfounded.

"When he took out the legal pad, what did he write?"

"You tell me. What did he write?"

"The letters T and P."

Before Rotelli could reply, Wood told him, "Just think about T and P."

Rotelli bolted up in his seat. "Tony Palmas. That ratfuck. I'll fucking kill him with my bare hands."

Wood reached out and pulled him back down in his seat. "It all makes sense now. With you gone, he was going to take over, but you have to be cool. Remember, he doesn't know you know and, keep in mind, he's a made-man, too. You're gonna need to get Chicago to bless it. That won't be a problem after you tell them what he did, but they need to okay it. While you're at it, my best advice is to get their blessing regarding the reservation as well."

"The reservation isn't anybody's territory. I don't need their approval."

"That's all the more reason to get it. Why would they oppose it?"

"Woody, tell me this, why does the government need my help in getting one person across the border?"

Wood seemed deep in thought before he replied. "That's what bothers me. It makes no sense at all."

After a prolonged silence, Wood turned to Rotelli. "Why do they want to avoid this prosecution?"

Rotelli shrugged. "Something to do with the election."

Wood shot back, "Everything to do with the election. They need the industry—its power and money. They need the reservation to stockpile illegal voters. So, what's the connection with this mystery man to the election?"

"You're the genius. What's the connection?"

"Let's play Sherlock Holmes. How do they know he's in Mexico if they didn't help him get there? If they got him into Mexico, why do they want to distance themselves from such a low risk action of getting him across the border?"

"Okay, Sherlock. You tell me."

"All right. Since everything else is about the election, the odds are, this is as well. Whoever this is, the government can't afford any hint of a connection with him. That explains why they were so anxious to provide the affidavit. I've got a bad feeling about this."

Rotelli was animated. "Hold on, hold on. Doesn't this mean we have something on the government?"

"If we're the only ones who know, it means we have targets on our backs."

"What do we do?"

"For starters, tell your coyote to get pictures—several pictures of the guy. Tell him to be discreet, that we'll pay for good pictures, but the guy can't know about it. Even better, tell him to try to get a fingerprint. Offer him five g's for photos and a print."

"Five g's for some pictures and a print?"

"What's your life worth?"

"You think we should make it ten?"

"Whatever it takes. Meantime, you need to catch a flight to Chicago."

CHAPTER TWO

Hill 666

Apache Dunes, Two Days Later

After receiving an APB for the Al Qaeda bombmaker, the sheriff was formulating a game plan on the go. He added his deputy, Homer, to the team, which made four. They piled enough weapons in the sheriff's truck to arm a small country and were getting ready to leave when his secretary, Rosa, came running out of the office with a note in her hand.

She said, "I thought you were gone. This man called. He said you would know who he was. He wants you to call him asap from what he said was a safe phone, whatever that means. Here's his name and number."

The sheriff looked at it before starting his truck. Buck Robertson and his area code 202 number. He smiled.

The ex-Chicago gang crimes detective, Max Sandowski, was riding shotgun. "What's up?"

The sheriff pulled out of the parking lot before replying, still deep in thought. "Either of you have a cell phone I can use?"

Sandowski's protégé, Manny Sandoval, handed him his phone.

"Buck Robertson is senior level CIA. We go way back to Nam. His given name is Bucknell and he was a West Point grad. Born with the proverbial silver spoon in his mouth, but a good man who came of age in country. I like to think that Dylan and I had something to do with that even though he was two years older than we were."

Sandowski turned to him, "Dylan?"

"Geronimo's dad. Big Dylan. Dial this number for me."

Robertson picked up on the second ring.

"Cappy, is that you?"

The sheriff laughed, "I was just thinking about you."

"You saw the APB?"

"Didn't just see it—my posse and I are headed to the desert as we speak."

"Cappy, can I speak freely?"

"The three others with me—I'd trust with my life."

"You know that's good enough for me. Cappy, we've got a fucked up situation here. A seriously fucked up situation."

"I thought you were going to retire a couple of years ago."

"I was, and only stayed on because of what I'm about to share with you. Cappy, the Company has been totally politicized and at the highest level. It's even worse with the Fibs. The two heads are bad guys. Bad and dangerous guys. I'm not sure who they're serving, but it's not the country's best interest."

"Whew, I pick up snippets here and there, but didn't know it was that bad."

"It's worse. We're at a dangerous point."

"What's that got to do with the bombmaker?"

"Everything. The two agents who were pursuing him—one of them was like a son to me. It was a total black op. Fewer than a handful of people knew about it and I can clear everyone except the highest level."

"What can I do?"

"You have to find the guy. He's the only connection to the Al Qaeda head in the US, a mysterious woman, believe it or not. We think she's connected by blood to Bin Laden. Extract as much intel as possible and then … and then it's Hill 666. You read me?"

"What happens if they find him first?"

"Little chance of that. In the event that did happen, they'd vacation him at Gitmo with three squares and access to lawyers. We're pretty sure they're planning something to disrupt the election. He's the critical link."

The sheriff paused, "Call this number if you need me. We're on it."

"Cappy, I owe you my life. Mine and several others. I'll never forget that. I need you one more time."

"I'll keep you posted. Re-confirm: Hill 666."

"Hill 666."

When he hung up, you could hear a pin drop in the truck. The others had overheard the conversation as it was on speaker.

Sandowski broke the ice, "That's some heavy shit. What's this Hill 666 all about?"

"It's a bit of a long story."

"What better time than now?"

After a pregnant pause, the sheriff replied, "The myth was that all combat Marine forces had left Nam in '71, but in early '72 Dylan and I were first looies, each in command of a platoon of approximately forty Marines engaged in counter-insurgency ops with, so called, ARVN pacification units. The handwriting was on the wall with the Peace Conference scheduled for early '73, but Charlie's mission was to capture as much new ground as possible to increase their leverage at the talks.

"Our secondary mission was to assist the ARVN efforts to hold the line. Our primary mission was to not sacrifice any more of our Marines in a hopeless cause. Rumor was that we, too, were about to be pulled out of that hellhole, but that would have been good news—there was no good news in Vietnam.

"Reality was that a Charlie company had infiltrated into Quang Tri province and were entrenched on a hill that came to be known as "The Devil's Hill". We simply called it 666. The news got worse when a total psycho—I mean the guy probably whacked off to pictures of Patton— was charged with cobbling together a company of Marines to take back the hill. Like we learned nothing from Hamburger Hill and all of the other fucking hills in that godforsaken place. Let me amend that. They learned nothing. Dylan and I were both Civil War buffs and we had spent countless hours discussing the Battle of Gettysburg, which was all about strategy involving hills. We had different ideas.

"The Gettysburg battlefield was a series of hills on one side separated from the other side by a vast expanse of field with little, or no cover—a perfect killing field.

"The two armies literally bumped into each other in the town, where the Rebs were looking for a shoe factory. Neither Lee, nor Meade knew the other was in the vicinity.

"The convenient history is that Meade reacted first and occupied the high ground, as military strategy dictates. Lee was, supposedly, indecisive, and allowed him to do so, because Jeb Stuart, Lee's eyes and ears, was off 'joy riding,'

"After a few random probes of the Union positions, we all know the story of Pickett's ill-fated charge across the killing field and into Meade's artillery. It was a suicide mission that effectively led to the end of the war and the Union victory."

"Here's what we think happened, mind you, Lee was a master strategist. He let Meade have the high ground—you'll see how this connects to Hill 666. Once Meade was entrenched from Cemetery Ridge down to Little Round Top and Big Round Top, he wasn't going anywhere. It was more like having a cat up a tree.

"Lee's forces were sick, tired, and hungry—many without even shoes. They had the countryside to themselves to forage, with Meade besieged in the hills. They could have rested and healed out of artillery range while Meade had to worry about supplies.

"I think it was General Hood who suggested that Lee's forces do an end-run around and march into Washington virtually unopposed. Lee had the outcome of the war in his hands."

Sandowski piped up, "Then, what the hell happened?"

"My guess, our guess, is that Lee had seen too much bloodshed and suffering and knew that a Confederate victory would not mean the end of the union, rather a continuation of the conflict that had already destroyed much of his beloved Virginia, and the South."

"What was Pickett's charge about then?"

"Our guess, it was Pickett's call and a suicide mission. It was 103 degrees on July 3, 1863. Their muskets weighed forty-pounds each and their uniforms were flannel for all seasons. They had to charge almost a mile without cover into heavy artillery. Regardless, neither Dylan nor I, could forgive Lee for letting them sacrifice their lives needlessly. If you want to fight, move on to more advantageous terrain. Meade wasn't coming off that hill until Lee departed. Now, to connect the dots with Nam.

"We had the bad fortune of a 'Captain Strangelove', with whom we'd had a history of selecting our platoons for his company. We would be two of four platoons with approximately 150 to 160 Marines, total. He was still dreaming of medals. We were dreaming of home.

"We had forty-eight hours to rendezvous with the other two platoons, two clicks from the hill. We were able to secure some pretty good maps of the area from the ARVN units we'd been supporting. When we saw the map of Hill 666, we said in almost unison, 'Gettysburg!'

"Our next thought was that our C.O. probably thought that Pickett was a hero. We had a problem. We knew that he was going to charge their entrenched positions, even though it was suicide. We, knowingly, incurred his wrath and possible consequences by arriving on the third, not the second day. We guessed he wouldn't wait for us and we guessed right. By the time we arrived, the other two platoons—one commanded by Lieutenant Bucknell Robertson in his very first taste of battle—had been decimated and the C.O. was literally screaming at us to continue the attack.

"Instead, we left our troops out of artillery range, and made our way to the C.O.'s makeshift command center, a tent halfway up the hill. What we found was disturbing. The C.O. was totally out of control and devoid of any connection to reality, and Bucky was a nervous wreck. Bucky reported that at least half of his men were killed, maybe twenty, and several others were wounded. They were pinned down by withering enemy fire.

"When we asked the status of the other platoon he just shook his head. That meant that as many as sixty beautiful young Marines had sacrificed their lives—and for what? A fucking piece of ground that would mean nothing in a few months. Ignoring the C.O.'s rant, Dylan exited the tent. There was only one thing to do.

"The bullet came through a slit in the tent's opening and removed part of the C.O.'s skull. He was dead before he hit the ground. Lieutenant Bucky was shaking uncontrollably when Dylan calmly re-entered. He knelt down in front of Bucky and told him the C.O. had been killed by an enemy sniper and died a hero. He then said that he and I would be acting as co-C.O.'s and that I would give him his new orders.

"It turned out, we not only had a history with our C.O., but also with the Charlie commander, Colonel Gi. We had been involved in two bloody firefights with him and, based upon that experience, guessed that he would allow us to withdraw our dead and wounded if he was confident that it wasn't a ruse. It wasn't. We had no intention of sending any of our Marines up that hill.

"I ordered Bucky to withdraw the dead, wounded and remainder of his force to a position a little over a click from the hill. We would call in the Hueys to evacuate them. He asked what we intended to do then. Dylan replied, 'Kick some Charlie ass. If you want to stick around and watch, you're welcome.'

"As we hoped, Gi let us withdraw, suspecting that was the end of the battle for Hill 666. Bucky would later say that he had already died once that day and wanted to see why we were so stoic amid the carnage. Gi didn't know about our two platoons, which we then moved, through the cover of jungle, to create a perimeter around the vacant killing field. With our friendlies away from the hill and the clouds breaking, we called in an air strike that set the hill ablaze with napalm. I'll never forget that smell.

"As Charlie exited the hill, helter-skelter, they flooded into the killing field. Dylan had directed us to hold fire until they were away from the hill and its cover. When we opened up it was a massacre. They had less of a chance than our troops had on the hill. We didn't suffer a single, major casualty. There was a long break in between the end of fire and their attempts to evacuate their dead and wounded. When it became apparent to Gi that we were reciprocating his mercy, he strode to the middle of the killing field and saluted our position. Dylan moved out to within ten yards of him and returned the salute.

"We had a photographer embedded with us and he captured that moment. He said it was his Pulitzer Prize photo, but he was censored by the brass who had announced that all Marine combat forces had been removed months earlier. Dylan and I were promoted to Captain, hence the 'Cappy' and that was the last combat any of us saw in country.

"When Bucky left the military, he joined the CIA and we've kept in touch over the years."

Sandowski breathed out. "I wanna buy the rights to that movie."

The sheriff smiled. "Sorry, I wasn't even supposed to talk about it, but now you understand what a Hill 666 solution is."

Sandoval said, "Our Arab friend is gonna die a hero from a sniper's bullet?"

The sheriff laughed. "This is Apache country. I have a better idea, but first we have to find him. I have a plan."

CHAPTER THREE

Time For A Change

Los Angeles

Math may not have been Carlos Garcia's strongest subject. In fact, Dylan/Geronimo opined he didn't have any strong subjects, but he could read the writing on the wall. That writing said that with the recent loss of eight more soldiers, the once feared Garcia cartel was a cartel in name only. It was time to swim away, but do so in a way that he wouldn't wind up shark bait.

The first order of business was to mend the fence with his estranged mother in L.A. Maria Garcia was a proud and capable, even forceful woman. She had been the favored subject of the Ninth lineal Marques of Andalusia. The original Marques had immigrated to Mexico to oversee the Mexican gold and silver mines in the north for the Spanish Crown. In its day, before the mines played out, the Garcia estate had entertained royalty and nobility from around the world. Its library was a noted center of learning.

Unfortunately, the Marques' noble wife was barren, which put the dynasty in peril. As a Catholic, the Marques could not divorce his wife. Thus any solution was imperfect. His wife returned to her family in Spain and his subject Maria bore him two sons out of wedlock. The sons, Roberto and José would be denied titles. In fact, would be subject to whispers of bastardo, but they could be granted title to the estate upon the Marques' death.

The Marques doted on Roberto, Carlos's father, who handled the situation with uncommon aplomb for a young man. Not so for José, who rebelled and hated his father for not acknowledging them publicly. It's easy to connect the dots on how their very different personalities developed from that troubled beginning. Roberto's nickname was "Ambajador," the Ambassador, and it was apt. His movie star good looks, superior intellect, and uncommon grace and manners would have allowed him to succeed at any venture, but he remained deeply devoted to his wife and the families who relied upon the estate for their existence.

José's anger and resentment would become cancers that would eventually destroy him and many of those around him. Roberto was one of the first to suffer his calculating wrath and died in the crash of a plane José had sabotaged.

Roberto's untimely death came when he was on the cusp of exiting the cartel—José could have it—and arranging for a better life for his wife and son. To do so, he had patiently and adroitly amassed a secret stash of tens of millions of dollars in off-shore accounts to provide for his family and sustain the estate. His plan was to move his family to L.A. and get involved in financing movie projects. He thought this would appeal to the young and impressionable Carlos. He purchased a mansion in Holmby Hills and established contacts at the highest level of the movie industry.

Had Roberto not perished in the plane crash, it was likely that he could have persuaded Carlos of the wisdom of his plan, but, as they say, "Man plans and God laughs." Unaware of the extent of his father's plans and being drawn to the drug life like a moth to a flame, Carlos eschewed the life prepared for him in L.A. and sought to take his father's place in the "family business." It was a decision that almost cost him his life.

It was time for him to reach out to his mother who, although estranged, was likely his only ally at this pivotal moment in his history and that of the estate. He diverted his jet to L.A. after reaching an accord with Jake/Cochise in regards to the "missing" thirty-million dollars of cartel funds. Carlos received nine-million dollars via wire transfer. His plane touched down as the gun battle raged in Apache Dunes. By the time the limo delivered him to the mansion in Holmby Hills, his eight soldiers were dead and with them any semblance of a cartel. It was time for a change.

His mother was waiting to receive him in her study when Carlos was ushered into the mansion. As was her wont and nature, she wasted no time in taking charge of the situation. Carlos was mystified at how she knew about the debacle in Apache Dunes even before he did, but that only added to her mystique. Maria didn't rise to greet him, or offer any insincere gestures. She simply motioned for him to sit in one of the overstuffed leather chairs and immediately got down to business.

"My son, your father has provided us with ample tools to survive this test, but the next few days may determine our fates and that of the estate, of which you are now the sole heir. We have a very delicate task ahead of us. Quite simply, we are without any semblance of an army to resist the other cartels who are now circling our bloody carcasses. Our only hope is to declare victory and withdraw from the playing field. To do so will require an Academy Award-winning performance, but I know how to arrange such a show and money is not our problem, as you will soon come to learn."

"Mother, I too, have some money and there is a safe house at the estate that contains millions of dollars."

Maria digested that information before replying. "That's good as the money at the estate can stay with the estate." She stared at him until he had to avert his gaze.

"Carlos, it is the province of youth to make mistakes, but until you can demonstrate good judgment I am in charge, and you will do as I say. Is that understood?"

Carlos could only nod his agreement.

"All right. Here's what we're going to do. We will return to the estate and stage a funeral for the dead soldiers, worthy of Hollywood, which is where it is now being planned. It will be a fiesta like never seen before. All of the other cartel leaders will be invited to attend. To do otherwise, is to appear to be hiding our situation. Instead, we will flaunt it. I will remain with the estate and manage it for the rest of my days while you will take my place here in L.A., where all doors are open to you. We will meet with the cartel leaders and announce our decision to turn over our territories and connections to them. In exchange, the estate and our environs will be off limits to them. Oh, and they will buy their marijuana from our fields in the high valley. It is the best anyway. Your father never wanted to be in the cocaine and meth businesses and now you can see his wisdom in that regard.

"The soldiers' families will be without fathers, but I will provide for them and the education of their children. We will also restore the mission and get a priest back to the estate. I will be available to you for advice at all times and have arranged for a support team of advisors for you."

She stood.

"Now let's see how the planning for the funeral is going."

CHAPTER FOUR

Man Plans

Apache Dunes

The first stop was a small building with a make-shift hangar, wind sock and one airstrip. The sheriff parked the truck and turned to Sandowski, "Gents, welcome to Apache Dunes International Airport."

Only Homer laughed, understanding the inside joke. Sandowski and Sandoval were trying to process the scene.

Max broke the ice, "I always wondered what became of Orville and Wilbur. They must have left their plane at Kitty Hawk."

The sheriff smiled. "The plane is in the hangar, but you're not far off as to its age. The pilot might be even more famous. His name is Snoopy."

Max replied, "If there is a cake inside that says 'Eat me,' I'm outta here."

The sheriff and Homer laughed. "Max, I'm impressed by your knowledge of literature. Let me give you a little background before we go inside. If we're to have a chance of finding our man, we need some aerial surveillance and this is it for the desert. The pilot's nickname is Snoopy because his pride and joy is a WWI Sopwith Camel bi-plane. Don't let either confuse you. He was a decorated pilot in Nam and he takes immaculate care of his plane."

"He flew in country?"

"He was an ace, but after the war wanted to get as far away from society as possible."

"Join the club and score one for him."

"We all agree on that. Which is why I thought you two might have something in common."

Sandowski opened his door and started to exit, but hesitated when he noticed the sheriff hadn't moved. "Is there something else?"

The sheriff smiled and Max could see that Homer was smiling too.

"There is one little thing you should know. Snoopy likes to fly high and I'm not talking altitude. He is generally stoned out of his gourd when he's up there. That's why we can't rely on him to do the surveillance. That's where you come in."

"I did my last suicide mission in Nam. That and traveling with Sandoval here." They all laughed.

The sheriff touched his arm. "You have nothing to worry about safety wise. Trust me."

"You know how they say fuck you in Chicago? 'Trust me'."

The sheriff smiled. "Okay, fuck you. You happy now?"

Max smiled back. "At least we're being honest with each other. Let's go meet Snoopy." He turned to Sandoval. "Linus, are you coming?"

Sandoval snapped back. "Hey, Max, trust me!"

The sheriff made the introductions and briefed Snoopy on the mission. Then Snoopy took them to the hangar to inspect his baby.

The sheriff looked at his watch. It was a little after ten a.m.

"Snoopy, take Max up and check out the desert. Radio me if you see anything. I'm going to take Manny to the Oasis to check on vehicles coming in to the area. I'll have Homer do the same in the east, though it's doubtful anyone would come from that direction. I'll check in with Michael, Chief Taza, at the reservation and see if we can get some trackers. Snoopy, if you don't hear differently, meet us at the Oasis around thirteen-hundred hours."

"Roger that."

As he drove away, the sheriff pondered what he had just done.

"What could go wrong?" He asked himself.

His alter ego answered quickly, "What could go wrong with letting Max go up in a World War I bi-plane, piloted by a guy called Snoopy who was stoned out of his gourd during his waking hours? Gee, I can't imagine."

CHAPTER FIVE

Significant Others

Las Vegas

Bobbie had mixed emotions as she gazed out on the Vegas Strip from Sonny's Penthouse apartment at the Pompeii. If this was indeed her new home, it was by far the best home she'd ever had. However, she was angry with herself for being deluded into what her life with Sonny was going to be like. The truth is, she had never really lived, only survived, and then by a combination of wits and sex. She wasn't a natural cynic. It's just that she'd been lied to, too often.

Bobbie had never had anyone take care of her, truly take care of her, but when Sonny swore he was going to do so she had uncharacteristically listened to her heart and let herself dream that he meant it. Two nights ago, on the way to Vegas, they had slept together and Bobbie couldn't remember the last time, if ever, she had willingly slept with a man. It wasn't the sex that was so memorable. In her life, sex had been a weapon, more than a need or desire, but it was definitely the first time that she had fallen asleep and later awakened in a man's arms. Even two days later, she could close her eyes and feel his warmth and strength.

But, like they say, "That was then and now is now." When they arrived at Sonny's apartment, he placed her bags in one bedroom and his in another. Last night they'ed slept apart, and today at breakfast he set up a lunch date with another woman, and right in front of her. It was clear that Sonny had brought her to Vegas for a reason, to replace the Asian dominatrix. She'd overheard Sonny's conversation with Joey C. about how much Suzy something was missed.

Maybe Kelsey was right. Maybe some people aren't meant to rise above their station in life. Dishing out discipline and pain to willing men, willing men who would pay for it, was a role she could play without acting. Maybe it's just back to the future.

She heard Sonny come in.

"Sonny, some guy called for you (she looked at her note) Vito Rotelli. He wants you to call him back asap. His number is there."

As she turned to walk away, Sonny called to her, "Where you goin? I wanna talk to you about somethin".

"You want to tell me about your nooner?"

Sonny winced. "My what?"

"Don't they call it a nooner?"

"They call it lunch. You got a problem or somethin?"

"No problem. I forgot for a moment why I was here. I'll just go to my room."

"Time out. Sit the fuck down and tell me what the problem is."

Bobbie started to tear up. "It's just, after we made love—not had sex, not fucked, made love—I guess I just hoped that maybe things would be different."

"Different how? I feel like I'm talkin to Vinny. We've only been here a day. I don't understand what the problem is."

"Let's start with we didn't sleep together last night and then, this morning, you make a lunch date with another woman right in front of me. Fuck me."

Sonny started to laugh.

"And you think this is funny!"

"Let me start with the sleeping arrangements. Bobbie, I'm old enough to be your father and I know I'm no sexual athlete. You deserve better."

Bobbie was now crying. "Sonny, sex isn't my objective in a relationship, and age is a state of mind. I fell in love with you dammit. I don't want anyone else."

Sonny waited for her to collect herself a bit and reached out to her with a business card in his hand.

"What? What's this?"

"Read it. This is from my, whatta ya call it, nooner."

The card read: Beth Simons Designs with a Las Vegas address and phone number.

"Who's Beth Simons?"

"Remember when you told me you always dreamed about being an interior decorator? Well, Beth Simons is THE interior decorator in Vegas. She did the Pompeii for us and is the go to decorator in Vegas. I told her about you and she's looking forward to meeting you and taking you under her wing. Call her when you're ready."

Bobbie couldn't have been more shocked, or delighted.

"You mean … you mean you didn't bring me to Vegas to replace the Asian gal? I heard you talking to Joey C. about her."

"Joey C. said they missed her and asked how she could be replaced. I said, 'You never know.' That's all. When I said I was gonna take care of you that didn't mean I was gonna let you sell yourself. Those days are over."

Bobbie ran into Sonny's arms. "Sonny, I do love you. Oh, you have to call that guy. Who is he?"

"Vito's a wiseguy from L.A. who controls all of the unions for the movie business. Most people would be more than satisfied with that, but he's not most people and doesn't seem to ever be satisfied. I know what he's callin about. There's a big fight at Caesar's Saturday night. He's probably lookin for tickets and a comped suite."

"You can do that?"

"It's what I do."

Just then the phone rang. Sonny looked at the number. It was Joey C. in Chicago.

"Joey, How ya doin?"

"I'm doin okay, Sonny. Listen, have you talked to the guy from Hollywood yet?"

"Funny you should ask. I just walked in. He called while I was out and wants me to call him back. I was just getting ready to do so. He probably wants tickets to the fight."

"He wants more than that. He flew to Chicago yesterday to meet with the Old Man."

"How's he doin by the way?"

"He's recuperating and fuggetaboutit. He'll never change. Anyway, our friend from L.A. wanted the Old Man's blessing on some things including a takeover of some Indian reservation in Arizona."

"Whatta you mean, take over a reservation? You mean for a casino?"

"A casino don't make no sense there. If it was a casino it would be a front. He's got other ideas. Apparently, the feds don't have no jurisdiction on reservations, or so he says."

"What did the Old Man say?"

"That's why I'm callin. The Old Man says he has to get your blessing. From now on, you call the shots for that area."

"I call the shots? How did that happen?"

"The Old Man thinks that you're responsible for Bellini's death. This is your reward."

Sonny digested the information before replying, "Help me out here. What should I do with the guy from L.A.?"

"If it was me, they'd find him in his hotel room with a plastic bag over his head and his hand on his dick."

Sonny laughed. "So you don't believe that's what happened to Johnny B.?"

"I'll make you a deal. I'll believe it, if you send Pompeii's jet to pick me up, get me two seats, and a comped suite for the fight Saturday."

"When do you want to be picked up?"

After hanging up with Joey C., Sonny dialed Vito's number. He put the phone on speaker. Vito picked up immediately.

"Sonny, how ya doin? Hey, by the way, who was the dame who answered the phone?"

"The lady who answered the phone was Bobbie."

"Sorry, I meant lady. Anything serious?"

Sonny smiled at Bobbie, "You never know. What can I do for you? You want tickets for the fight and a suite?"

"That would be great. My wife loves being with the celebs, but I got something else that I need to talk to you about. It so happens I'm in town today. How about you and me have dinner tonight at Carlucci so we can talk? Say, six o'clock? How's that sound?"

"Sounds like a plan. What about Saturday?"

"We'll get in by one or two. How about dinner with the girls before the fight?

"That works for me," he said, looking over at Bobbie. "I mean for us. Your suite will be taken care of."

"Thanks Sonny. We got lots to talk about."

After he hung up, Bobbie said, "Sonny, I don't have anything to wear Saturday and I need to get my hair and nails done."

"Well, if I was you, I'd get my little white ass down to the shops in the lobby and get yourself something to wear and then make an appointment for the spa. Just sign my name."

CHAPTER SIX

And God Laughs

Apache Dunes

Max and Snoopy had a lot to talk about, both being veterans of that damned war, but with different perspectives. Max had seen Nam from ground level, while Snoopy had been the Animals proverbial "Sky Pilot." The jungle looked a lot better from the air.

Max watched as Snoopy went through his diligent pre-flight routine. Snoopy then handed Max two different headsets.

"What's the deal with these?"

Snoopy held each one up, separately. "This one is for us to communicate in flight. This one is for the tunes."

"The tunes?"

"Dude, this is a carefully choreographed experience. How do the Moody Blues, Stones, Dire Straits, Dylan, Fleetwood Mac, and a little Warren Zevon, thrown in, sound?"

"Works for me."

Snoopy opened a painted, tin container. "I'll make it work even better if you join me."

Max instantly recognized the incredible works of art contained inside the tin. Thai sticks, were expertly rolled, potent marijuana joints coated with opium, which he hadn't seen since being in country.

"Where the hell did you get these?"

Snoopy just smiled. "After our tour was up, a buddy of mine and I flew for Air America, the CIA front, and we ferried illegal contraband for the Company. I came home, but he married a Thai girl and decided to stay. He's now some type of asset, because I get a package via the diplomatic pouch every couple of months. Now, if you'll join me, I'll make this a day you won't forget."

Lost in the moment, Max threw caution to the wind and it felt good. He remembered the incredibly mellow high that Thai sticks provide and he wasn't disappointed.

They got situated in the plane, Max behind Snoopy. Snoopy motioned for him to put on the tunes headphones first. The song was Warren Zevon's classic, "Werewolves of London" with a howl, ow -woooo, they were airborne. Reality was soon thousands of feet below.

The Oasis

After dispatching Homer to cover the road from the east, which was doubtful, the sheriff got Sandoval situated at the Oasis. It was the only gas station in the area. Odds were that the bad guy's contact would be coming from the west and either pass by the Oasis, or top off their gas tanks there.

They put "out of order" signs on the gas pumps. Sandoval was to be the attendant who would bring gas to the vehicles. The manager, José, would signal when the customers were locals and Sandoval would use his instincts with strangers. They were looking for only one contact, but had no idea who it might be.

If Sandoval thought he had a hit, he was to fill the tank with a watered-down mixture that would soon stall the vehicle.

Before leaving to return to his office and coordinate the search, the sheriff called Chief Michael Taza at the reservation.

Michael recognized the number. "Hey Tom, what's up?"

"Michael, I may need your help. We're searching for a bad guy, a very bad guy, who crossed the border last night and is expecting to be picked up by his contact."

"What can I do to help?"

"Just stand by for now, but I may need some trackers."

"Just let me know. Oh, Tom, while I have you—do you remember the last time you were at the reservation? We were having a discussion with a guy from L.A. who wanted to do some type of project on the reservation. I didn't get a good vibe from him and it wasn't just me. Problem is, he doesn't seem to understand that we aren't interested and it's getting a little contentious."

"Keep me in the loop."

"Will do."

Sandoval waited for more than two hours before an alien vehicle pulled into the station. It was a Toyota Tundra with California plates, with a dirt bike lashed down in the back. He was unnerved when he approached the driver's side as the driver was a stunningly beautiful young lady wearing a scarf. She smiled as he approached.

"Hey, the pumps say: out of order. I need some gas."

Completely off balance, he fumbled his reply, "No— no problem. We just— we just had a problem with some of the gas. I'll get some good gas from the back."

She got out to stretch as he poured the gas. "You don't look like a gas station attendant."

"Actually, I'm just helping out. What do I look like?"

She pretended to study him and smiled. "You look like, maybe military or even maybe police. Something like that."

Under her spell, Sandoval came close to disclosing his true identity, but something held him back.

"When you live in the desert, I guess you have a little edge."

"Maybe, but you don't have a local accent."

"I wasn't born here, but enough about me. What's a young lady like you doing out in the desert?"

She flashed a beguiling smile. "I'm a grad student studying geology. I come out to the desert periodically."

"What's the dirt bike for?"

"There are some places that my truck can't go."

While they were conversing, a late model Volvo with Arizona plates pulled in to the pump area. Sandoval glanced over and noticed the driver was a dark complexioned, thirty-ish man with a beard.

He turned back to the young lady as he emptied the second five gallon container in her tank. "That should get you on your way."

"How much will that be?"

"I think ten dollars will cover it considering the inconvenience."

The man in the Volvo honked for attention. Sandoval scowled at him.

The young lady smiled. "Looks like you're busy. Maybe we'll see each other again."

Another honk.

"I'd like that."

She smiled as she drove away with Sandoval's heart in tow. He approached the impatient customer, who fit the middle-eastern racial profile.

"What's the rush?"

The driver appeared nervous and animated. "Look, I'm in a hurry, okay? I have to be somewhere and I need some gas. What's the problem with the pumps?"

Sandoval milked the situation, sensing he might have his man. "We had some bad gas. No problem. I'll get some gas from the back. How much do you need?"

"I need at least another ten gallons to get me where I'm going and back."

"You're in a hurry, huh?"

"You know, I would love to hang out and chat with you about the weather or whatever, but I really need to get where I'm going."

Sandoval just smiled and took his time. He returned with two five gallon gas cans. Each were at least half water.

After the impatient suspect pulled away, Sandoval radioed the sheriff, as per protocol. "Sandoval here. I think we have our man."

"Did he gas up?"

"Roger that, but he's not going far."

"Sit tight. I'm in the area. I'll radio Snoopy and Max."

While Sandoval was briefing the sheriff on his encounter with the suspect, Snoopy and Max were approaching the Oasis. The relatively hard and flat desert surface near the Oasis provided a natural landing strip.

What bothered the sheriff most, was the apparent ease, thus far, of the operation. Had he really planned the operation so well that there were no hiccups or Murphy's Law?

The answer came quickly when Snoopy executed a fly-by that included a barrel roll and a loop. Sandoval rushed out to meet them when they landed and just as quickly rushed back to deliver the news to the sheriff.

"I think they found the guy and he's dead."

"They told you that?"

"Not exactly. It seems like they're celebrating. They keep singing that he's dead."

"Who's dead?"

"Timothy Leary. They keep singing Timothy Leary's dead."

"Can I give you some advice?"

"Sure. What?"

"Don't be standing in front of the Twinkies display when they enter the station."

CHAPTER SEVEN

Let the Dead Bury the Dead

Northern Mexico

Hollywood can do amazing things when money is no object. The spectacle of the mass funeral and celebration of life, for the eight dead Garcia soldiers, was itself worthy of an Academy Award in several categories. Each gleaming brass casket was borne atop an antique mahogany carriage pulled by a matched pair of perfectly groomed white horses. The path of the cortege, from the freshly painted mission to the estate's manicured cemetery, was strewn with rose petals.

The Archbishop of the Archdiocese of Guadalajara presided over the funeral Mass.

After the burials, the grounds of the estate were transformed into an al fresco banquet, replete with mariachi bands and piñatas for the children. The celebration would last into the wee hours.

Carlos and his mother returned to the Hacienda where they would have a face-to-face meeting with the leaders of the Gulf and Sinaloa cartels and the Zetas.

While they were awaiting their arrival, Carlos queried his mother.

"Mother, I still don't understand why it was necessary to spend a fortune on a funeral for dead soldiers. Some of them, no, most of them were very bad guys."

"My son, there is an old saying, 'Let the dead bury the dead.' This production wasn't for the dead. It was for the living and, particularly, you."

Carlos looked incredulous. "How is this about me?"

"It was obvious to the other cartels, and we didn't attempt to hide it, that we no longer have enough soldiers to defend our territories. We had two choices. We could either spend a fortune on assembling a new army, or demonstrate that we have buried not just our soldiers, but all remnants of our cartel. The other cartels understand only power and, more often than not, power is defined by numbers of soldiers and quality of arms. Today's production, however, displayed another form of power and one that none of them possess. They wouldn't have a clue how to stage such an event.

If we waited for them to make the move, we would be dealing from a position of weakness. By summoning them to meet with us, after witnessing the spectacle, we are in control."

"And just what are we going to tell them?"

"*We* aren't going to tell them anything. *I* am going to tell them that the Garcia cartel was also buried today, and that we will leave it to them to divide up our territories as they see fit, with only two conditions. You personally, and the estate, are off-limits from this day forward. You are leaving for California to be involved in the movie industry and I am living out my days here at the estate. The only commerce the estate will be involved in will be the sale of marijuana from our fields in the high valley. They can have first rights to all of that product."

Maria had learned well from her husband Roberto and commanded the meeting with aplomb. Her strategy was brilliant. She gave them what they coveted before they could take it by force, because it fit her plans, not theirs.

Carlos returned to L.A. via private jet. The mansion was incredible and he was truly excited about getting involved in what everyone called "the business". The first step would be to enroll in some industry related courses at USC.

CHAPTER EIGHT

The Scarf

Apache Dunes

It was clear to the sheriff that Sandowski was "eight miles high" and not likely to land for several hours. That left the sheriff and Sandoval to follow up on their prime suspect for the contact. It was unlikely that his car made it very far with the watered-down petrol mixture.

Snoopy and Max were sharing a nuked pizza when they left them at the Oasis. Prior to departing, the sheriff and Sandoval donned protective vests and checked their weapons and ammo.

"Manny, if this is our guy, assume he's armed and dangerous. One false move and we take him out. Understood?"

"Roger that."

"When we find the car, we split up and keep a safe distance. Follow my lead."

As expected, the car was pulled over on the shoulder and the suspect was sitting half-in/half-out of the driver's seat. The sheriff stopped his truck approximately fifty-feet away and stood behind his opened door with a bullhorn. Sandoval scrambled out the other side with rifle aimed at the man.

When the suspect exited his car and turned toward them, looking perplexed, the sheriff screamed in the bullhorn. "Stop right there. Don't move a fucking muscle. Put your hands in the air."

The sheriff and Sandoval inched closer with weapons leveled on the suspect. He raised his arms.

"Oh. I get it. You gave me bad gas so you could hold me up. Well I've got some disappointing news for you. I don't have anything of value."

"Shut the fuck up and turn around and put your hands on the car. Manny, frisk him. Buddy, if you move a muscle I will shoot you."

"Are you guys nuts? What's this all about?"

Sandoval patted him down and retrieved his wallet. He tossed the wallet to the sheriff. "He's clean."

The sheriff motioned the suspect away from the car and told him to kneel down.

"Manny, check the car and watch out for booby traps."

The suspect looked at the sheriff. "Booby traps? Are you guys insane?"

Sandoval reported that the car was clean. Just an open box that appeared to contain file folders.

The sheriff studied the driver's license and I.D. "Who are you and what are you doing?"

The suspect looked up. "Can't you read? I'm exactly who it says I am and when did it become illegal to drive?"

"Do NOT get smart with me."

"My name is Stuart Eisenberg. I'm a lawyer with Meyer and Langdon in Tucson. I have to get those files to an attorney in Four Corners by four today."

"Who's the attorney in Four Corners?"

"Don Jennings."

The sheriff turned to Sandoval.

"Keep your gun on him. I know Don. I'll call him."

The sheriff took out his cell phone and called his office to get the law firm's phone number. Then he dialed the number and spoke with Jennings, who confirmed the story.

He walked back over to Sandoval and told him to put his weapon away. He reached down to help Eisenberg up, but the attorney brushed him away. "Look, I'm sorry. We made a mistake. You fit the profile of a guy we're looking for."

"Sorry doesn't cut it. I've been working eighty hour weeks and this is my first weekend off in over a year. I've been trying to get a date with a girl for two years and she finally agreed to have dinner with me in Tucson, but thanks to you, there's no way I can get to Four Corners and back to Tucson in time for dinner."

The sheriff stepped away and called his deputy, Homer, on his cell. "Homer, I'm about five miles east of the Oasis. Meet me here asap. I need you to run something over to Four Corners for me."

He turned back to the young lawyer. "Look, I'm really sorry. We'll get you gassed up and headed home. My deputy will take the files over to Jennings." He then reached in his wallet and pulled out two, one hundred dollar bills. "I know this doesn't make up for it, but dinner's on me tonight."

At first the lawyer appeared not to want to take the money, but the sheriff insisted.

All of a sudden, Sandoval yelled, "FUCK!"

Startled, the sheriff and the lawyer looked at him.

"It was the girl!"

"What was the girl?"

"She had a scarf on. I should've noticed."

The lawyer motioned to the distance. "I passed her when she was pulled over. Looked like she was making a call. When my car conked out she drove right by and turned left into the desert about a mile or so up the road."

CHAPTER NINE

The Enemy of my Enemy

Las Vegas

Sonny Day and Vito Rotelli met for dinner at Carlucci as planned. Rotelli didn't know that Sonny had been briefed by Joey C. on the reason for the meeting. Sonny let Vito break the ice.

"So, Sonny, I understand you're movin up in the world."

Sonny didn't respond.

"I mean, I have an interest in a little project, nothing earth shaking, near the Arizona/Mexico border and Chicago says I gotta clear it with you. Go figure."

Sonny took a sip of his drink and still neglected to respond.

Vito was a bit unnerved. "I didn't mean no disrespect. You know. It's just— I always considered us friends, you know, but if you need to bless it— I'm good with that."

Sonny played dumb. "Vito, I don't have any idea what you're talkin about. What is it you wanna do?"

"Like I said, it's small potatoes. I hate to even bother you with it."

Sonny smiled. "Vito, the only thing I know is, if it was small potatoes you wouldn't bother with it."

Vito smiled. "Sonny, shame on me. Tryin to bullshit a bullshitter. No offense, you know."

"None taken."

"It's like this: There's an Indian reservation down near some one horse fuckin town called Apache Dunes."

Vito didn't notice Sonny shift in his seat and lean forward.

"So, get this, reservations are off limits to the feds."

Sonny chimed in. "I'm not so sure of that. What about the FBI?"

Vito laughed. "Fuggetaboutit. They're more corrupt than we are. The broad gets elected in November and everything's for sale. Get this, she sold uranium to the Russians! Can you imagine the balls on that broad? Now, I ain't no scientist, but uranium is what they make bombs out of."

"Yeah, well, the truth will come out someday."

"Sonny, you don't get it. They control the press except for that one network.

"What's this got to do with the reservation?"

"Sonny, we can do whatever we want there. Capiche? We just have to take care of our friends. Maybe even help with the illegals."

"What happens if our friends, so to speak, don't get elected?"

"There's no chance of that. The only one they fear is the guy from New York."

"Are you shitting me? That's just a P.R. stunt isn't it?"

"I don't know. There's some angry people out there."

"Why do they fear him?"

"Think about it. The fucking guy can't be bought."

"And that's a bad thing?"

"It ain't a good thing for the people in power, but its bein taken care of."

"Whatta you mean, its bein taken care of?"

"I mean … it's just a rumor, but I heard that something may happen to him."

"Vito, I hope to hell you don't have anything to do with that."

"You know what they say, 'The enemy of my enemy …'."

Sonny was now seriously unnerved and took his time replying. "Look Vito, I know a little bit about that area and my best advice is to forget about it."

"Sonny, I've got too much invested in this to walk away. There can be a taste for you, of course."

Sonny bought some time by savoring his drink before replying. I need to sleep on this."

It was clear, by his expression, that Vito wasn't pleased with Sonny's response.

"By the way, whatever happened to your friend Vinny and his nephew?"

Sonny understood the sentiment behind the question and just shrugged. Sonny also understood that Vito was a dangerous foe. He broke the ice on an uncomfortable silence. It was clear that neither person was happy with how the conversation had gone.

"What about Saturday?"

"Let me check with the wife and get back to you."

CHAPTER TEN

Mexizona

Apache Dunes

Despite the missteps so far, the good news is that the sheriff was pretty convinced that the contact was the young lady with the scarf. The ex-factor was that she was driving a truck with a dirt bike in back. If she was just picking him up, what was the purpose of the dirt bike?

Knowing the desert as well as he did, the truck would have to exit somewhere near the Oasis, while the dirt bike could handle any of the terrain. That narrowed the possibilities to them splitting up—one with the truck and one with the motorcycle.

The calculated guess was this: How proficient would an engineer, a bombmaker, be in unknown desert terrain on a dirt bike?

He turned to Sandoval. "We'll set up a road block five miles west of the Oasis. He's got to pick up the highway by then."

Abdullah al Somali

The connection in the desert had gone like clockwork. His contact had delivered the truck plus supplies and directions to follow. It was against his nature, if not Islam in general, to appear subservient to a woman, but this was the home of the Great Satan and even the Sheikh himself, had explained that he must follow her directions.

He had to laugh to himself. Throw logic out the window when dealing with infidels. They were fools. They had allowed over 80,000 Somalis to immigrate to Minnesota. Enough to guarantee them representation in Congress someday! He would complete his mission, inshallah, and seek out his cousins to plan more attacks on the non-believers.

He took time to study the documents he was given. If he was stopped for any reason, he was to hand them the ACLU's lawyer's card and tell them they had to speak with the lawyer. What fools! Put American in your name and people accept you are defending America, as opposed to trying to destroy it.

In the Great Satan, there was a thing called the Fifth Amendment which said you don't have to answer any questions if you think it might implicate you. Go figure. You don't answer questions in Saudi Arabia and it's off with your head.

He memorized the false driver's license. The truck was a rental with proper registration. He was to take the truck to the Tucson airport where he would find another vehicle in a designated space. He was to switch vehicles and follow the instructions contained in the glove box of the new one. How hard was that?

He exited the desert and traveled at least ten kilometers without a problem, but his growing sense of complacency was ended by the flashing lights, signaling a road block up ahead. He slowed down, breathed out and rehearsed his scripted response. Just be calm.

The sheriff and Sandoval saw the truck approaching. Sandoval confirmed it was the truck the lady with the scarf had been driving, but the driver was now an Arab-looking male. The sheriff had guessed right.

They approached the truck from both sides with their hands on their weapons. The sheriff approached the driver's side. The driver appeared stoic, showing no emotion or even questioned why he had been stopped. That was telling.

The sheriff tapped on the driver-side window. When Abdullah lowered the window, the sheriff asked him for his driver's license and registration, exactly as he had been told would happen. After a brief hesitation, he complied reciting his memorized lines.

"Is there a problem?"

The sheriff appeared to study the driver's license and then asked him to please step out of the truck.

Here's where things were getting a little off script and Abdullah panicked a bit and handed the sheriff the card of the ACLU lawyer.

Sandoval had now joined them.

The sheriff studied the card and looked at Abdullah. "What the fuck is this?"

"In America, I don't have to speak with you. It is an amendment." In his nervousness he forgot the number. "Please call my lawyer."

The first rule of holes is, when you're in one, stop digging. According to the laws of the desert, Abdullah had just confessed and the sheriff was going to make up for the angst of the earlier miscues. He winked at Sandoval.

"I'm sorry, did you say, 'In America'?"

"Yes, in America you have to talk to my lawyer."

The sheriff milked the situation with a pregnant pause before replying. "Mister, that may be true, but you appear to be lost. You aren't in America, you're in Mexizona."

Now Abdullah was in full panic mode, but there was no place to run to and, certainly, no place to hide. "But— I'm in Arizona and Arizona is in America."

"You're not listening. Arizona is in the United States, or as you say America, but this isn't Arizona. This is Mexizona. We seceded from the U.S. and we have our own laws down here. We're looking for a man of your description who allegedly killed two U.S. agents in Mexico. Manny, take this lawyer's card and check it with your DNA machine to see if we get a match."

Sandoval had trouble suppressing a smile as he got into the sheriff's truck and appeared to be deeply engaged. He exited the truck and gave the sheriff a thumb's up.

"We've got a match."

"Sir, turn around and put your hands behind your back. Cuff him Manny. Sir, you are charged with the murder of two U.S. agents."

Abdullah knew it was futile to resist and maybe damning, but he couldn't believe what was happening. No one had told him about Mexizona. He was pretty sure, but not certain, that there was no such place as Mexizona and he noted the Arizona plates on the Sheriff's vehicle. His mind was abuzz trying to process what was happening. He knew the supposed DNA test had been a joke, just not a funny one. He needed to keep his wits about him. His American friends were sure to find out about him. Weren't they?

Chapter Eleven

A Bedtime Story

Apache Dunes

With the prisoner secured behind bars and still cuffed, just in case, the sheriff called the number Bucky Robertson had given him. Not recognizing the number, Bucky answered cautiously. "Bucky here."

"Bucky, this is Cappy. I've got that package for you."

"Who all knows?"

"The um package, myself, and two deputies."

"Any resistance?"

"None."

"Is there a landing strip nearby?"

"A good strip and a wind sock."

"Good. I've got a Cessna and am officially on holiday, so I should be able to fly under the literal radar and get there sometime tomorrow. Can I reach you at this number?"

"That's affirmative."

"Cappy, good work."

Abdullah was angry with himself for not following the script, that he had practiced over and over. He had been led to believe that all he needed to do was present the lawyer's card and keep silent.

But he was now feeling a bit emboldened, knowing these two cowboys had gone rogue. Too many people were looking for him for them to hide him for long, whatever their plan was. Maybe it was money. That was all that mattered to infidels.

The sheriff and Sandoval returned from dinner and relieved Homer.

Abdullah called out to them, "You can't keep me here like this. People are looking for me."

The sheriff looked at Sandoval.

"Manny put some tape on his mouth. I've got a call to make."

Abdullah tried to resist, but it was useless.

Confident that the prisoner was muted, the sheriff put his radio on speaker and connected with the head of the Homeland Security Task Force charged with finding the Al Qaeda bombmaker, aka, Abdullah al Somali.

"Captain Bryson here."

"Captain, this is Sheriff Tom Ward, Apache Dunes, Arizona. In response to the APB on the fugitive terrorist, we conducted a very thorough search of the desert area around here and found no trace of him."

Abdullah jumped up and was trying desperately to reach the tape on his mouth, to no avail. Sandoval was loving it.

"Thanks, Sheriff. We're coming up dry also. Chances are he made his rendezvous and God knows where he is now."

"We'll keep our eyes open, but I didn't want you to waste any resources on a dead end."

"Appreciate it Sheriff. Thanks again. Over and out."

The sheriff casually approached the cell where a wide-eyed prisoner was starting to realize that the script that was playing out, bore no resemblance to the one he had so patiently rehearsed. The air was warm, cooled only with an electric fan, yet Abdullah was starting to feel the chilling effect of fear.

The sheriff motioned for Sandoval to remove the tape. Before Abdullah could speak the sheriff signaled him to be quiet. "From now on, you speak only when spoken to, or the tape goes back on. You understand me?"

"Abdullah nodded."

"Now, I gotta say, I'm impressed by your command of the English language, but it's not perfect yet and I'm gonna help you. You said I can't keep you here like this. Can means ability and I can do whatever I feel like with you and, as you just heard, if anyone is looking for you, they're looking in the wrong place. "

"What do you want from me? Is it money? I have twenty thousand U.S. dollars in my bag. You can have it."

The sheriff turned to Sandoval. "Check his bag."

Sandoval searched the bag and found the false bottom that concealed the cash.

"Bingo. He handed it to the Sheriff."

The sheriff approached the cell with the money in his hands. "I can have this?"

Abdullah shook his head yes. "It's yours, please take it."

The sheriff turned to Sandoval and then back to Abdullah. "Thanks."

Abdullah watched him walk away with the money and he appeared to split it up.

"Now will you let me go?"

The sheriff re-approached, but this time with a different demeanor.

"The only chance you have of leaving here alive, and it's a slim one, is if you tell us what we want to know."

"You can't make me talk."

The sheriff shook his head. "There you go again with can't. I CAN make you talk and I WILL make you talk. You'll wanna talk. Sandoval, put the tape back on. Cut a small hole for a straw for water."

The sheriff pulled his chair over near the cell. "Before we turn the lights out, I'll tell you a bed time story. It's about how the Apaches get people to talk. They dig a hole in the desert and bury their prisoner up to his neck. It's bad enough that the desert sun will bake the head, but the scent will attract all kinds of scary things: scorpions, snakes, centipedes, lizards, coyotes and, of course, the vultures. They will literally fight over the eyeballs, which are a delicacy to them. After the eyeballs are out they'll crawl through to the brain, while their cousins down below feast on the rest of the body. You have two options. Tell us what we want to hear before the varmints get to you or you become part of the food chain and die a death even worse than the one you inflicted upon our two agents. Sweet dreams…. Oh. Thanks for the money."

As the sheriff was about to turn out the lights he noticed that there was a puddle on the floor near the prisoner.

CHAPTER TWELVE

The Spider and the Fly

Los Angeles/Hollywood

Vito Rotelli was back in his domain, still smarting from the slight from Chicago and Sonny's condescending attitude. Who the fuck did he think he was? There was something wrong with this picture, but Vito couldn't put his finger on it. What did happen to Vinny and his idiot nephew? He's with Sonny all those years, and poof, he disappears? He disappears and Sonny is made boss of Arizona? Vito needed some leverage with Sonny. Maybe he was trying to see something that wasn't there, but maybe not.

The problem was, he'd told too many people about his "Arizona Pie" before it was baked and pocketed a couple of million bucks from investors to cover some gambling losses. There was no going back on the deal. He had to smile just thinking about its potential. Bring in some chemists and have a world class meth facility there. Cha-ching! Have a staging area for illegals, particularly around election time. Cha-ching! Build a casino as a front just to launder the profits from the drugs and the smuggling. Cha-ching! No fucking way that some dipshit Indian Chief was going to stand in his way. Sonny was more of a problem, but he would try "honey" first. If that didn't work, he'd do what he had to do.

His reverie was interrupted by his under boss, Paulie, who knocked once and entered.

"Sorry boss, there's somebody wants to talk to you."

"Somebody who?"

"The young kid who's over at CAA, the talent agency."

"Talk to him. Tell him I'm busy."

Paulie shrugged. "I told him, but he says it's important."

Vito shook his head and reached for the phone. "Who's this?"

"Mr. Rotelli, sir. This is Jimmy at CAA. You told me one time to keep an eye out for you."

"Yeah, I think I remember you. What's up?"

"Well, sir. I just had to set up a meeting with some of the big guns here and guess who they're meeting with?"

"Jimmy, I hope to fuck you don't think I'm gonna play a guessing game with you."

"Sorry. I'm just a little excited."

"Jimmy, you gonna tell me who it is and why I should care?"

"It's— it's Carlos Garcia!"

Vito looked at Paulie, who just shrugged.

"Who the fuck is Carlos Garcia?"

"He's the head of the Garcia cartel. The one on the Mexico-Arizona border."

Vito sat up in his chair and was now engaged. "Yeah, now I know who you mean. What was the meeting about?"

"I pretended not to listen, but I had to bring in some drinks and they were talking about him investing millions of dollars in some movie projects. His mother was one of the biggest investors in the business and now he wants to get involved. I thought you'd want to know."

"Jimmy you did good. You know where he's staying?"

"His mother has a mansion in Holmby Hills."

"You hear anything more, you let me know, okay?"

"Sure thing, Mr. Rotelli, sir."

Vito hung up and sat back in his chair with a smile on his face. The leader of a drug cartel with ties to Arizona wants to invest millions in movie projects. Movie projects that Vito's unions can shut down at his whim. He could hear his mother reciting her favorite poem, "Welcome to my parlor, said the spider to the fly…"

Welcome to Hollywood, Carlos.

CHAPTER THIRTEEN

Bad Company

Apache Dunes

The sheriff was waiting for Buck Robertson's Cessna at the Dunes air strip. Robertson was wired when he landed after flying fourteen hours, interrupted only by two stops to refuel the plane and his coffee thermos.

They did a man hug. "It's been too long Cappy and I'm getting way too old to pull a stunt like this again."

"I gotta say, you look like shit. Doesn't the CIA have a jet?"

Robertson looked at the sheriff. "I broke a few rules getting here, but you're the only one who knows I'm here and I want to keep it that way."

"Get some shut-eye on the ride in. "

The words had barely gotten out of the Sheriff's mouth and Robertson was out like a light. When they got to the jail the sheriff parked in back to let him catch a few zzzs. The prisoner wasn't going anywhere.

It was approaching mid-day when Robertson finally stirred, confused at first by the unfamiliar surroundings, but he quickly got his bearings and entered the jail. Sandowski also was well rested after some colorful dreams. He and Sandoval came over after breakfast. The sheriff had them bring a bacon and egg sandwich for Robertson that just needed zapping.

After introductions, the sheriff said it was time for the prisoner to be interrogated, Apache style. Robertson wondered if it was worth trying to get something out of him before any extreme measures, but the sheriff quickly overruled him. "His contact met him yesterday and expects him to be somewhere today. We need to find out where and we don't have time to waste."

They put a hood over the whimpering prisoner, whose attempts to resist were futile. They exited in the rear and put him in the back of the sheriff's truck. Sandoval had parked the prisoner's truck in his garage last night. Few words were spoken between the sheriff, Robertson, Sandowski, and Sandoval on the way to the desert. The prisoner's fate was sealed—each of them had killed before. When it ceased to be a time for solemn introspection—that was a time to worry.

The worst aspect was that they would give the prisoner false hope that if he gave up his secrets he might live. The chances of that were slim and none and Slim was on a train to the coast.

They agreed to take turns digging the hole and it went quickly. They didn't take the prisoner's hood off until he was in the hole. Abdullah resisted as much as possible, but again, to no avail. When he was buried up to his neck in the noon-day sun, they pulled off his hood. Fright doesn't do justice to describe the look on Abdullah's face.

The sheriff knelt down in front of him and gave him a drink of water. "

"Abdullah. I'm sorry we have to do this, but we don't have any time to waste and we have to know that you understand. If you want to live, you have to tell us what we want to know. If you don't, if you lie to us, we'll walk away. Just nod if you understand."

"Please, please don't leave me. I'll tell you everything."

"We'll see about that. Let's start with who the young lady is?"

"I don't know. I swear. It is against my religion to have contact with her."

"What happened to her?"

"She— she left on the motorcycle. She went through the desert."

The sheriff glanced at the others who collectively shrugged. Maybe yes. Maybe no.

"That's not a good way for us to start. Let me try this. What were your instructions?"

He coughed as some sand blew in his eyes and mouth. "I was supposed to take the truck to the Tucson airport and switch with a car parked in the space."

"What space?"

"It's— it's written on a sheet of paper in my wallet. A letter and a number."

The sheriff glanced at Sandoval who was already fetching the wallet from the truck.

"Got it."

"That's good. Then what?"

"Instructions are supposed to be in the glove compartment."

Robertson was now appearing to stare at Sandoval who felt his gaze.

"What?" asked Sandoval.

"Sorry. I was just trying to imagine you with a beard. You're about the same size as he is."

The sheriff turned to Robertson. "What do you have in mind?"

"If he doesn't switch cars, they'll know something happened to him. If we can make the switch today, maybe we can get those instructions and buy some more time. In the event they have someone watching the car, we need to disguise Manny, and I have a company kit in my plane. How long will it take to get to the Tucson airport?"

"To get you back to your plane, get Manny prepped, and get to Tucson is probably three hours. Manny, are you game?"

"I was undercover in Chicago. It's what I do, but remember his truck is in our garage."

The sheriff went back to the prisoner.

"Abdullah, unfortunately, we can't let you slide for killing the two agents."

The prisoner cried out, "I didn't kill them."

They collectively scoffed at his claim. "Abdullah, they were beheaded.

You beheaded them."

"But I didn't kill them."

The sheriff said, "That's it. Let's go.

He started to walk away and the prisoner cried out again, "I swear to Allah I didn't kill them!"

Sandowski pivoted and approached the prisoner. "If you beheaded them, how didn't you kill them?"

"Because, because they were already dead."

The response stopped everyone in their tracks and they moved toward the prisoner. Robertson knelt down and faced him.

"What do you mean they were already dead?"

"Water, water please."

They gave him some water.

"There were two men, two Americans, who got me into Mexico and past customs. They took me to a small village and arranged for a, they called him a coyote, to take me across the border after dark. They gave me some money and the phone and said my contact would call me. I was to wait in the desert. I was taking a nap in the afternoon, in a hotel in the village, when two other agents burst in. More water please.

"They put cuffs on me, gagged me and took me to their car. They put me in the back and headed for the border. On the way to the border a truck approached with flashing lights and the driver motioned for them to pull over. It was the two men who had been my guides. The agents seemed to recognize them and stopped the car. They all got out and appeared to be arguing when one of the men slipped behind the two agents and pow! pow! Shot both in the back of the head. It happened so fast. The other man was angry at him for killing them. He said I would have to behead them so they could get rid of the heads and no one would know they were shot. They said everyone would believe I killed them."

Robertson gave the prisoner another drink of water.

"Was there anything you remember about the two men? Can you describe them?"

The prisoner seemed to be trying to think and then said, "The one who was in charge … not the shooter, the other one … he had the lip, where it has been … How do you say, sewed up?"

Robertson turned to the others. "Stone."

The sheriff asked, "Who's Stone?"

"I told you this was fucked up. Stone is a contractor for the Company. He's a go-to assassin. He was born with a cleft palate."

Sandowski whistled. "Are you saying two CIA agents offed two others?"

"The prisoner is saying it and he has no reason to lie."

Sandoval looked at the others. "Speaking about the prisoner. What do we do with him? Does it make a difference that he didn't kill the two agents?"

Robertson replied, "Not really. He came here to kill Americans and he has blood on his hands."

Sandowski walked over, knelt down and shot him in the back of the head.

"Poor bastard. I hope for his sake all those virgins are waiting for him."

They covered the head as much as possible, but that wouldn't last long. They got back in the truck and headed for the airstrip and Robertson's kit. When they got in the truck, Robertson pulled out his cell phone and dialed a number. He put the phone on speaker. A man named John answered. "John, here."

"John, this is Buck."

"Buck, you're supposed to be on holiday? Where are you?"

"I am and you don't want to know where. Listen, do you happen to know where Stone is these days?"

"Don't you get the news?"

"I told you, I'm on holiday. What news?"

"Yesterday afternoon an aircraft registered to United Mining crashed near El Paso. Witnesses said it exploded in mid-air. Two execs of United Mining were killed. Get this, a Mr. Stone and a Mr. Weathers."

Robertson was silent as he digested the news.

"Buck, what's going on?"

"We didn't have this conversation. Watch your back and I'll be in touch."

When Robertson ended the call, the sheriff asked, "What's United Mining?"

Robertson replied, "One of the CIA's fronts. Weathers was Stone's partner. They only handled the black ops."

"So, what happens now to the guy who planted the bomb? Where does it end?"

"It was likely a contractor who knew nothing about what happened to the other agents. No way to connect the dots to Abdullah."

"Are you cool?"

Robertson smiled. "I'm on holiday. What do I know?"

CHAPTER FOURTEEN

The Sheikh

Los Angeles

Among the many misconceptions about Islam is that the honorific title Sheikh is exclusively for males, as females are clearly second-class citizens in the faith. Fatima was an exception, like Sheikh Hasina of Bangladesh. At USC, she was known as Fatima Hassim, one of her many aliases. In reality she was the daughter, one of the many children, of an infamous Saudi businessman and arms dealer.

She hardly fit the profile of a reactionary. Her life had been one of uncommon privilege. She had grown up in villas with breath-taking views, multi-million dollar yachts and private jets surrounded by the rich and famous. It was almost unfair that she happened to be blessed with uncommon beauty and grace.

Privileges and gifts, however, are sometimes respected and valued by their costs and hers were free.

What she lacked, thus coveted most, was power. Islam is a male dominated world. The truth is, if she had a cause celebre, it was feminism, not Islamic Jihad. She had been very close to her mother and countless times listened by the bedroom door to her father's pathetic supplications for her mother's gifts, only to later ignore her in public.

When she thought about it she had to laugh. In her home country she couldn't even drive a car, yet she was waging a war against a culture where the feminist movement was a vibrant force. She was uncomfortable, as we all are, when forced to confront our personal demons and their twisted logic.

Her aphrodisiac was power. Power, ironically, over males. It was neither unique, nor esoteric. Freud identified it as a "father-complex." Perhaps, left to her own devices, she could have learned to deal with it, but there were too many "young Jihadis" out there who instinctively hated the Great Satan and would gladly go to their death, if ordered to do so. That symbolism and power were stronger than fentanyl and she was addicted.

She had just returned from her rendezvous in the Arizona desert with the Al Qaeda bombmaker. It took all of her resolve not to leave him stranded there. Him with his condescending, orthodox attitudes toward women. She could feel it, but an even better feeling was the orgasmic motorcycle ride through the desert, knowing that she was about to shape history.

As she drifted off to sleep, her thoughts went to the young man at the gas station in Arizona. There were many things that puzzled her about that encounter. She had been uncharacteristically caught off-guard. He presented several anomalies. He exuded a natural confidence and power, but he was deferential to her and not under cover of darkness. She had to admit, if he was unnerved, so was she. She willed her heart, that feminine curse, to be quiet as she relived the moment. It was akin to trying to put a square peg in a round hole. He wasn't a gas station attendant, but who was he and why did she care?

She needed a good night's sleep. Tomorrow, the bomber would be directed to the second stage of this carefully planned operation. The separate stages were designed on a need-to-know basis. In that way, only she knew the entirety of the plan and she had developed contingencies for the corruption of any single stage.

CHAPTER FIFTEEN

The Doppelganger

Apache Dunes and Tucson

On the way to the Dunes airstrip and Robertson's kit, they formulated a plan. It was all contingent on the vehicle for the switch still being at the Tucson airport, as almost a full day had elapsed. The only hope of getting the instructions for Stage Two and keeping the ball in play resided with the vehicle. Robertson spoke first, "If it's still there, and there are a number of reasons for a delay, it's likely that there's a tracking device. That's s.o.p. for the Company and I have a detector in my kit. The wild card is if someone is watching the car. That's why the switch has to be executed swiftly with as little facial exposure as possible."

The sheriff inquired, "How do we handle the tracking device?"

"We don't, at least not until he reaches his next destination, as expected. We'll have to adjust on the fly after that. If they think he's alive, they'll be looking for him if he drops off the grid. "

"What's the plan?"

"I'll need some time with Manny plus a long-sleeved shirt and a baseball cap for him. He has to drive the truck, so someone has to bring it to the airstrip. It'll be best if Max and Homer can go ahead and discreetly check out the scene. Tom and I will tail Manny in a separate car and keep in touch by cell phone. Our two cars must be unmarked and you're gonna have to ditch the badges."

"No problem. We'll swing by and get the truck and Homer's car on the way. Homer, you and Max take your car to Tucson. When we're finished at the strip, Bucky and I will take my wife's car."

Apache Dunes Airstrip

It was obvious that Robertson knew what he was doing and had the right gear. After a little over forty-five minutes, Manny was almost a doppelganger for the terrorist. By that time, Max and Homer were well on their way. The sheriff and Robertson followed Manny to the Sheriff's house where they switched vehicles with his wife.

After confirming that there was no tracking device on the terrorist's truck, The sheriff and Robertson trailed Manny to the Tucson airport maintaining periodic communication with the team to ensure all lines were open and operable.

Tucson Airport

Max and Homer arrived almost an hour before the others and conducted a discreet surveillance of the area. The car was in its designated space and they didn't detect that it was being watched. They had taken Robertson's gizmo and did confirm that a tracking device was attached to the car, but, as directed, simply took note of the fact.

When Manny arrived, he made the switch with ease, taking care not to appear being rushed. He exited the airport with both tails within sight of his car. At the first stop light he made contact with the sheriff and Robertson, who patched in Max and Homer. "Guys, we've got a problem. I opened the glove compartment and there are what appear to be instructions, but, if so, they're in some type of code."

Robertson quickly took charge. "Shit. There has to be a key. Where's his bag?"

There was a pause while everyone waited for the other to respond. It became apparent it was left at the sheriff's office. "Okay, we have to adjust. Head north and take the first exit that has a McDonald's. Max, you and Homer take the lead and we'll bring up the rear. No, better yet, slow down and let us both pass. When you arrive, go straight to the rest room and I'll be waiting for you. Slip me the instructions. I'll try to get some help with the code while you take your time with your meal. Max, you and Homer see where Manny parks and sit where you can keep an eye on his car. If I get something, I'll text you. When I do, Max and Homer head for your car, but let Manny exit the parking lot first. We'll bring up the rear."

Mickey D's

The relay of the coded instructions went off without a hitch. Robertson went outside and called his friend John. He answered quickly, "Buck, are you okay? There's some strange shit going on."

"I'm okay, but I need your help and as discreet as possible. For your eyes only."

"Roger that. What do you need?"

"I'm going to take a picture of a coded document and then e-mail it to you. The code looks familiar, but I need it decoded asap. If you can help me, let me know, again asap. Highest priority. Afterwards, erase the document from your phone."

"I'll stand by. Buck, watch your back."

"You too. This conversation never took place."

By the time Robertson finished his fish sandwich and fries, his phone buzzed. He recognized John's number and answered. "Can you help?"

"Buck, I've got good news, but I have a question. The good news is that I was able to decode the document and will forward after we hang up."

"That's great. What's question?"

"Buck, there was an APB out on an Al Qaeda terrorist, but it seems he disappeared. May I ask where you got the coded document?"

"John, bear with me for the time being. I need to sort some things out. In the meantime, we didn't speak and you have no idea where I am.

And, for God's sake, wipe your phone."

"Roger that."

When Robertson got the decoded instructions, he forwarded them to the team. Stage two directed the terrorist to a house in Henderson, Nevada, a suburb approximately fifteen minutes from Las Vegas. The text stated that he would be contacted there with further instructions.

Robertson then texted the team that he was going to rent a room at the Hampton Inn on S. Tucson Boulevard. He would text them the room number and they should regroup there and plan their next move.

CHAPTER SIXTEEN

A Dubious Beginning

Los Angeles

Prior to seeking a mediated sit down with Sonny, in re his grand designs for the Apache Reservation in Arizona, Vito Rotelli had a few relevant items on his to-do list. First off, he wanted to explore possible synergies with the new industry investor, Carlos Garcia. Rotelli assumed that Garcia was still involved in the drug trade and had some first-hand knowledge of the reservation itself. He whiffed on the former, but was accurate on the latter, although it wasn't the response he was hoping for.

Carlos wasn't offended by the query, but was clear that his cartel days were behind him and would remain so. He was truly excited to be involved in the movie industry and was planning on taking some introductory courses at USC. When the subject turned to the reservation and the Apaches, Carlos tried to warn him that the desert was a dangerous and unforgiving place. It had secrets that only the Apaches understood and could exploit.

Rotelli scoffed at the caveat, explaining that the notorious Asesino MC would be a partner in the venture. Carlos wished him well, but said he would willingly take the other side of that bet.

"Geronimo and just thirty braves held off a force of ten thousand U.S. and Mexican soldiers for months in the nearby hills."

Rotelli replied, "But, my friend, that was then and now is now."

Carlos just shook his head, "Little has changed. I witnessed the Garcia cartel get wiped out in two separate battles with the Apaches. My uncle believed like you do."

Rotelli was pissed that his vital counsel, Wood, had begged off on being present for that meeting. "Vito, how many times do I have to tell you? I can't be present when you're discussing breaking the law."

"But, I need you with me when I meet with the bikers as we'll be discussing our terms. You know, the split."

"Just tell them upfront that we will be discussing the Apache reservation venture. It isn't necessary to get into specifics. It's implicit what the roles are. Just like when you and I discuss our real estate joint venture."

Rotelli heeded that advice because, truth was, the bikers scared the shit out of him. Wood asked, "What's the proposal?"

"I tossed out 75/25. I expect they'll counter, but no way they get more than 40 percent or I look elsewhere for the muscle."

"For the help."

"Sorry. For the help."

"Now, I suggest we invite two or three of their leaders to my office for the discussion. No way am I going to their club house and be surrounded by a dysfunctional mob."

The two apparent leaders entered the office later that day. Their escort of twenty of so club members idled on their bikes outside. The meeting was brief and to the point. The leaders agreed to the proposed 75/25 split with no comment. Rotelli interpreted that as a positive sign. They were content with 25 percent. Wood sensed a totally different meaning. After the labs were up and running, the bikers wouldn't need Rotelli. They might have agreed to 90/10 just to get in the door.

The only condition they sought, was being provided with military hardware and equipment. Their wish list was for AR-15 rifles, accessories and tactical gear including body armor. When the subject was broached, Wood quickly excused himself and left the room. In the meantime, Rotelli expressed his confidence that his friend (Mr. Wolf) could deliver the goods as he had done for Barry Seal.

After handshakes on the agreement, the bikers departed and Wood re-entered the office. When Rotelli explained what the bikers were seeking, Wood cautioned that a piece of the puzzle with the government was still missing. The identity of the person they helped cross the border into Arizona, had yet to be disclosed.

Wood had taken a leap of faith by contacting the DOJ attorney, Hayes, with whom he had enjoyed a cordial dialogue. He guessed correctly that Hayes was out of the loop, which Hayes himself had admitted, and asked if he could help identify a man in a photo, believing he may be on a watch list. Hayes' reward for doing so would be the steak dinner at Musso and Frank which they had talked about.

Except for Wood's awkward and evasive answer, as to why he was interested in what turned out to be an infamous Al Qaeda bombmaker, the meal and the evening were very enjoyable for both.

Realizing that Rotelli's tangled web now involved Apaches, a biker gang from East L.A., a corrupt government agency and an Islamic terrorist, Wood presented Rotelli with a new document the following morning.

Rotelli glanced at it. "What's this?"

"It's just an amendment to our real estate venture. Just sign where indicated. I've already signed."

"What am I signing?"

"It's nothing. It just allows us to purchase key man insurance policies on the principals. Our insurance agent said it would be a good thing. Sign it and then I'll reach out to Mr. Wolf in regards to the ... um ... equipment."

Wood would sleep much easier knowing he had a three million dollar life insurance policy on Rotelli. His only restlessness was caused when he wondered why he hadn't made it more.

CHAPTER SEVENTEEN

The Next Move

Tucson

Robertson texted his room number at the Hampton Inn to the team. Within forty-five minutes they were all re-united to discuss the next move. Before Robertson took the floor, Sandowski spoke up.

"Buck, if you don't mind, I'd like to send the coded document to one of my assets back in Chicago. He's a Chinese genius, Jimmy Chu—not to be confused with the shoe guy. Jimmy was on a work visa when he was busted for bank fraud years ago. So much of the gang communications were encoded, he evaded jail time by doing some work for us and there was no code he couldn't crack."

"Max, John is with the Company. He cracked the code."

"Buck, humor me. First of all, the Company seems to be part of the problem, but more importantly, if you're gonna need any more help from Manny, I don't want to leave anything to chance."

"Fair enough. It can't harm anything if he's discreet."

"Trust me on this."

"Done."

Buck, e-mailed the coded message to Max's phone and he, in turn, forwarded it to Jimmy Chu, with a message to call Max's phone upon receipt.

Buck pulled a chair up near the beds. "Before we get started, I have a charger cord over there, if anybody needs to charge their phones. Okay, here's the way I see it. The Company suspects that the terrorist disappeared. That's according to John."

The sheriff raised his hand. "Why would they think that if Manny picked up the car? "

"That's a good question. John asked how I got the coded doc."

"What did you tell him?"

"Nothing. I said he needed to bear with me for a bit."

Max spoke up, "Look, the mission, as I understood it, was to get the bad guy and eliminate him. You referred to it as a Hill 666 solution. Well, mission accomplished, in my book. The coded document was icing on the cake, but it just tells you to go to some house in Nevada where you will be contacted. They have things compartmentalized, which is smart. I don't see much more that you can accomplish."

The sheriff seconded Max's comments. "I have to agree with Max. Regardless, Homer needs to get back to the Dunes, as I do. Homer, why don't you take off? I'll be along."

Homer said his farewells and headed back to the Dunes.

The sheriff turned to Buck, who seemed deep in thought. "Buck, what more can you accomplish?"

"I don't disagree with anything you've said, but since we've come this far, I'd like to scout out the house in Nevada. If we don't find anything, we cut bait."

"Who's we?"

Robertson looked over at Manny. "If anyone is watching, the bomber is alive and well and following instructions. Plus, I can use the back-up. Just in case."

Max turned to Manny. "It's your call. We're a little out of our league here. With all due respect to Buck, I'd prefer you take a pass on this one."

Manny took his time before replying, obviously debating it internally. "Here's what I'll do. I'll take the next step with you, but no promises from there."

Buck stood up. "I really appreciate it. We'll get going then. Everybody get your phones and stay in touch."

CHAPTER EIGHTEEN

The Sit Down

Las Vegas

Joey C. called Sonny to tell him that he would be flying in early, because Vito Rotelli had called the Old Man and requested a sit down over this Arizona business. Joey C. had replaced Bellini as the spokesman for the Don and was designated to mediate the dispute. They were to meet at Joey C.'s suite in the Pompeii at five.

There was a noticeable chill in the air when they assembled as planned. Each person feigned collegiality with the requisite "How ya doins", but a sit down is never a lovefest.

Joey C. was seated in the middle and, as protocol dictated, opened the dialogue. "Just to be clear. I'd rather be getting one of them proctoscopes than be doin this, but Don Anthony told me to mediate this dispute and I do what I'm told to do."

Sonny raised his hands, "Somebody please clue me in. What's the fucking dispute?"

Vito leaned in. "Sonny, I came to you like a man to ask your approval for my move in Arizona. Why? Because Don Anthony told me that I needed your approval. Now, I gotta be honest, I don't understand what the fuck you have to do with it. I'm kicking some serious tribute to Chicago. You want to make a movie in Chicago, you gotta deal with my unions. My unions. Now, I know Vegas was the big prize at one time, but so was Rome."

Joey C. motioned for Vito to tone it down and then motioned for Sonny to respond. Sonny collected his thoughts and sipped at his water before replying.

"I counted about three separate things. So let me try to address them all. First, it was the Don who said you needed my approval. I didn't ask him for that authority. Joey can attest to that. I was more surprised than anyone. Having said that, like Joey said, I'm also gonna do what I'm told to do. If you got a problem with that, take it up with Chicago. Don't bust my balls. Second, I didn't deny your request outright. I told you that I have some knowledge of the area."

Vito interjected, "How the fuck do you know anything about Apache fucking Dunes, Arizona?"

Sonny again threw up his hands, exasperated. "I'm gonna ignore the insinuation, for old time's sake, but I'll explain. There was a problem with a gambler who lived there and Johnny Bellini sent Vinny and me down there to collect some money."

"Is that the same Bellini who died under mysterious circumstances which made you the new king? And whatever happened to Vinny and his nephew? Did they just disappear?"

Sonny took another drink of water and exchanged glances with Joey C., "That's the second time I'm gonna ignore your insinuation, but, and hear me good, there is no third time. Capiche?"

Joey jumped in, "Let's everyone calm down and, Vito, we're here to talk about Arizona. Nothing else. Now, it's not my job to be partial, but I gotta say, you aren't doin yourself any favors, so far. Go ahead Sonny."

"I was gonna answer his comment about Vegas. The 'that was then' comment. Let's take a little trip down memory lane. Vegas was the Golden Goose of Golden Gooses. Everybody got fat and we made more money than we could spend. You know what happened? One guy. One guy who I knew when he was in diapers. He had it all. Money, broads, respect. You name it. But, it wasn't enough for him. He was never satisfied. You know what he did? He organized a crew that robbed the gamblers who made us a fortune and businesses on the Strip. On the fucking Strip! He brought so much heat on Vegas that it finally imploded and took a lot of people with it. And for what? Because his fucking ego could never be satisfied. Now, the reason I tell you this story is that I don't know why you want to fuck around with an Indian reservation in Arizona when you've got all anyone could ask for in L.A. and fucking Hollywood!"

Joey C. held up his hands. "Vito, I gotta say that I agree with what Sonny said."

"I get it, but if the Arizona deal blows up, who's that hurt besides me?"

Joey turned to Sonny. "Sonny, it's your call. Are you opposed to Vito's move in Arizona?"

"Joey, I never said no. I said I wanted to sleep on it. It's like this: if Vito can convince the Indians to go along with the deal, I'm okay with it. But, if this involves force or worse yet, bloodshed, it will bring too much heat and Vegas is too close. The other possibility is for Chicago take back the authority, so if this blows up it's not on me."

"That ain't gonna happen. Vito, I think Sonny's conditions are reasonable. You get the Indians to go along and no one will interfere. Capiche?"

"Capiche. Listen, Sonny, I'm sorry for getting a little heated. It's just business. Are we good?"

"I think we understand each other."

Joey shook hands with Vito and turned to Sonny. "Sonny, hang on for a minute."

After Vito left, Joey turned to Sonny. "How many times did we try to warn our friend, whose name we can't mention anymore, but he wouldn't listen. We shoulda known how it would end. We got a problem here. Are there any cornfields around here?"

Sonny laughed, "No, but there's plenty of desert. Even more in Arizona."

Joey C. smiled, "I need a drink. How about dinner at Carlucci? Hey, does Bobbie want to join us?"

"I'll ask."

CHAPTER NINETEEN

God Protect Me from My Friends

Returning to Apache Dunes

The sheriff and Max were on the road for more than thirty minutes before either spoke. The sheriff broke the ice. "Max, what's eating at you?"

"Tom, I'm gonna share a secret with you. This burned out detective began his career with the FBI. I went from the Marines to college on the G.I. Bill and right to Quantico and the Fibs. I was part of a special op group. We were renegades. In fact, they had a nickname for us, 'The Hole in the Wall Gang'. We didn't need no stinkin badges. We broke every rule in the book, but we swore an oath of loyalty to each other. As long as we had each other's backs no one could touch us. I would have taken a bullet for each one of them."

"What happened?"

"What happened is that one of them got leaned on and was afraid of losing his job, his benefits and his pension. I get it. I was single, but he had two kids with a third on the way."

"You have doubts about Buck's fellow agent?"

"I'm just sayin. Four agents, we know of, are dead. If this goes all the way to the top, as Buck suspects, what can two agents do? I don't know this John guy, obviously, but he's got a lot to lose. Not to mention his life."

Just then Max's phone buzzed. He put it on speaker. It was Jimmy

Chu. "Max, I decoded the message. I've seen this code before."

"And did it say to go to a house in Nevada?"

"Yup. Spring Valley."

The sheriff and Max looked at each other. "Jimmy, you said Spring Valley. You sure it wasn't Henderson?"

"Max, how can you confuse Spring Valley with Henderson?"

"Jimmy, you're positive?"

"When have I been wrong?"

The sheriff pulled off on the shoulder. No sooner had he done so than another phone buzzed, but neither reached for it. Max had his phone in his hand. He looked at the sheriff.

"Aren't you going to answer?"

That's not my ring. He then felt the vibration in his coat pocket. He must have picked up Buck's phone by mistake. They were the same model. The text message was from John. *Text me when you arrive.*

The sheriff took out his wallet and retrieved Sonny's business card. He called his cell number. "Sonny here."

"Sonny, this is Tom Ward. The sheriff of Apache Dunes."

"We didn't do it and I have an alibi."

The sheriff laughed. "This is a social call. I need a favor."

"I'm just finishing dinner. What can I do for you?"

"I don't have time to explain. You need to trust me on this. Are you familiar with Henderson, Nevada?"

"Sure. It's a suburb of Vegas."

"I have two friends, one of them you met. One of the guys from Chicago. I need someone to pick them up as soon as possible. I'll text you the address in Henderson. Then, I need somewhere they can stay for a couple of days. Completely off the radar screen. Can you help me?"

"I'll take the hotel limo to pick them up. I'll leave now. I'll put them up in a suite. No sign in or anything."

"Thanks, Sonny. What can I do for you?

"Give me four hundred bucks for the busted tail lights. Capiche?"

The sheriff laughed. "Capiche. Call me when you have them."

Max called Manny's cell phone. "Hey Max. What's up?"

"Manny, listen to me. You and Buck have to get out of that house. We have a limo coming to pick you up."

"Whoa, Max, what's happening?"

Buck's cell phone buzzed again. The text said, *Are you there?*

Max screamed in the phone. "Get the fuck out NOW! You hear me? Call me when you're at least a block away."

The sheriff and Max were on edge until Manny called. "Okay, were out in the street. What the fuck's going on?"

"Are you at least a block away?"

"A block and a half and we're still walking. By the way, do you have Buck's phone?"

"That's affirmative. Stand by."

The sheriff typed in a reply to the text. *Arrived and in bed.*

They could hear the explosion over the phone.

Manny called, "What the fuck is going on? How did you know?"

"Are you both okay?"

"Pretty shaken up. Both of us were knocked down. I think I see a limo coming now. Hey Max, I guess John wasn't a friend, huh?"

"An old Jewish gentleman once told me, 'God protect me from my friends. I know who my enemies are'."

CHAPTER TWENTY

High Heels and Backwards

Los Angeles

The Sheikh was more pissed off at herself than anyone else. She knew the moment she met the Al Qaeda bomber that he wasn't up to the task. It took him an entire day to switch cars and get the next instructions. That should have taken three hours, at most. Then he was a no show at the safe house in Spring Valley, Nevada. To further complicate matters, news reports said that there was a massive explosion at a house in a nearby suburb with several dead and missing.

She couldn't rationally connect the dots, but didn't believe in coincidences. The Americans must have intervened and screwed everything up. She thought, *Good riddance.* Now, she would do it her way, with her people and the job would get done right. Power was her aphrodisiac and she was now empowered.

It would continue to gnaw at her, however, that something didn't add up. The Americans were the ones who wanted the terrorist attack. They were the ones who benefitted from the candidate's death. Why would they muck it up?

She tried playing the Devil's advocate and it gave her pause. What if someone else, or others, had discovered the plot? What if they had eliminated the bomber? The bomber couldn't have revealed her identity as he had no clue who she was or where she lived. And, even if they followed the instructions, they would get no further than stage three.

She had been wise in compartmentalizing the master plan.

In fact, she had made no mistakes. It was the egotistical and condescending males who screwed things up. She smiled as she recalled something she had read, *Ginger Rogers could do everything Fred Astaire could do. She just did it in high heels and backwards!*

CHAPTER TWENTY-ONE

The Debriefing

Cia Safe House in Northern Virginia

The Deputy Director of the CIA, Aaron Nolan, and Agent John Morgan's immediate superior officer, Barrington "Barry" Stanton, had arrived by helicopter early at the remote farmhouse in Northern Virginia. They met while at Yale together and had been close friends ever since. Nolan had always been the more political of the two.

Agent Morgan was expected shortly for a debriefing on the Buck Robertson affair.

"So Barry, what do we know?"

"You mean other than this whole thing, not just Robertson's involvement, has been a clusterfuck? Five good agents are dead so far, assuming Robertson is dead."

"Implying that number might grow?"

"I truly hope not. It depends on what Morgan knows. Remember, he followed the book and reported to me immediately."

"That's good enough for me, but the people calling the shots, no pun intended, are leaving a bloody wake and seem not to care. What's Morgan working on now?"

"The staffer who is feeding files to Wikileaks."

"I thought he had him."

"He does. He's just checking to see if anyone else is involved."

"And?"

"Nothing, so far."

"Okay, here's what we're going to do, regardless of the outcome of the debriefing. Turn the staffer over to the Fibs. Let them get some blood on their hands."

"Sir. With all due respect. We may not have handled this matter as well as we should have, but they fuck up everything. FBI stands for Full Blown Idiots."

Nolan laughed. "True, but how hard is it to take out one low level staffer with all the violence in D.C.?"

"I'm on record. They'll fuck it up."

Nolan saw the car lights approaching through the window. "This must be him. Give me a brief bio on Morgan."

"Nothing remarkable. Good agent, thus far. No bad habits we know of. Likes to run marathons. If he drinks at all, it's very rare. Partial to La Croix sparkling water."

"Married?"

"Separated, no kids."

"No reason to drink."

They both laughed.

"Where did he go to school?"

"Brigham Young."

"Fucking Mormon. Worse yet, he has some ethics. Why don't we stick with the Ivies?"

Morgan parked and was greeted by Nolan's "man Friday" Agent Schneider. Morgan knew the drill. He left his phones, gun, and watch in the car. Schneider escorted him inside where he was given the once-over with the wand.

Stanton then greeted Morgan warmly and ushered him into the living room, where the deputy director rose to shake hands.

"John, we were getting ready to have a drink. Will you join us?"

"Just water for me, please."

"How about sparkling water? We have some La Croix."

"That'll be perfect. Thanks."

Nolan smiled at Stanton. He'd done his homework.

Drinks were poured and they settled in. After some polite chit chat, Stanton took the floor.

"John, thanks for coming. The purpose of this meeting is simply to try to figure out what Buck Robertson was up to in this puzzling affair. We note that you followed protocol by advising me of his contacts with you. Now, we just want to fill in the gaps of which there are several. Why don't we let you lead off?"

Morgan cleared his throat. "I received a call from Buck, Agent Robertson, asking me if I knew where Stone was."

Stanton interrupted. "Did he tell you why he was asking?"

"No. He just said that something was amiss in so many words."

"And, what did you reply?"

"Simply that it was reported that Stone and Weathers had died in a plane crash."

"Had you had any contact recently with either Stone or Weathers?"

"The only contact I ever had with them was several years ago in Panama."

"Do you have any reason to suspect that the plane crash was suspicious?"

Morgan appeared nervous as he took a sip of his water before replying.

"Only that witnesses said there was an explosion. Truth is, I never gave it any thought."

"Did Robertson say where he was calling from?"

"He confirmed he was on vacation, but he said I didn't want to know his location and told me the conversation never happened."

"According to your report, the next contact was in reference to an encoded document."

"He asked for my help in decoding it. I immediately contacted you and followed your instructions."

"You asked him how he got the document?"

"I mentioned that a terrorist on our watch list had disappeared, as per your instructions, and asked him how he got the document."

"And?"

"He gave no response to the news of the terrorist and said he wouldn't disclose how he got it. At least for now."

Nolan and Stanton glanced at each other before Nolan spoke, "John, how much do you know about the terrorist?"

"Only his name. I checked the recent traffic and noticed an APB was issued for him in the Mexico/Arizona border area. He was alleged to have killed two of our agents. One of whom I knew very well."

"John, we're going to take you into our confidence because we know this affair has been unsettling. The terrorist was responsible for the deaths of the two agents. We don't have a clue what happened to Stone and Weathers. The NTSB tells us it was a fuel tank that ruptured. It happens. The terrorist's work wasn't done yet. We had intel that he was traveling to Nevada to plan a major bombing that could have killed hundreds, if not more. We were monitoring his every move from crossing the border to switching cars in Tucson, where he got the encoded instructions for his safe house in Nevada—Spring Valley, Nevada."

Stanton took over. "We knew he had a contact in the U.S., but we didn't know who it was. As much as we hated to admit it, all signs pointed to Robertson."

Morgan shook his head. "I— I still can't believe it."

"Believe it. You ever hear of Benedict Arnold? Alger Hiss? The Rosenbergs?"

"But— but why would he need me to decode the message if he was with the terrorist?"

Nolan and Stanton exchanged glances.

Stanton answered, "Look, here's what we know. The terrorist picked up the vehicle at Tucson airport. Robertson contacted you to decode document, which he could have only gotten from the terrorist. Maybe the bad guy lost the code. Who knows? Maybe it was misdirection from

Robertson to see if we knew anything. Regardless, the only reason for them—them—to proceed to Nevada was to complete their mission. We couldn't let that happen. If Robertson was on our side, he would have prevented that from happening, but we know that two men arrived at the Henderson location, believing it was the right destination."

There was a protracted period of silence before Deputy Director Nolan looked at John. "John, are you okay? Maybe you need a rest. We've decided to transfer the DNC staffer to the FBI."

"That's a bad idea. I mean, with all due respect, that's probably a death sentence. What I'm really struggling with is the family next door who were killed in the explosion."

Stanton replied. "Collateral damage is a fact of life in any conflict. The terrorist would have killed many, many more. If the target was Las Vegas—pick a number."

"I guess a rest wouldn't hurt. This is the first time that I was the one who pulled the trigger, so to speak."

The deputy director stood up and was followed by Stanton and Morgan. "You did your job. For that we're grateful. Take some time off and check in with Barry in a couple of weeks. Needless to say, this meeting never happened."

After Morgan left, Nolan and Stanton loosened their ties and replenished their drinks.

Nolan went first. "So, what do you think?"

"What I'd like to think is he's going to deal with it and move on. What I believe is that the loose ends and inconsistencies are going to eat at him. He began as an analyst. It's what they do. In retrospect, it was a mistake for him to trigger the explosion."

"I agree. We got sloppy."

"Here's the bigger question, did Robertson and the terrorist die in the explosion? Further, was it really the terrorist? What do we know?"

"The site is a mess. There are body parts everywhere, but, so far, no DNA matches to Robertson. A man down the street was headed to the bathroom when he heard his dog barking a few minutes before the explosion. He thought he saw someone in the street, but he wasn't wearing glasses and can't be sure. As for the terrorist, we've blown up the pics of him switching cars at the Tucson airport. Get this. An Arab terrorist was wearing steel tipped cowboy boots."

"So the terrorist must have been eliminated. That would explain why they didn't know the code. Did you check the taxis and Ubers for the area?"

"Checked them all. No one was picked up in the neighborhood that night. It's a bedroom community. The explosion was massive. Odds are they were killed."

"Well, nothing we can do until we know more. At minimum, the terrorist was eliminated."

"By the way, how did he get across the border?"

"A biker gang. The Wolf traded them some weapons and military gear."

Nolan shook his head. "So, where does that leave us? "

"If the terrorist is dead, the "Red Queen" is going to be on the warpath. We haven't told her about identifying the staffer yet. Worse yet, the "Sheikh" will go to Plan B, if she hasn't already, and we won't be in the loop."

"What about Morgan?"

"The line that sticks out in my mind is when he said this was the first time he pulled the trigger. That's a lot for anybody to deal with and he is the last person connected to this disaster."

"Aaron, may I ask you a personal question?"

"Shoot."

"What's happened to us? We're killing federal agents, arming biker gangs and protecting terrorists. What's wrong with that picture?"

"Barry, don't repeat that to anyone else. We've got the proverbial tiger by the tail. The question is, how do we let go without getting eaten by the tiger? Let's see what Schneider has for us."

Stanton called for Schneider.

"Anything to report?"

"Just this. In addition to his cell phone, he has a burner. Here's the number."

"Good work. Get the chopper ready."

After Schneider departed, Stanton turned back to Nolan.

"What do we do?"

"Monitor the burner and his every movement. His fate is in his hands. Sooner or later, every man must die."

CHAPTER TWENTY-TWO

The Gray Lady

New York City.

One side of Morgan had been fearful that he wouldn't return from the debriefing. He had survived, but would replay the meeting several times in his mind. He would take the suggestion of some time off, but stay close to home and run as much as possible.

It was already clear that his conscience couldn't bear the added weight of the death sentence for the staffer on top of the innocent victims in Nevada. He had spent over twenty-five years with the Company more than arm's length from any killing, but now bodies were piling up and he was complicit. It became clear to him that his continued silence was a crime in itself. He couldn't bring back the lives of the Nevada victims, but he might be able to save the life of the young staffer.

He read the *Wall Street Journal, The Washington Post,* and *The New York Times,* daily, finally deciding that "The Gray Lady" had a better history of disclosing explosive stories while protecting their sources. Within the *Times,* he chose the popular but controversial, investigative journalist, Howard Sternberg.

After a sleepless night, he summoned up the courage to make the call. He crossed his Rubicon.

"This is Mr. Sternberg's secretary. How may I help you?"

"I'd like to speak with Howard Sternberg."

"May I ask the purpose of your call?"

"Is he there?"

"Let me explain how this works. I'm the gatekeeper. What's the purpose of your call?"

"I have a story I think he'll be interested in."

"Okay, that's a start. What's the nature of the story?"

"I'd rather speak directly with him."

"And I'd like to be on a yacht with George Clooney."

"Fair enough. The story has to do with corruption at a very high level of government. A very, very high level."

"We're making progress. And, who may I ask are you?"

Morgan paused before replying.

"Are you there?"

"I'm a Government Agent."

"Which branch?"

"Due to the sensitive nature of my position, I'd like to divulge that to Mr. Sternberg."

"Do you have direct knowledge of this story or is any of it hearsay?"

"Very direct."

"Are you currently employed by this agency?"

"Yes."

"Did you sign an NDA when you joined the agency?"

"Yes."

"How long have you been employed there?"

"Over twenty-five years."

"And your name is?"

"Smith."

"Of course. Okay, Mr. Smith. Due to the sensitive nature of your employment, as you say, you're going to have to speak with our legal department before we can proceed. That conversation will be protected. Would you like me to transfer you?"

After a brief hesitation, Morgan replied, "Please."

After a few minutes of being repeatedly thanked for his patience, he was connected to the *Times'* legal department.

"Eli Waters, here. Who am I speaking with?"

"Is this conversation protected?"

"As much as legally possible. Now, what do you have for us?"

"I'm a career officer with a government agency."

"What agency?"

"The CIA."

"Your name?"

"If you don't mind, it's Smith for the moment."

"And where are you?"

"The D.C. area."

Waters paused. "Okay, Agent Smith, for the moment, tell me about the story."

"I know who leaked the DNC files to Wikileaks and I have reason to believe his life is in danger. I also have some other sensitive information about the Company. About the CIA."

Waters needed to process this information. If true, it was a potential bombshell. Another way to characterize it would be a potential gold mine.

"May I ask you to hold for a minute? I need to do something."

He made some quick notes and returned to the call. "Sorry about that. Now you have my complete attention. Can you provide documentation for your claims?"

"I can and I will, if I'm assured that my identity can be protected."

"Agent— er, Smith, if your identity is leaked it won't be by us. Here's what I suggest. First, can you give me a phone number where you can be contacted?"

"I can."

"Good. I gotta tell you. We get a lot of calls a week like this. My job is to separate the wheat from the chaff, and my gut reaction tells me that this merits follow up. The next step will be an in-person interview with someone from our legal department. Let me be perfectly clear. At that time there has to be full disclosure on your part. Plus, we'll have to see as much proof as you can provide. Are we clear?"

"Would the interview be in New York?"

"I don't think it's a good idea for you to come to New York. At least, not yet. Here's what we'll do. I'll have a member of our legal team contact you. They'll fly into Dulles and arrange to meet you near the airport. If you're good with that, give me the contact number."

Morgan gave him the number of a burner phone and went for a long run.

CHAPTER TWENTY-THREE

The New World Order

Langley, Virginia

Waters wasn't as burdened by ethical issues as Morgan. Waters was a graduate of Yale Law where he was a classmate of the Clintons. Another classmate was Aaron Nolan, Deputy Director of the CIA. He debated where the information would prove most valuable. The DNC or the CIA? Since the agent claimed to be currently employed by the CIA, he decided to open the bidding with them.

Nolan recognized the name and took the call immediately. "Eli the Eli. To what do I owe this pleasure?"

"Is this a secure line?"

"As secure as it gets."

"Good. I have a gift for you. A very valuable gift."

"A gift or a trade?"

Waters laughed. "Semantics. As it turns out, I can use your help on a separate matter, but one that's not pressing."

"I'm all ears."

"It so happens that a man called the *Times* today seeking to speak with Howard Sternberg. Sternberg's secretary ran interference and referred him to me to sort out some potential legal conflicts, as per our protocol."

"What type of conflicts?"

"Well, this man claimed to be a career employee of the CIA and he claimed to know the identity of the staffer who leaked the DNC files to Wikileaks. He further claimed to have knowledge of corruption at the highest level of a government agency."

"Nolan knew the identity of the agent, but asked anyway. Does this person have a name?"

"He said it was Smith for now."

"What was your response?"

"I discouraged him from coming to New York. I said that an attorney from our legal department would fly into Dulles and arrange to meet him somewhere near the airport. I cautioned him, however, that there would need to be full disclosure including evidence at that interview."

"How is he to make contact?"

"He gave me his phone number. Do you have a pen handy?"

Nolan recognized the number of Morgan's burner.

"What's your plan?"

"Me? I don't have one. You see, we're a little stretched right now and his story is a bit fantastic. I thought maybe you'd like to follow up. Seems like you're the logical party. I thought about calling another old classmate of ours, but the thought brought back some unpleasant memories."

"You did the right thing. Now, what's this issue that you need help with?"

"Like I said, it's not pressing. Next time I'm in Foggy Bottom let's have dinner—on you."

"It's a deal. This is new to me—the CIA and the press on the same team."

"Get used to it. It's called the 'New World Order'."

After Nolan hung up from Waters, he texted Stanton to come to his office. When he arrived he noticed Nolan deep in thought. "What's up?"

"Guess who just called me? Eli Waters."

"In college that generally meant he wanted to borrow money."

They laughed. "Actually, this time he delivered a gift. A very valuable gift. It seems that Morgan contacted the *Times* today to speak with

Howard Sternberg."

"That dumb son of a bitch. Sternberg is an egotistical prick."

Nolan motioned for him to calm down. "Fortune smiled on us today. Sternberg's secretary routed him to the *Times'* legal department due to potential conflicts. Eli Waters took the call."

"Waters must want something in return for him to give up Morgan and the story he could tell."

"He didn't get Morgan's name. Only that he was an employee of the CIA and the outline of the claims. Waters agreed to send an attorney to interview him in D.C."

"How do you know it was Morgan?"

"He gave Eli his cell number."

"The burner?"

"Yep."

"What's Eli want from you?"

"TBD."

"What's the play?"

"Give this to the Doctor. He'll need a business card for the *Times'* legal department. Create a file that connects Morgan to the investigation into Chinese opiod shipments. Poor schmo sampled the evidence and o.d.'ed. It's an epidemic. Afterwards, have his house scrubbed."

Breaking the string of total screw ups; the operation went like clockwork. A Chinese-American agent rented a room at the Westin near the airport using a fake I.D. and prepaid credit card. The "Doctor" called Morgan's cell and gave him the room number at the hotel.

If Morgan was nervous, it didn't show after the Doctor presented his *New York Times* business card stating that he was Morris Adamson, Senior Legal Advisor to the *Times*.

After some polite chit chat, the Doctor offered water to Morgan. He had a choice of Ice Mountain or La Croix sparkling water. Morgan chose the latter, as they knew he would.

What Morgan wasn't aware of, was the minute hole near the rim of the can made by a syringe which dispensed enough fentanyl to kill a horse. It was a perfect pairing. Fentanyl's slight metallic taste was masked by the carbonation of the sparkling water.

After a couple of sips, the opioid did its work. When asked how he felt, Morgan uttered his very last words, "Never better." Dr. Kervorkian would have been impressed.

The Doctor removed the tainted La Croix can and replace it with another that was half-full. He then removed any prints and departed, making note that there were much worse ways to die.

The body wouldn't be discovered until the following morning. By that time all computers, cell phones, records and files had been removed from Morgan's house and his house had been professionally scrubbed.

The police contacted the CIA after seeing Morgan's I.D.s. The Company quickly took possession of the body and the investigation. One of the young agents was tasked with delivering the sad news to the deputy director. He was impressed with how stoically the deputy director received the news. When the young agent departed, he almost collided with Barry Stanton who was entering with a sheaf of documents.

Nolan motioned for him to sit. "What's up?"

"We lost a good agent."

"I just got the news. I mean, officially."

"That's not what I meant. I had Morgan's computer delivered to me." He handed over the papers.

Nolan glanced at them. "What am I looking at?"

"When Robertson first contacted him, he refused to divulge his location. Whether by instinct or training, Morgan tried to figure it out on his own and he did some remarkable work."

"I'm all ears."

"Okay. He started with the assumption that Robertson was at his vacation home in the Outer Banks. Since his wife died several years ago, he was spending a lot of time there. His second good guess was that Robertson had flown there from Virginia in his Cessna, as per usual. He called the nearest airport to Robertson's vacation house and they confirmed that he had flown in a week earlier, but had left abruptly without filing a flight plan, which was unusual."

"He didn't want anyone to know where he was going and he could fly under the radar."

"Bingo. The next brilliant stroke was that he guesstimated from the APB, where the terrorist crossed the border into Arizona. Here's his map. He circled two small towns near the border." Stanton squinted at the map. "Four Corners and Apache Dunes. They each have a landing strip."

Nolan swiveled in his chair, deep in thought. "We know Robertson drove to Nevada. What we don't know is if he survived the explosion. If he did, it follows that he would return to his plane."

"Makes sense to me."

"Find out if the Cowboy is still in Texas. Regardless, have him pay a visit to those airports or landing strips. Brief him on his mission."

"I'm on it."

Nolan started to laugh.

"What's so funny?"

"It's not funny. It's actually sad. It would take a hundred FBI agents with computers to figure out what Morgan did on his own. We did, indeed, lose a good agent. You know what Waters calls it? The 'New World Order'."

"Do me a favor. If you find a way for us to get off this ship before it sinks let me know."

"And vice versa."

CHAPTER TWENTY-FOUR

The Reservation

Apache Dunes

The sheriff and Sandowski returned to Apache Dunes exhausted, both physically and mentally, from the events of the past forty-eight hours. They met for breakfast the following morning before heading to the Sheriff's office. When they arrived at the office, a large letter postmarked from L.A. was on the Sheriff's desk along with a note to call Michael, Chief Taza, asap.

The letter was from Carlos Garcia and was part greeting and part mea culpa. He wanted the sheriff to inform Dylan and Jake that he had heeded their advice and retired from his former pursuits, in favor of enrolling in USC, to take some courses for his new career in the film industry. He invited everyone to visit. He had plenty of room and left both his land line and cell numbers. Enclosed was a picture of Carlos astride his motorcycle outside one of the campus buildings. The sheriff smiled as he pinned the picture to his bulletin board.

That would be his last smile of the day, as the call to Michael proved problematic. The sheriff and Sandowski left immediately for the reservation. On the way, the sheriff tried to tell Max what he knew about the Chief, the tribe, and the reservation.

When they arrived, Michael was waiting for them outside the school where some of the tribe members were sweeping up broken glass from the shattered windows. The sheriff and Michael shared a man-hug before he introduced Max. He then took in the scene at the school. "Michael, what the hell happened?"

"That's what we need to talk about."

He pointed to a picnic table under a shade tree that was out of earshot. "Let's sit down. I've got a lot to tell you."

After they were seated, the sheriff motioned for Michael to continue.

"I don't know if you remember, but when you came to pay your respects after my father died, I was engaged in a conversation with a man."

"The guy with the Cadillac."

"The guy with the Cadillac. In the beginning, he portrayed himself as a real estate developer from L.A. who was interested in building some buildings on the reservation."

The sheriff furrowed his brow. "What type of buildings? For what?"

"That's the point. He was always evasive. Problem is, he doesn't seem to understand when I told him, as politely as possible, that we aren't interested. Not to mention there is plenty of cheap land available nearby."

The sheriff turned to Max. "What's your gut tell you?"

"Indian reservation in the desert near the Mexican border? It's not a Walmart. My guess is some type of drug facility—maybe meth. I'm no legal scholar, but I believe that reservations have some autonomy. Guy probably feels the feds can't touch him there. If he's right, it's clever."

"Well, like I said, he won't take no for an answer. He's even offered a small fortune and a piece of the business, whatever it is. Two days ago he, abandoned the carrot for the stick. He showed up with one of his associates. When I repeated my position, he motioned for his associate to open his trunk. Inside were body armor, AK-47 rifles and plenty of ammo. He said the next time he came, he was coming with forty East L.A. bikers all fully equipped with the armor and weapons. His associate gave a demonstration of the AK-47 on the school house windows."

Max said, "An offer you can't refuse."

The sheriff was pensive before replying. "Michael, you have to notify the State Police. I'll do it for you, if you'd like."

Michael stood and paced for a bit before turning to the Sheriff. "I can't do that."

"What do you mean you can't do that? I'll do it for you."

Michael was clearly conflicted about something. He sat back down and looked directly at the Sheriff. "Tom, I need to tell you something that needs to stay confidential. Can I speak freely?"

"Michael. Nothing you sat here will ever be repeated. I trust Max with my life."

"That's good enough for me. I need to tell you some history of the reservation that you don't know. The reservation was given to the tribe as part of a treaty negotiated by Cochise, who was Chief at that time. After Cochise's death, his son Taza, my namesake, became Chief and everything was fine until a deadly conflict between the tribe and some settlers. They had been selling whiskey to the tribe. The reservation was abolished and the Apaches were split up. Some were sent to Ft. Sill, Oklahoma and some to San Carlos reservation. Neither were welcoming places. Over the years a few escaped from their new homes and found their way back to the desert. Eventually that number grew to the present population."

The sheriff couldn't have been more surprised. "Wait. Hold on. Are you telling me that the reservation was never formally re-established?"

Michael nodded. "That's what I'm telling you. When I was much younger, a government lawyer came to visit my father. He had discovered the oversight, but was sympathetic to our plight. He promised my father that if anyone found out, it wouldn't be from him."

"So, your dilemma is if you disclosed that to the guy from L.A.—does he have a name?"

"Vito Rotelli."

"Sounds like a wise guy. If you told Rotelli, it would solve one problem, but could put the entire tribe in jeopardy."

"Precisely."

"When do you expect them to return?"

"Soon. Do you know how to contact Geronimo? I really need him."

"I'll try, but no promises."

"I understand. He came to me for help with the Garcias and I was there for him. It's now me who needs the help."

The sheriff and Max drove back to Apache Dunes in mostly silence. Both were lost in their thoughts.

Max broke the ice, "Unless there's something I'm missing—our friend is fucked."

The sheriff replied. "The numbers, the armor and the rifles are problems, but the desert belongs to the Apaches."

"Some problems. I think Manny and I better go back to Chicago where we can get some peace of mind."

"From what the Police Chief told me, you're not welcome anymore."

Max smiled. "There is that."

CHAPTER TWENTY-FIVE

The Scorpion

Arizona Desert

Rotelli left the sit-down with Sonny and Joey C., and had Paulie drive him directly to the Apache reservation. His goal was to secure the Chief's cooperation and return to Las Vegas for the big fight, where he could announce his success to both Sonny and Joey C. That success was going to come one way or another. He was prepared to offer the Chief one million dollars in cash. There was no way in hell that the Chief would ever see the money, but it was the thought that counts.

Failing that approach, he would give the Chief a taste of what was to follow if he continued to refuse Vito's proposition.

Unfortunately, for Vito, the Chief repeated his mantra that the Apaches weren't interested in the idea. At Vito's direction, Paulie delivered the "taste" by turning an AK-47 loose on the school house windows. It would have been an impressive display of force to most people, but Vito was a bit unnerved by how stoically it was received by the Chief.

It appeared that Vito was going to return to Vegas empty-handed and that was problematical. Why, was everything associated with this deal such a pain in the ass? His attorney advised against it, his muscle, the Mexican biker gang, didn't act like they understood the concept of minority partnership, and it had placed him in an adversarial position with Sonny Day.

The more pertinent question would be: Why a guy, who had the world on a string in L.A. and Hollywood, with more money than he could ever spend and all the trappings of success, would risk it all on what appeared to be an ill-fated venture? Regardless of the potential.

Occam's Razor posits that the simplest explanation is most likely the right one. When Sonny had pondered that very question, it was the auto-didactic Bobbie who came up with the simplest explanation.

"Sonny, did you ever read the fable, 'The Scorpion and the Frog'?"

"If it ain't part of the 'Daily Racing Form', I musta missed it. Is it new?"

Bobbie laughed. "It's more than 2500 years old. Proof that human nature hasn't changed and never will."

"Do I have to hear it?"

"Does someone need a little discipline?"

"I'm all ears."

Bobbie smiled. "Good. There was a Scorpion who wanted to cross a river and approached a Frog for help. The Frog initially refused, fearing the Scorpion would sting the Frog during the journey and both would drown. The Scorpion convinced the Frog that he understood and would never commit suicide, but halfway across the river, the Scorpion did sting him and both were doomed. The Frog cried out, 'Why did you sting me? Now we are both going to die.' The Scorpion replied, 'I can't help it. It's my nature.' So you see, it's Vito's nature and that will be his downfall."

The Desert

It was obvious to Paulie that his boss was in a funk after leaving the reservation. "Hey Boss, I got an idea to cheer you up. Let's stop for an early dinner at Villa Roma. It's just up the road a bit."

Vito looked at Paulie. "The only place within fifty miles of here is that cowboy joint and last time I was there, I thought we were going to have to shoot our way out."

"That's the place, but they ran the cowboys out and got this new Italian chef. They changed the name to Villa Roma. I stopped there last time you sent me to meet with the Indians. I'm tellin you—I had the best Veal Parmigiana I've ever had and the place was packed, but we'll be early."

Vito's stomach growled, answering for him. "We gotta stop and eat somewhere."

"Trust me on this one. The new chef is fantastic."

"Paulie, why would a great Italian chef want to work at someplace in the fucking desert? Does that make sense to you? You were just lucky that time."

"Maybe, but maybe we'll get lucky again. The Veal Parm was the special. You know what they say—always order the special."

When they pulled into the parking lot it was almost full even though they were early. Vito noted that late model automobiles had replaced the pickup trucks and motorcycles. Both signs were encouraging.

They both ordered the special, Veal Piccata al Limone. Vito said that would be a good test as that was his go-to dish at his favorite Italian restaurant in L.A.

It was either lightning striking twice, or the chef was incredibly talented. It was the subtle nuances of the seasoning that made the difference. When the owner came over to inquire about their dining experience, Vito was effusive with his praise. "I gotta tell you, I got talked into coming here. I was here when it was a cowboy saloon and it wasn't a pleasant experience. It wasn't that long ago. I can't get over the change."

The owner smiled. "It was God working in strange ways. The cowboys had run off my original chef and I was an inch within giving up when some guys from Vegas happened by and one of them knew how to cook. He stayed and is now my partner. He's the one with the golden touch in the kitchen."

Vito's ears perked up. "You said, some guys from Vegas. That must have been not too long ago. How many guys were there?"

The owner seemed a bit nervous at the question. "Uh— there were three as I recall."

"You know, I would really like to personally compliment the chef. Maybe even give him a tip. This is the best meal I've had in a long time."

"Well, I guess that would be okay. Follow me to the kitchen."

When they entered the kitchen, the chef was in conversation with his sous chef and didn't notice their entrance. Vito, however, knew immediately who the new chef was and couldn't believe his good fortune. Paulie could sense his change of mood, but was oblivious as to the reason.

Vito called out, "Petey", and Petey instinctively turned, but, just as quickly, realized his potential mistake in doing so. Vito sensed that and disarmed him with a huge smile and a one-sided man hug.

"Petey, it's me, Vito Rotelli. Your uncle Vinny and I are good friends. Sonny told me you were here, so I stopped by for dinner and the Veal Limone was to die for. I never knew you were a chef. Here, say hello to Paulie. Paulie, Petey's uncle and I go way back."

His machine gun like banter served to disarm not just Petey, but the owner as well. "I'll let you and Christopher—I mean Petey—get caught up. Thanks again for coming and come again."

"No, thank you. Like you said, 'God works in strange ways'."

Vito then turned back to Petey. "Listen, Petey, there's something I want to show you. It will only take a half hour, if that. Can you break away?"

Petey had been ambushed, but he was too naïve to understand.

"Gee ... I don't know. Will it only take a half hour?"

"Probably less. You gotta see this."

"Okay, but I can't be gone too long. Here, we can go out the back."

They drove about five miles and turned onto a rutted path that led into the desert. Vito could sense that Petey was starting to get nervous and laid on the charm. His demeanor changed after he told Paulie to pull over and they all exited the car. Vito surprised even Paulie, who remained clueless, when he pulled his gun and trained it on Petey.

Petey was sure he was going to die and started to cry.

"Petey, listen to me. No body's gonna harm you if you just do what I say. You understand me?"

Petey brushed away his tears and nodded.

"Paulie's gonna tape your hands and feet just so you can't get away. Where's your uncle?"

"Sonny said he's in Mexico."

"It's like this. Sonny and me have a little disagreement about something. I'm hoping that you can help me resolve it. If you can, you can return safely to your job and we'll pretend nothing ever happened. You understand?"

Petey nodded, although he didn't understand anything.

"Petey, trust me. I hate to have to do it, but it is what it is."

After they had Petey bound and back in the car, Vito pulled Paulie aside and explained everything to him.

"But, Boss. What do we do with him in Vegas?"

"We don't. Call a couple of your guys. Two of your best. They can't fuck this up. Having them meet us and take Petey to L.A. Now, Paulie, listen to me. You listening?"

"I'm listenin."

"I don't want a mark on him. They treat him with kid gloves. Give him anything he wants. Just don't let him out of their sight and don't let him make any calls. How hard is that?"

"Boss, this is good news, right?"

"Let's put it another way. Sonny Day just became my bitch."

CHAPTER TWENTY-SIX

The Cowboy

Apache Dunes

After two days ensconced in a suite in the Pompeii, with every whim catered to, Robertson and Sandoval wondered if they had died and gone to Heaven. However, when Sonny told them their suite was booked for the night of the big fight, they chose to head back to Apache Dunes rather than change rooms. After what they had been through, the luxurious respite had been more than therapeutic. An added dividend was that they got to dine with Sonny and Bobbie and that was world-class entertainment.

Everything taken into consideration, they were still glad to be heading "home." Sandoval, because he was, frankly, in over his head. Robertson, because he was officially a "ghost," with many people believing he was dead. He needed time to ponder what possible advantage that might provide in this game of deceit.

Sonny went the distance in arranging for one of the hotel's drivers to take them back to Apache Dunes.

They were dropped off at the Sheriff's office where the sheriff and Sandowski were waiting for a debriefing. After coffee was served, they were ready to be seated when Sandoval appeared fixated on Carlos Garcia's photograph on the bulletin board. All of a sudden, he twirled around spilling part of his coffee in the process. "Holy shit! Holy shit! That's it! That's it!"

The thought briefly crossed Sandowski's mind that the mercurial Sandoval had finally cracked. He moved a chair over for him.

"Sit down and catch your breath. What's it?"

Manny wasn't sitting. He was animated, pointing at the picture. "The girl! The girl!"

"What girl? Manny, you're starting to scare us. There's no girl in the picture. Sit down and take a deep breath."

He did sit down and did take a deep breath, but he took the picture down from the bulletin board before doing so. When he finally composed himself, he pointed to the picture.

"The girl in the desert. The one with the scarf, who delivered the truck to the bomber. She had a motorcycle in the back of the truck. That's how she left the desert."

Max handed him a glass of water. "Slow down. We know all that. What about her?"

There was something on the motorcycle. A decal that I didn't recognize, but there it is."

He pointed to the USC parking sticker with the Trojan helmet logo on Carlos's motorcycle.

The sheriff took the photo and peered at it. "Are you sure?"

"I'm positive. It's been bugging me. I remembered something distinctive, but couldn't visualize it. It's been driving me nuts, but there it is."

Robertson glanced at the photo. "It makes sense. USC is on the west coast and has a huge foreign enrollment, particularly from the Middle East. Each student has to have a photo I.D. Manny, could you identify her?"

"Trust me. I will never forget that face."

"She has to suspect the bomber is dead, but what concerns me is the compartmentalization of the instructions. That can only mean she was aware that the original plan might not succeed. If that's the case, there has to be a Plan B and she's the key to it."

Robertson looked at the Sheriff. "Cappy, I'm sorry. I didn't mean to disrupt your peaceful existence."

Sandowski almost fell out of his chair, he was laughing so hard. "The definition of peace around here is a nuclear war. Tom, why don't you bring them up to snuff?"

The sheriff recounted what they had learned from the Apache chief. For what seemed like a protracted period of time, the only sound from the office was the whir of the fan as they each digested the news.

Robertson broke the silence. "I have to follow this lead. It's what I came for. I hate to ask, but, Manny, you're the only one who can identify her. I can use your help."

The sheriff glanced at Sandowski, then back to Robertson.

"Buck, you and Manny go ahead. That is, if Manny's in."

Manny chimed in, "I'm in."

"Good. You guys go ahead. Max and I have a battle to plan. In that regard, I have to try to reach Geronimo."

With no time to waste on either end, man-hugs were given and Buck and Manny prepared to leave when the Sheriff's phone rang. He answered and appeared pensive as he motioned for everybody to stay put. After he ended the call he motioned for everybody to sit back down.

"That was Snoopy. There's a cowboy, he swears is a Fed, checking out your airplane."

"Tell him not to say anything."

The sheriff smiled. "Trust me. He does a great Sergeant Schultz impression."

"It's the Cowboy."

"What do you mean, the Cowboy?"

"He's a company contractor. One of the best. My money says he's the one who took out Stone and Weathers."

"So, they don't believe you died in the explosion?"

"They would have scoured the site. They found the plane. His mission is pretty clear."

The sheriff took the lead. "Okay, here's the plan. Homer will take you and Manny to Tucson. Charter a plane to L.A. Use Abdullah's cash. I'll call Carlos and take him up on his invitation. That way you're under the radar. Max and I will deal with the Cowboy."

Robertson looked concerned. "Cappy, keep him on ice if you can. I may need him, but he's dangerous. Don't let your guard down for a minute."

"I already have an idea."

CHAPTER TWENTY-SEVEN

Fight Night

Las Vegas

The owner of the Villa Roma was concerned when he learned that Christopher, née Petey, had left with his supposed friends, but that concern turned into panic when he failed to show up for work the next day. He found Sonny's card and called him.

It was the call Sonny half expected someday, but still dreaded. He blamed himself. Apache Dunes may have been in the middle of the desert, but it was still too close to Vegas. The owner recounted what happened to the best of his ability.

"Did you get either of the guy's names?"

"Yeah. The one who did most of the talking was Vito something. He called the other guy Paulie—I'm pretty sure. Listen, Sonny, I'm real sorry. I didn't know what to do."

"It's not your fault. I'll take care of it."

"Sonny, will Christopher be okay?"

"If I have anything to say about it, he will."

After he hung up, Sonny realized he was on the very real horns of a dilemma. It was transparent what Vito had done. He would use Petey to blackmail Sonny into approving the Arizona deal. Petey was leverage because Chicago had issued a contract on him and it was Sonny's responsibility to carry it out. If that wasn't bad enough, which it was, Rotelli would hold that over Sonny's head even after Sonny acquiesced to the deal. It would only be cancelled when one of them was dead.

Bobbie knew something terrible had happened. The only time she had seen Sonny like this was when he found out Vinny had been killed.

"Sonny, baby, you're all I have in the world. You have to confide in me. We're in this together."

Sonny did his best to explain the gravity of the situation. The final arbiter would be the Old Man in Chicago. The key word might be "old". Tradition was just another word to the "Young Turks", but to the "Mustaches" an order was an order. Period. Full stop.

They finally agreed that Sonny should try to explain the situation to Joey C., realizing the danger in doing so. The greater danger was that Vito would beat him to the punch. Joey C. and Sonny went back a long way, but that was then and now is now. If Joey knew that Sonny ignored an order and misled the boss about it, he was just as guilty. Sonny's choices boiled down to terrible and worse. He opted for the former and called Joey C.

"Joey, I need to talk to you. Can you come to my place?"

"Sonny, I'm about to get a massage and a blow job. Can it wait?"

"Joey, I really need to talk to you."

Joey could hear the despair in Sonny's voice. "Sonny, are you okay?"

"You'll have to decide."

"What the fuck does that mean? Okay, I'll come over."

When Joey arrived they went to the study where Sonny poured each of them a Scotch on the rocks.

They sipped their drinks in silence until Joey said, "Okay, let's have it. What the fuck is eating you?"

After Sonny related what happened to Petey, Joey was enraged. He jumped up and pointed his finger at Sonny.

"You motherfucker. You motherfucker. You lied to me. You told me that Petey and Vinny were dead."

"I didn't lie to you. I told you, you wouldn't hear from them again."

"What are you, a fucking lawyer now? Guess what, I'm hearin from them again."

"You're hearin from Petey. Vinny is dead."

"You whacked Vinny?"

"I didn't, but he's dead."

"So, how come the idiot nephew is alive?"

"Look, Joey, I know this is bad."

"You know this is bad? Bad doesn't do it fucking justice. You disobeyed an order from the boss. That's a death sentence. Now that I know, if I don't rat you out, I'm a dead man, too. Thanks, pal."

"Just hear me out. Please."

Sonny proceeded to tell Joey about how Petey wound up at the restaurant. He didn't explain that it was after Sonny decided not to whack him in the desert.

"Joey, Petey was never cut out for this life. If Rotelli hadn't stumbled into him, you wouldn't have heard from him again."

"If. If your aunt had balls she'd be your uncle. You swear that Vinny's dead? Dead, dead. Not dead, like I won't hear from him again."

"I swear."

"Look, Sonny. Vito's a prick. Make that a worthless prick, but if he goes to the Old Man, I can't save you."

"He did this just to get my approval for his deal. If I give him the okay, he's got no reason to rat me out."

"Maybe not now, but you ready to live the rest of your life with him holding this over you?"

"Joey, I just need some time to figure things out."

"What's to figure out?"

"He'll be here tonight. I just wanted you to hear it from me first."

"Look, Sonny, I'm pissed at you and I got a right to be, but you did the right thing to tell me. Let's see how he plays it. The smarmy fuck. What he doesn't know, and what I never told you, is that there are people in Chicago that wouldn't mind see him buy the farm. Capiche?"

"Capiche."

"I've got an idea, but I ain't sharin it. You owe me big time for this one."

Later that Day

Sonny knew this was a deadly game and that each move had consequences. He upgraded Rotelli's suite and told the desk to notify him when he arrived.

When he went to the lobby to greet him, he was surprised that Vito's wife had been replaced by his lieutenant, Paulie. The requisite embraces and kisses on the cheek were exchanged. To the un-informed bystander they would have appeared to be best of friends.

"Welcome to Vegas. I thought your wife was comin."

"Something came up at the last minute. You know how broads are. Sonny, you've met Paulie before."

"Yeah, how ya doin?"

"How ya doin?"

"Listen, Sonny, I need to talk to you about somethin. Why don't I let Paulie get us situated and you and I find someplace to talk?"

"We'll go up to my place. Bobbie is out somewhere."

No words were exchanged on the elevator. The tension was palpable. When they arrived at Sonny's suite, Sonny took Vito into his study. Vito noted that two empty rock glasses were on the bar.

"Looks like you had company."

"Bobbie and I had a drink before she went out. What'll you have?"

"Scotch works for me. With a splash."

Sonny served the drinks and sat down across from Vito. "So, Vito, whatta you want to talk about?"

Vito took a sip and measured him. Did he really have no clue? If not, he was a good actor. "Sonny, I want to help you out of a ... a situation."

Sonny feigned surprise. "What situation is that?"

"Sonny, remember when I asked you what happened with Vinny and his nephew?"

Sonny nodded. "I don't remember answering that question."

Vito laughed. "No you didn't, but that's what got me wondering. See, I knew there was a contract out on them."

"There was a contract out on Petey. Bellini called off the one on Vinny."

Vito milked the situation. "Okay, so there was a contract on Christopher. I mean Petey."

Try as he might, Sonny couldn't mask his unease at hearing the name Christopher, but neither did he reply.

"By the way, I heard Vinny is in Mexico."

"Vinny's dead."

Vito raised his eyebrows. "That doesn't help you. The guy who is supposed to be dead is alive and the one who's supposed to be alive is dead."

Sonny stared at him. "I think it's time to cut to the chase."

Vito smiled. "Trust me. I'm enjoyin this after you busted my balls on my deal with the Indians."

Both voices were raised. "How did I bust your balls? I told you I wanted to sleep on it and then Joey C. told you to get their approval. You said you would."

"Yeah, well the fucking Indians won't give me their approval. I even offered 'em a million bucks."

"You were gonna give 'em a million bucks?"

"Of course not. I said, I offered it."

"So, you've got Petey and you want me to approve your deal?"

"Sonny, you may be King of Vegas, whatever that means these days, but don't play fucking high and mighty with me. If I tell Joey C. that you didn't honor the contract on Petey, you're a fucking dead man. I'm trying to do you a favor and you're treating me like an asshole."

"Where's Petey now?"

"He's safe and sound and nobody's laid a hand on him. He's a great fucking cook, by the way."

"So, if I approve the deal, you let Petey go. Is that it?"

"That's a good start."

"Whatta ya mean, a good start?"

"Just what I said. You're no good to me dead. Capiche?"

If there had been a way for Sonny to whack him then and there, he would have done it, but what would happen to Petey? Vito was way too smug. He'd come to the same conclusion.

"I don't see I have much choice. How you wanna do this?"

"Let's have a drink with Joey C. before the fight and we can announce the good news together. If that goes well, I'll have Petey delivered to you tomorrow. You tell me where."

"I'll reserve a booth at Carlucci at six. I'll call Joey."

They both stood. Vito was like the cat who swallowed the canary.

"See, that wasn't so hard. Look at it this way. You're working for me now, but at least you're alive."

After Vito left, still smiling, Sonny called Joey C. and recapped his meeting with Vito.

"He said that to you? You're workin for him, now?"

"His words."

Joey was quiet for a moment. "Here's the problem. That's enough to get him whacked, but you'd have to go too."

"I can't do anything until I get Petey back."

"Okay. Here's what we do. We meet with him as planned and I don't know nothin. It'll be all nicey nice. Did you say he had a guy with him?"

"His name is Paulie. He's his guy."

"Get a couple of your best girls for them for after the fight. I'll see you at six."

CHAPTER TWENTY-EIGHT

Eight Miles High

Apache Dunes

The Cowboy emerged from the hangar and approached what served as the office. Snoopy had been observing his movements, but pretended to be occupied when the Cowboy entered after a brief rap on the screen door.

"Howdy."

Snoopy acted surprised. "Oh, sorry. I wasn't expecting anybody. I don't get a lot of visitors."

"Seems pretty quiet hereabouts. I guess I should have checked in first, but I'm looking for an airplane and noticed the hangar was open."

"It's a free country and I got nothing to hide. Did you find what you're looking for?"

"As a matter of fact, I did. The Cessna. And, by the way, what's the story with the bi-plane? That's a real beauty."

"It's a Sopwith Camel that I restored."

"You fly it?"

"Every chance I get."

"Forgive me. I didn't introduce myself, I'm Hank, but people call me Cowboy."

Snoopy stuck out his hand. "Mike, here. People call me Snoopy."

The Cowboy laughed. "Snoopy. I get it. You ever run into the Red Baron?"

"I look for him every day."

"That's good. Where'd you learn to fly?"

"Air Force. I was in Nam and then did a stint with Air America."

The Cowboy raised his eyebrows. "Air America, huh. Wasn't that a CIA front?"

"Not a well-kept secret."

"I suppose not. What'd you do after the war?"

"You're looking at it. I tried to get as far away from so called civilization as possible."

"Looks like you did a good job. Aren't you gonna ask why I'm interested in the Cessna?"

"I figure you'll tell me if you want me to know. I'm not what you call a curious sort. I try to mind my own business."

"I'm actually looking for the owner of the plane. It's a private business matter."

"Sorry, I can't help you there."

"You mean you don't know who the owner is?"

"That's what I mean. The plane was parked when I showed up several days ago. I put it in the hangar."

"Somebody just parked their plane and left without even leaving a message."

"In case you didn't notice, this isn't a real busy place. I built the strip so that I could fly. Private planes will fly in occasionally, but I find it's best not to meddle in other people's business."

"Yeah, I get your drift. Being so close to the border."

Just then, the sheriff and Sandowski pulled up in the Sheriff's truck with the bubble lights.

"That there's the sheriff. Maybe he can help you."

The Cowboy appeared a bit unnerved. "You call him?"

"Why would I call him? He's a friend. Stops by every now and then to shoot the breeze."

The sheriff and Max entered.

"Hey Tom, Max. Say hello to Cowboy here."

They all shook hands.

"Cowboy here is lookin for the owner of the Cessna."

The sheriff played dumb as per the plan. "What Cessna is that?"

"I guess I didn't mention it, but why would I? Anyway, I came in a few days ago and a Cessna was sitting there. I put it in the hangar."

The Cowboy's instincts told him something wasn't right, but it was clear that things were different here.

"Sheriff, you have any idea who the owner might be?"

The sheriff smiled. "The only one of my friends who owns a plane is Snoopy, here. Having said that, and why we dropped by, we got a call from the reservation. They said there's at least one Anglo, maybe two, out in the desert. A couple of the young Apaches stumbled across them, but didn't know what they were up to. Feared they might be lost. I thought maybe you could take Max up with you and do a little recon."

Max chimed in. "If I go with you, we'd need to leave now. I don't have much time."

The trap was set perfectly.

Snoopy grimaced. "That's a bit of a problem. I'm going to need some time to prep the plane and fuel up. I was just taking my time today."

The Cowboy jumped in to the web. "If you need someone to do a little recon, I got nothin to do. I'd be happy to help out. Who knows, maybe it's my friend."

The sheriff shrugged, "If you don't mind. Maybe it is your friend. Regardless, you're in for a treat. You staying around here?"

"Not really. Just in and out."

"Well, enjoy your stay. Snoopy, call me if you find anything."

"Roger that."

After the sheriff and Max departed, Snoopy brought the Sopwith out of the hangar and proceeded with his pre-flight checklist.

The Cowboy had started to relax, but noted that Snoopy hadn't fueled the plane. "I thought you said you had to fuel up?"

"I just remembered I topped off after I landed yesterday."

Snoopy handed him the two head sets and explained one was for tunes and one communication.

"I hope you have some Willy Nelson or Garth Brooks."

"I got just what we need. He showed him The Highwaymen CD and *Nashville Skyline*. We'll start with Dylan and Cash. Now, if you'd like to join me—I have to fuel up myself."

Snoopy opened the Thai stick box.

The Cowboy, like most people, had no idea what he was looking at.

"What's this?"

"You ever smoke weed?"

"Who hasn't?"

"Well, you see how thin these are? This is a real mild high. I highly,– no pun intended, recommend it."

"Are you okay to fly with this?"

"It's the only way I fly."

Seeing no harm in doing so, the Cowboy took one of the Thai sticks and became mellow real quick. By the time they were aloft, he was in the clouds. Higher than he'd ever been before and in an incredibly pleasant zone.

As per plan, Snoopy only stayed aloft long enough to make sure that the Cowboy was stoned out of his gourd. The Cowboy was tripping on Dylan's first foray into country music and seemed oblivious to time and everything else. He wasn't going to the "North Country Fair," he was already there.

Had he been sober, the alarm bells would have been going off when he saw the sheriff and Max waiting for the plane. However, Sober Street was in the rear view mirror and he was unable to process what was happening.

The sheriff and Max each had guns drawn as he almost fell out of the plane. The sheriff barked the orders. "Face down on the ground with your hands spread. You make one false move and you're a dead man."

Max frisked him and then knelt on his back and cuffed him. The Cowboy was totally at sea and wondered if this was all a bad dream. If it was a dream, it was a nightmare.

With Snoopy's help, they got him in the back seat of the sheriff's truck. Max sat in the back with him, aware that the Cowboy was a pro and not to be taken for granted.

The Cowboy made an effort to speak. "What's going on? What did I do?"

"What's going on is, this might be your last rodeo. It's not what you did, it's what you came here to do. You came here to kill a friend of mine. Until he returns, your ass belongs to me."

When he started to emerge from his fog, he realized he was in a jail cell. The cobwebs prevented him from recalling the name of this godforsaken town. This wasn't the first time he was in a dire situation, but this time felt different. He had walked into a well-orchestrated trap and his captors were serious, maybe deadly serious. He made a half-hearted overture.

"You can't keep me here. I work for the government. I'm on official business and they know where I am."

The sheriff looked at the Cowboy, then glanced at Max. "Max, would you like to respond?"

Max walked over to the cell. "Fuck you. And, from now on, you speak only when spoken to or we tape your fucking mouth shut."

"I'm entitled to one call."

"Max, get the tape."

CHAPTER TWENTY-NINE

Our Thing

Las Vegas

All of the actors were well rehearsed for what was, ostensibly, a casual get-together for cocktails prior to the big fight. Vito was convinced that he had an inherent edge in the acting department by virtue of his association with the industry, which had no connection to the art. His goal was to make it clear to Joey C., and by extension Chicago, that he was now the dominant player in the West and that included Las Vegas. Sonny Day would have to eat humble pie and like it. He was now Vito's bitch. That is, unless he wanted Chicago to find out that he had disobeyed a direct order.

Joey C. simply had to pretend that he was totally oblivious and appear to be pleased that Sonny had blessed Vito's deal, avoiding potential conflict. Joey was pissed that Sonny put himself in this position. Joey knew he, too, could easily get ensnared in that web. He wouldn't mind seeing Sonny do a little penance by having to take shit from Vito. He deserved it. But, Joey had to consider the bigger picture with an eye to self-preservation. Sonny had been right to wonder what possessed Vito to risk a life others could only dream about in exchange for what? More power? It was the proverbial "Spare the rod and spoil the child" conundrum. If he was allowed to effectively take over Vegas, would he be content? Or, did he have even bigger aspirations knowing that, although he survived the failed assassination attempt, the Old Man was long in the tooth?

Joey C. was putting all of his chips on the fact that Vito was never going to be content, thus needed to be stopped. The question was, how? An idea was brewing in his mind. He hoped that Vito would bring Paulie with him tonight. Normally that would be a breach of protocol, as Paulie wasn't a Capo. However, if Joey was right about Vito's true aspirations, he might try to deliver a message by acting as if he was the final arbiter of protocol, snubbing both Sonny and Joey C. in the process.

Sonny had to prepare himself for something he had never done in his life, knowingly eat shit and act like it was caviar. To do so in front of Joey C. made it doubly problematic. Pussies don't last long in the mob. In that regard, he had to hope that he had built enough good will over the years to let this one slide. It all came down to one question. Was Sonny's ego worth Petey's life? That gave him pause. Something must be happening to him. Before meeting Bobbie he would take the ego and lay the points. Go figure.

Carlucci

Joey C. and Sonny each arrived shortly before six. Joey bet Sonny a c-note that Vito would be at least ten minutes late—on purpose. He arrived at quarter past six with Paulie in tow.

It was a bit awkward as the requisite hugs and kisses were exchanged between Vito, Joey, and Sonny as Paulie stood by, not entitled to the same show of respect.

"Joey, Sonny, you've met Paulie before. He's going to the fight with me so I invited him to join us. I mean, since this is a happy occasion, right?"

Joey tried to be stoic, but seethed inside. Vito invited Paulie to join them? Like this was Vito's show. His suspicions were confirmed. He'd let Vito have his day, but he swore on his mother's soul that this wasn't going to become a habit.

Though he wasn't party to Joey's innermost thoughts, Sonny knew that Vito had pushed the envelope way too far and they had yet to sit down.

Both nodded to Paulie, but neither said anything. That threw Vito off a bit, but he quickly recovered as they took their seats.

"Joey, I don't know if Sonny told you, but he's on board with my play in Arizona. If I need him for anything, I'll let him know."

Joey feigned surprise and looked at Sonny, who simply nodded.

"Well, if Sonny's on board, that's good enough for me."

Sonny started to speak, but Vito interrupted him.

"He's on board."

"As long as you two work things out."

Once again Vito cut Sonny off before he could reply. "We'll be fine. Right, Sonny?"

Sonny wasn't going to give Vito a hat trick of interruptions. He simply gestured with his hands.

After a very pregnant pause, Vito stood up and Paulie followed. "I guess we're finished for now. We're gonna hit the tables a bit and then get our seats at the fight."

Joey looked at Sonny. "Sonny, did you arrange for the ladies after the fight?"

Sonny replied, "Two of our best. A blonde and a redhead. Here are their room numbers."

Vito looked surprised and pleased. He took the number for the blonde as Joey took note. As he started to leave, he turned to Sonny. "Oh, Sonny, I'll have that package delivered tomorrow."

After they departed, Joey and Sonny were silent for a bit as they pretended to savor their drinks.

Joey spoke first, "You know what has to be done, right?"

Sonny nodded. "I know."

"And you're not gonna fuck it up this time, right?"

"Did I fuck it up with Johnny Bellini? I didn't fuck up with Petey. I told you what happened."

"Could've fooled me."

"I have to get Petey back first."

"Is that the package?"

Sonny nodded.

"Okay, here's what I'm gonna do. I'm gonna have a talk with Paulie. Try to explain about Our Thing. You've got a week. I can't help you after that."

"Thanks, Joey. I owe you."

"Tell me something I don't know. Is everything set up with the dealer?"

"I'm headed there right now."

Later that Evening

The redhead's name was Bridget. She was majoring in business at UNLV, but already making more money than most young Ivy League MBAs. Sonny had instructed her to text Joey when Paulie arrived after the fight. She was to make drinks and engage in small talk until Joey showed up.

After receiving the text, Joey took the elevator to her room and knocked gently on the door. Paulie appeared stunned when Joey entered the room. Joey told Bridget to pour him a Scotch and disappear for thirty minutes. He slipped her a c-note as she departed.

No sooner had the door closed than a visibly nervous Paulie blurted out, "Joey, if this has anything to do with the guy—the cook, I didn't know nothin about it."

Joey raised his free hand. "I didn't ask and I don't wanna know. I'm just here to talk to you. So, relax."

They both sat down and Joey savored his drink for a moment before continuing. "You came to Chicago with Vito, right?"

Paulie nodded.

"You know why Vito came to Chicago?"

Paulie, still nervous, replied, "He was askin permission for his deal with the Indians."

"You're exactly right. He had to ask permission because anything he does outside of L.A. needs approval. Paulie, do you know who I am?"

"You're— you work for the boss in Chicago."

"Let me put it another way. When I speak, I speak for the boss. You understand?"

Paulie nodded again.

Joey stood up and motioned for Paulie to follow him out to the balcony where they had an incredible view of The Strip.

"Paulie, you may be too young to remember, but it wasn't that long ago that we didn't just run this town, we owned it. Lock, stock and barrel."

Joey sighed. "And you know what happened? One guy, one fuckin guy—a friend of mine—brought so much heat down that we lost almost everything. It affected everybody. Las Vegas, Kansas City, Milwaukee, Cleveland, and Chicago. My point is, one bad move on just one guy's part can affect a lot of people and that includes you. Maybe you most of all."

Joey turned and walked back inside and topped off his drink.

"Paulie, apparently Sonny has given this Arizona deal his blessing, but I gotta tell you—it makes the boss nervous and when he's nervous, we all should be. Capiche?"

"Joey, are you askin me to spy on Vito?"

"Not at all. If he's gonna go ahead with this, I hope he succeeds, but, since this can affect us all, I need to know what's goin on. Especially if there's any problems. And, Paulie, if something happens to Vito, we're gonna need you in L.A."

At that, Paulie to perked up. Just the thought of him running things in L.A. made his head swim.

"Joey, just tell me what you want me to do."

"It's simple. Here's my card. Anything happens, you call this number. But, Paulie, this is just between you and me, Capiche?"

"Capiche. Yeah, Capiche."

Joey stood and smiled. "When you're through with Bridget, which should be about ninety seconds, take her down to play a little blackjack. Ask for the dealer called Wall Street. Tell him that Sonny sent you. He's got five thousand in chips for you. After you win ten thousand, you're on your own. Oh, and take good care of Bridget."

Paulie was beaming. "Thanks, Joey. You can count on me."

Sonny hesitated as Bridget knocked gently on the door.

"We'll see."

CHAPTER THIRTY

The Gathering Clouds

Apache Dunes

The sheriff was able to reach Dylan and, as expected, he responded immediately to Chief Michael Taza's plea for help. He would fly non-stop from Madrid to Chicago and charter a plane to Apache Dunes. After the settlement of the missing cartel funds, money was no object. Jake had also expressed a desire to come, but they both understood that someone needed to stay with Dusty and Ashley.

The sheriff and Max knew it was problematic to keep the Cowboy at the jail for any length of time, but the sheriff had an idea what Dylan's suggestion would be in that regard—the cave.

Los Angeles

Holmby Hills, on the west side of L.A. is one of its most affluent areas. At times it was the home of a veritable Who's Who of Hollywood including, Bogie and Bacall; Walt Disney; Barbara Stanwyck; Robert Taylor; Bugsy Siegel; Jack Benny; Gary Cooper; Lloyd Bridges; Bing Crosby; Jean Harlow; Alan Ladd; Aaron Spelling; Claudette Colbert; Barbra Streisand; Frank Sinatra, and the iconic Playboy Mansion—to name just a few. The Garcia mansion was one of the largest and most valuable properties in Holmby Hills.

Carlos had been in residence for weeks and still hadn't visited all of the rooms. He was flush with cash from his nine million share of the cartel funds, plus millions more from the Garcia stash in Mexico, but he had yet to understand how much money his father had salted away before his death in the suspicious airplane crash. He never asked his mother and she never informed him. He got an inkling when he probed the family's accountant about a possible investment in a motion picture. When he said he might need to tap into the family funds for the investment, the accountant inquired how much that might require. When Carlos dangled the figure of ten million, the accountant simply asked if that would be check or cash.

He was doubly pleased when the sheriff accepted the offer of his hospitality on behalf of Buck Robertson and Manny Sandoval. In addition to having company, he would be helping the sheriff, and on the right side of the law for a change.

They say that opposites attract and, although they were both young and Hispanic, Carlos' and Manny's upbringings couldn't have been more different. Carlos had taken for granted the wealth and love his father had showered on him, in favor of the allure of the wild side of the street. Manny, in contrast, had grown up fatherless and the wild side of the street was the only side he knew until Davey, and eventually Max, came into his life.

Regardless, each found in the other the companionship and fraternity that both had lacked and yearned for. In contemporary parlance, it was a bromance from Jump Street.

As if things couldn't get even better, CAA, covetous of the fortune that Carlos now controlled, sent over a bevy of aspiring starlets to keep them company. When they found out that Buck wasn't interested in the young blood, a fiftyish former child star showed up to keep him company in the vast swimming pool.

Manny had to laugh to himself at how his uncharted journey with Max had turned out. After leaving Chicago under duress, after a seeming death-wish type mission, he had been ensconced in Jake's incredible home in Apache Dunes, enjoyed a comped suite overlooking the Vegas

Strip and, now, was living in Shangri-La. When he had admired Carlos' Harley Softail, Carlos picked up the phone and ordered one for Manny to be delivered the next day. If this was a dream, he didn't want it to end.

They were there on business, however, and even Carlos was looking forward to their quest.

Across town, the "Sheikh" was totally unaware that she had become the prey rather than the predator. In truth, she had never really gotten over her brief interlude with Manny at the Oasis and might have relished the sport. However, she was consumed with a different problem—her mission. It was obvious that the bomber was either dead or co-opted. Her immediate disdain for his misogynistic attitude, not something uncommon in the Kingdom, clouded her judgment and she wrote his disappearance off to incompetence. In doing so, she never considered that she was now on the defensive.

The question was, how had this development influenced her collaborators in the CIA? She didn't believe the explosion a few miles away from the safe-house was a coincidence, coming on the very night that the bomber was to arrive. It was time for her to make contact with her government counterpart, Mr. Hayes. He was the one who had recruited her and conceived of the mission. She retrieved his card which read Asian-American Logistics, Inc. with an office in Newport Beach. She was mildly concerned when she was informed that the number she dialed was not in service at this time. It had been almost a year since they had met at his office. Maybe the number had been changed. She would take a ride over to Newport Beach.

What she found, or rather, didn't find, was troubling. Not only was the office no longer at that location, there was no trace of either the company or Mr. Hayes. In fact, the current occupant claimed that they had been there for five years and was certain that the young lady had the wrong address. One thing was certain. It wasn't the wrong address.

Her anger had nothing to do with being used. She understood that from the beginning. Rather, it appeared that her co-conspirators had abandoned the mission. That was something she wasn't prepared to do. The silver lining in that cloud was that there was no one now to hinder or muck up her plans. She actually got a rush of adrenaline. This was now her mission, her fate and she had no intention of failing. She laughed to herself. She had the perfect foil, Saleh. He was totally egocentric, while fashioning himself a true believer and a jihadist. The chink in that armor was how his eyes betrayed his virtue when they lingered on her. It was the classic question: Who are you going to believe, me or your lying eyes?

That thought only served to elicit another. It was easy to understand why she detested misogynistic men. It seemed ingrained in her DNA to resent so-called alpha males and their supreme confidence. What was it that kept reminding her of the man in the desert? Her eyes could see that he was confident and secure in his being. She even asked him if he was a cop, but her eyes also detected a vulnerability that confused her. It was something that she had never experienced with a male. Ah well, that would remain a mystery as she would never return to the desert.

Las Vegas

When Sonny returned home, he carried the weight of the world on his shoulders. Bobbie had waited up for him.

"Why aren't you in bed?" he said. "It's late."

"I was waiting for you and the a/c went out in my bedroom. We'll have to share a bed tonight."

"I'll go check it out."

Bobbie stood in his way. "You'll do nothing of the sort. It's too late. We'll get it checked tomorrow. Go sit down and I'll make us a night cap."

"I could use the whole bottle."

"That bad, huh?"

"It's not good. Wait—there is good news. Vito is going to deliver Petey tomorrow."

"You mean Christopher."

"Petey, Christopher, whatever. I shoulda whacked him in the desert. None of this would've happened."

Bobbie helped him off with his sport jacket and gave him his drink.

"By the way, I'm sorry about the fight. There'll be another one."

Bobbie shrugged. "Sonny, I was just going for you. I've been fighting all my life. I don't need to see another one."

Sonny said, "You know I don't deserve you."

"I know."

"You wasn't supposed to say that."

"You want me to lie to you?"

"No, well maybe—yeah, sometimes."

They both laughed.

"So what's the plan?"

"Joey's gonna talk to Vito's guy Paulie. Try to find out what Vito's up to. Joey said I have a week to get rid of Vito."

"Get rid of—like whack him?"

"Unless I can talk him into committing suicide. You see, now I got Joey involved and Vito will hold this over our heads for the rest of our lives."

"How about I do it for you?"

Sonny jumped up. "You ain't gonna take the Asian broad's place and you damn well ain't gonna whack anybody. I told you I was gonna take care of you."

"But why? I can help you."

"Just because."

"Just because why?"

"You're given me a fuckin headache. Just because. Period."

"Why can't you say it?"

"Say what?"

"You know what. Why can't you say I love you? Is that against your religion or something?"

Sonny sat back down and looked like he was ready for a root canal.

"You know how I feel about you."

"Will you just fucking say it? You can mumble it if you want."

"Bobbie, you know I don't deserve you."

"I think we already agreed to that."

After a long pause, Sonny mumbled, "Okay … I … I love you. You happy?"

"Rock Hudson was more convincing and he was gay, but I'll take it."

"Bobbie, look at me. If I don't get rid of Vito, I got no place to hide. Even if we ran, I got some cash stashed away, but it won't last us forever."

"It will if forever is a week."

"Bobbie, this is no time for jokes."

"Sonny, I have an idea about how to get some, what do you call it? Fuck you money."

"What, was you watchin, *Ocean's Eleven?*"

"Nothing like that. Hear me out."

"I think we both need another drink."

After topping off their drinks, Bobbie said, "I was just thinking the other night. Kelsey always said her husband had a fortune stashed off shore, but he never told her where."

"So you're thinkin about holding a séance? Get him to tell us?"

"Sonny, I'm deadly serious. Listen to me. He had to have kept the records somewhere."

Sonny jumped up and spilled some of his drink in the process. "The safe room. The fucking safe room."

Bobbie got up, too. "Has to be, and we're the only two people who know about it. The Feds couldn't even find it when they were looking for the guns."

"We gotta be talkin about millions, but how can we be sure we'll find it? What if it's on one of the computers in some kinda code?"

"Number one, Del wasn't that bright, but, if need be, we can hire a teenager hacker to break in into his computer. Keep in mind, he was confident that no one other than himself and Kelsey even knew about the room, and he wasn't worried about Kelsey."

"A near fatal mistake."

"Everyone makes them. Vito will too."

CHAPTER THIRTY-ONE

The Missing Link

Los Angeles

Since Manny was the only one who could identify the mysterious "Sheikh," and because Carlos was registered as a student at USC, they left Buck behind and rode their motorcycles over to the campus. Buck did help them narrow down their search. To create a profile, he started with the presumption that she was a practicing Muslim by virtue of the scarf. Combined with the fact that she appeared to have ample funding and that fifteen of the nineteen 911 perpetrators were Saudis, pointed the arrow toward the Kingdom. That she could not just drive, but ride a motorcycle—and in the desert—seemed to be anomalies, but the hypocrisy of the Saudis was well known to anyone who ever flew first class from Riyadh to London. After takeoff, the burkas quickly gave way to designer clothes and top-drawer Scotch replaced the soft drinks.

Buck was able to learn from the Office of International Services at USC that of the approximately 8,000 foreign students, only approximately 150 were from Saudi Arabia. He was unable to learn how many of those students were female, but it was a good bet the majority would be male.

When they arrived on campus, Carlos and Manny started their quest at the Office of International Services since they had been somewhat helpful so far. Aware the much of the staff would be students who were working for a reason, Carlos brought a wad of "Benjamins" with him to, hopefully, grease the skids so to speak. As fate would have it, the person they were directed to was not a student, rather a clone of Nurse Ratched and deeply suspicious of their motives.

However, while Carlos fumbled at describing the young lady's appearance, and the fact that she rode a motorcycle, Manny noticed that a young man, who appeared to be of Indian nationality, had moved to within earshot and was doing a terrible job of pretending not to eavesdrop on the conversation. Manny nudged Carlos who picked up on it right away. He made eye contact with the young man as they departed the office after conceding defeat to Nurse Ratched. Lifelock couldn't have protected identities any better.

Their instincts bore fruit when the young man approached them outside. "I couldn't help but overhear your conversation. Are you really in the movie business?"

Carlos replied, "I'm an investor who is enrolled in the film program."

Carlos could swear that the young man's eyes got big when he heard the word investor.

"My name is Amit. I may know who you are looking for."

Carlos pulled the wad out of his pocket and peeled off a c-note. "Amit, I'm Carlos and this is Manny. We're kinda pressed for time. I'll help you (dangling the bill) if you can help us."

Amit snatched the bill. "If it's who I think it is, every guy on campus dreams about her. The tip-off was when you said she wore a scarf and rode a motorcycle."

Carlos gestured for him to continue, but realized it was a mistake to have displayed the wad.

"I— I'm having trouble remembering her name (said staring intently at the cash)."

Carlos peeled off one more bill and this time did dangle it. "Tell me if you can recall it."

Amit reached for the bill, but Carlos held fast until Amit spoke. "Ah yes, it's just now coming to me. Her name is Fatima."

"What's her last name?"

Amit frowned and then looked at his watch. "Good sir, that I don't know, but I do know where she might be found."

Manny shrugged as Carlos sighed while handing over the third hundred dollar bill.

Amit was now animated. "You see, I had a class with her last term. After the class she would go to a group study room on the second floor of the library. The same one every day."

"I know where the library is. Which study room?"

Amit smiled as he nodded his head sideways in Indian fashion.

Carlos just shook his head. "Okay, here's the deal. You take us there and you get one more. Period. You're starting to piss me off."

Amit nodded again and smiled. "Follow me good sirs."

USC Leavey Library

The Leavey Library is on the northeast corner of the USC campus. Upon arrival they went to the second floor study room where Amit thought she might be found. There were several students there, but not Fatima. Amit looked at his watch. "We must wait about fifteen minutes as classes are just letting out."

Carlos sat and motioned for Manny to join him. He turned to Amit. "We'll wait. In the meantime go find a book to read. Look under E for extortion."

Amit just smiled as he drifted out to the hallway.

It was only shortly thereafter that Amit rushed back in the room and was animated. "She is coming. I told you she would be here."

Carlos and Manny were fixated on the doorway when she entered with a backpack and plastic water bottle. She took a quick glance around the room before deciding where to sit and noticed the giddy Indian, who seemed familiar, and his two friends. It was then she did a double take and made eye contact with Manny.

Manny's knees got weak as he grasped for his chair before diverting his gaze. He had been dreaming of this moment and, now that it was here, he felt dizzy.

Fatima was no less confused about her feelings and she, too, had to sit down.

Resting her head in her hand, she peered through her fingers and saw the other man appear to give the young Indian some money. He then spoke with his friend and both he and the Indian departed.

Manny reached for a book that someone had left on the table and pretended to be interested in it. Her heart was beating a mile a minute.

Fatima tried to collect her wits. She was certain it was the young man from the desert. The one who had been haunting her dreams inexplicably. She tried to make sense of it and therein was the rub. His sudden appearance on the heels of the disappearance of the bomber couldn't be a coincidence. How could the bomber have led him to her? Try as she may, she couldn't make that connection. But, he was real and he was here, and there had to be a connection.

An even more relevant question came to mind. If he had been searching for her, and found her, why hadn't he approached or apprehended her? And, why wasn't she trying to escape?

The tension was palpable as both tried to regain control of their emotions. She caved first and walked over to him.

When she spoke aloud one of the other students gave a reproaching, Shh. He motioned for them to go out into the hallway.

Even alone in the hallway, there was a pregnant pause before either of them spoke. She said, "Haven't we met before?"

He smiled, "I could never have forgotten your face."

"In the desert. In Arizona."

He shook his head. "My name is Manny. What's yours?"

"Fatima."

"Are you a student?"

"No, a friend of mine is. I'm staying with him."

"Does he live on campus?"

"No. He has a home in Holmby Hills."

She raised her eyebrows. "He must be very wealthy. What does he do?"

"He's in the movie business. He's an investor."

Perhaps this was just a coincidence. Regardless, she felt a definite attraction to him.

"Well, maybe we'll see each other again."

As she turned to walk away, Manny replied, "I'd like that."

She stopped in her tracks and turned to face him. "That's what you said the first time."

"Was it?"

"It is you. What do you want with me? Am I under arrest or something?"

Manny feigned a look of surprise. "Have you done something wrong?"

"Why are you here?"

"I'm not sure I understand myself."

Fatima had completely lost her edge, if she ever had one. "I— I don't understand."

Manny smiled. "Then that makes two of us. Hey, I have a great idea. My friend's chef is preparing a special feast tonight. Why don't you come with me? When you want to leave I'll send you home in his limo."

Her mind was bombarding her with reasons to say no, but, and to her surprise, her heart spoke louder.

"We rode over on our motorcycles. Mine's brand new. Are you cool with that?"

"I have a motorcycle, myself. Or, did you forget?"

It dawned on her. The motorcycle. The parking sticker. She had been careless, but if that had been careless, what's this? It's exhilarating— that's what it is. Just then, she realized she had agreed to meet Saleh tonight. The thought of humiliating him turned her on even more. She wouldn't even call.

One of two things was happening. Either she was actually attracted to this man, or he was a more competent foe than the previous men in her life, but still a foe. She wanted to believe the latter and chose to proceed accordingly.

"As long as I may leave when I want, I'm game."

CHAPTER THIRTY-TWO

An Unexpected Gift

Las Vegas

Sonny and Bobbie were both home when Christopher, née Petey, was delivered unharmed as promised. He expected Sonny to be angry at him for the problems he created, but both Sonny and Bobbie appeared to be relieved that he was safe.

"Sonny, I'm sorry. You shoulda killed me that day in the desert."

"Don't remind me. That option remains."

"It's just— it's just that I'm not smart like you. Uncle Vinny said I musta fallen on my head as a baby. I dunno, maybe I did."

Sonny held his hands out. "Calm down and tell us what happened."

"It— it just happened. I was in the kitchen with my back turned talking to my sous chef when the owner brought them into the kitchen. He said they wanted to compliment me. Then Vito, he says 'Petey' and I turned around without thinking. He knew I was nervous then, so he said he was a good friend of Uncle Vinny and he said that you told him I was there. I didn't have a reason to doubt him."

"I understand."

"But, Sonny, you told me never to answer to Petey and I forgot. You said I was stupid and I guess you were right."

Bobbie frowned at Sonny.

"Then what happened?"

"They drove me out to the desert. Vito said they wanted to show me something. When we got there, he pulled out a gun and I thought he was gonna kill me. I was really scared. But, he said they wouldn't harm me, if you and Vito took care of some problem you had."

Sonny motioned for Bobbie to get Petey a glass of water.

"Sonny, I guess I really screwed up this time."

"It's not good, Petey."

Petey took a long drink of water and then looked up sheepishly. "May I ask a favor?"

Sonny and Bobbie appeared puzzled. Sonny nodded.

"I really like the name Christopher. Petey even sounds stupid."

Bobbie attempted to console him. "Petey— I mean Christopher, we've all done some dumb things at times. It doesn't mean were stupid."

"Yeah, well. I only know about two things, cooking and computers."

Sonny was having a glass of water, as well, and almost spilled it when Christopher mentioned computers. Bobbie's eyes lit up as well.

Sonny patted his shirt and sat forward. "Christopher, you said computers."

"I said cooking and computers. That's all I know."

Bobbie was engaged. "What do you know about computers?"

"What do you want to know?"

Sonny interjected, "Slow down. Where did you learn about computers?"

"When we first came here, after Uncle Vinny sent for us, I didn't speak English. The school put me in a class they called special, but it was really for dumb kids, like me. There was only one other student. His name was Alex and he was artistic or something."

"Artistic? You mean autistic. Don't you?"

"That's it, autistic. Anyway, we became friends because we only had each other and even the teachers left us alone. But Alex wasn't stupid, he was really, really smart. He was constantly playing with computers and he knew things the teachers didn't even know. If someone was mean to either one of us, he would hack into their computers and create all kinds of problems for them and they never knew who did it."

Bobbie and Sonny looked at each other before Bobbie turned back to Christopher. "And he taught you about computers?"

"I'm not as good as he is, but no one is."

"Do you know how to get into someone else's computer without knowing their password?"

"It's pretty simple. It just takes trial and error. See, the server tells you to make passwords as difficult as possible, but, in reality, most people will create a password that they will remember. That's usually names and numbers that are important to them. If you know something about the user, you can generally figure it out."

"What happened to Alex?"

"We talk from time to time. He has a huge ranch in Montana that he bought with bitcoins he got from hacking computers. It's called ransomware. He doesn't like people—except for me."

No one spoke for a bit.

Sonny said, "We have a computer in Apache Dunes that we need to get into. The owner is dead. If you can help us, maybe everything will turn out all right."

"Sonny, am I supposed to go back to the desert?"

"Not yet, if ever. In the meantime, I'll get you a room here. Hey, maybe you can help in the kitchen at Carlucci?"

"That would be great. Sonny, I'm really sorry for all the trouble I've created."

"It ain't over 'til it's over."

Sonny had a separate suite at Pompeii reserved for his guests. The same suite that Buck and Manny had been lodged in. He took Christopher there to get him situated after which he would swing by Carlucci and inquire about Christopher working in the kitchen.

When he exited the elevator in the lobby he was somewhat surprised to see Vito's lieutenant, Paulie, seated off to the side as if he was waiting for someone, he was, for Sonny. Sonny was aware that Paulie had delivered Christopher, but was puzzled as to why he had lingered afterwards.

"Sonny, any chance that we can talk somewhere?"

Still on guard, Sonny motioned toward the lobby entrance to Carlucci. "I was gonna stop by Carlucci. I'll buy you a drink."

There was a special booth in the bar area reserved for Sonny and VIPs. Sonny called it his office. They sat down and ordered drinks. Sonny told the waiter that he wanted a word with the manager, Zak, before he left.

After the drinks were served, Sonny motioned to Paulie. "You have the floor."

Paulie couldn't hide the fact that he was nervous. "Sonny, first of all, I didn't have nothing to do with Petey. I never even heard of him before that night. And, and I made sure that nobody laid a hand on him."

Sonny just nodded. "So, what can I do for you?"

"It's actually Joey C. that I was tryin to get in touch with, but I keep callin and nobody answers."

"That's because it's his anniversary and his wife wanted to go on a Mediterranean cruise. He won't be back 'til next week."

"I figured something like that, so I thought I better tell you instead."

"Tell me what?"

Paulie fidgeted. "Sonny, what I'm about to tell you ain't ratting on Vito. I ain't no rat."

Sonny motioned for him to continue.

"I don't know if you know that Joey C. came to my room after the fight."

Sonny gave no indication either way.

"Well ... we had a long chat. Actually, he talked and I listened. He talked about Our Thing and about how he was concerned about Vito's Arizona plans because, if something goes wrong it can affect other people who weren't even involved—particularly Las Vegas."

Sonny appeared wistful as he savored his drink before replying. "Paulie, you're being a stand-up guy by comin forward. We used to run this town. I mean everything. You needed to take a shit—you used our toilet paper. Now we have crumbs and you know why? Because one fucking guy—a guy I knew when he was shining shoes as a kid on Grand Avenue in Chicago, he had it all and he wasn't satisfied. He ended up ruinin it for everybody. And I mean everybody. I got nothing against Vito, I mean other than his bullshit move with Petey— with Christopher, but he's got the world by the balls in L.A. What the fuck is he messin with a bunch of Indians in Arizona for?"

"Sonny, I hear ya and that's why I'm here, to keep you informed of what's goin on."

Sonny motioned for him to continue.

"There's a couple of things that concern me. The biggest one is that Vito got in bed with an East L.A. biker gang. These fuckin guys scare me, but Vito's blind. He wants their muscle, but he thinks they're just gonna walk away afterwards. I can tell that ain't what they're thinkin, but Vito won't listen. And these guys have weapons and body armor. Get this, it was supplied by the government for help on some secret deal. Talk about doin business with the Devil. Now, Sonny, I ain't no choir boy and never pretended to be, but I'm a fuckin American."

"I hear ya, and I told Vito, but like you say, he don't listen."

"Any way, the bikers are gonna go to the reservation and blow up the school to start with. The Indians got this beautiful school that some millionaire built for them."

"Do you know when?"

"Soon, but I'll find out and let you know."

"Paulie, you said there were a couple of things that concerned you. Is there something else?"

Paulie paused to collect his thoughts. "Maybe this is something, but maybe not. I just don't understand why the Indians, if they're protected on their reservation, haven't gone to the police or the government. We've destroyed property, tried to bribe the chief and threatened them, but they don't appear to have done anything about it. Does that make sense to you?"

Sonny pondered the thought. "It's strange to say the least."

After Paulie departed, Zak came over to Sonny's booth. Sonny motioned for him to sit down. "Zak, I got a favor to ask. You know who Vinny's nephew is. Well, it turns out he's a great cook."

Zak raised his eyebrows. "Sonny, are we talking about the same guy – Petey?"

"He calls himself Christopher now."

"That's a start, but you know what they say about putting lipstick on a pig."

"I hear ya, but you gotta trust me on this one. No one was more surprised than me."

"Sonny, obviously I can't say no to you, but if this doesn't work out you gotta understand."

"Completely. Trust me, you're gonna be surprised."

"We can agree on that."

Sonny's next stop before home was Christopher's suite. Christopher was surprised to see him. "Sonny, is everything okay?"

"Christopher, I just need a minute. If I needed some information about a treaty, could your friend get into the government archives? It may be public information, but it would be old."

Christopher smiled. "Sonny, I might even be able to do it. "

"Even better, but here is the big issue. If we need to alter a document can we do it?"

"Probably, if it's old, but it depends on how much you need to change."

"We'll talk tomorrow. And, Christopher, I'm glad you're okay."

Christopher misted up as they said good night.

Chapter Thirty-Three

Closing The Loop

Holmby Hills

B uck Robertson was a master of his craft and had a suitcase full of the electronic tools of his trade. He had been helpful in profiling the mystery lady, which facilitated the "accidental" meeting on the USC campus. Although he considered it a long shot that, even if the meeting took place, Manny would be able to persuade her to come to Carlos' Holmby Hills mansion, he formulated a plan for that possibility and forced Manny and Carlos to practice it repeatedly, as if a movie production.

The plan was a simple one, but it had a very narrow time window with which to execute. It went like this: upon arrival at the mansion, Manny would give her a brief tour of the lower level and the grounds, during which time Buck would be out of sight.

Manny and his guest would be served dinner in the gazebo. Just the two of them. Bottled water would be poured for both, but hers would contain a opiate-based sedative that should act like an anesthetic. The trick was to use the minimum dose necessary for her to be asleep for no more than thirty to forty-five minutes. It had to appear that she had simply fainted.

During that time, Buck would photograph every document in her purse and/or backpack and install tracking devices where possible. When she regained consciousness, Buck would be introduced as Dr.

Russell, a neighbor whom they had summoned after she fainted. The doctor would tell her that all of her vital signs were good and ascribe the fainting spell to either low blood sugar level and/or excitement, both of which were plausible.

It was a name and phone number scribbled on a memo pad that closed the loop on the CIA's involvement in this plot. That had never really been in doubt, but now all of the dots could be connected. The name was Hayes, the nom de guerre of one of the Company's two most feared assassins. His specialty was explosives, while his counterpart, the Cowboy, made death more personal.

The CIA involvement was clear from the involvement of Stone and Weathers in getting the Al Qaeda bomber into the country. Their elimination, after they had killed two other agents; the explosion at the supposed safe house near Las Vegas; the mysterious female who had delivered the vehicle to the bomber; and Hayes' connection to her, had closed the loop.

Forget the romantic version of the 00 British agents who had licenses to kill, wore tuxedos, and drank martinis—shaken, not stirred. Hayes and the Cowboy were psychopaths with few social graces. They didn't need no stinkin badges! They acted with impunity and violence.

Unbeknownst to the powers that be, the Cowboy was in custody somewhere in/near Apache Dunes. If Robertson could find Hayes, almost the entire "A-Team" of CIA black ops agents, in one disastrous and sinister plot, would be eliminated. The only one left standing would be Robertson, himself. The proverbial snake might not be dead, but it would be severely wounded.

Fatima awoke from the sedation, naturally confused, but feeling fine otherwise. The doctor spoke first.

"Fatima, I'm Dr. Russell. I'm a neighbor. Your vital signs are fine. I think you just fainted because of low blood sugar, maybe combined with excitement. Have you had anything to eat today?"

Still muzzy headed, she shook her head no. "Only coffee and a croissant. I— I don't eat much."

"Well, that must be the problem and it's not uncommon. I suggest you have something to eat. Maybe some soup and tea or coffee with sugar or honey. Then get some rest."

The doctor and Carlos then departed, leaving Manny and Fatima alone. She immediately panicked. "Where is my backpack?"

Manny pointed to one of the chairs. "Right where you left it."

She grabbed it and looked through it, retrieving her phone, which she also appeared to inspect. Nothing seemed out of order.

Manny held his hands out in a calming gesture. "You need to relax and, more importantly, get something in your stomach. How about some soup and maybe a 7 Up?"

At the mention of a 7 Up, she looked at her water glass, which had been switched in the interim, "It was the water. You put something in my water!"

Manny smiled to himself at the brilliance of Buck's plan as he grabbed her glass and downed the remaining water in one gulp.

"There was nothing wrong with your water. What is your problem? Let's get something in your stomach and I'll have the driver take you home."

Now clearly puzzled, Fatima looked at him. "You're going to let me go?"

Manny feigned shock. "I'm beginning to wonder about your sanity. Why wouldn't I let you go? "

"Why did you track me?"

"Track you? I didn't track you. I told you—I'm visiting my friend who goes to USC and I remembered your parking sticker. It was a shot in the dark."

"But ... what did you want with me?"

Manny appeared exhausted. "Did, is the key word. I'm male and you're female. The birds and the bees?"

"It wasn't about the man I met in the desert?"

"You met someone in the desert?"

"You don't know?"

"Why would I ask you if I knew?"

Fatima's mind was in overdrive. Could this just be an incredible coincidence? If so, what happened to the bomber? Who switched vehicles at the Tucson airport? What was the explosion in Nevada about?

Manny tried to snap her out of her trance.

"Do you want to tell me what's going on? About the guy in the desert?"

Fatima scrambled to collect her thoughts. "There wasn't anyone in the desert. It's my head. I'm still confused."

"Imagine how I feel. Let's get some food."

"I'll have some soup, maybe bread if they have any, and a 7 Up. That works for me. What about you?"

"Are you kidding? I'm having the Lobster Thermidor they prepared for us. And, a glass—make that a bottle of chardonnay."

Fatima finally smiled, but it was a sad smile. "And then, you just let me go?"

"Why would I want to keep you here?"

"Why do you ask me, if you know?"

He smiled. "Touché."

They ate in mostly silence although the tension was palpable. Fatima had two bowls of minestrone soup, a generous amount of warm, freshly baked sourdough bread with butter, and a 7 Up. She found she was famished and as to excitement—duh! Also, for the first time in memory, her heart was trying to overrule her mind and convince her to stay.

She wasn't alone in her turmoil. While Manny was totally impressed with Buck's plan and its flawless execution, his heart was also engaged in battle and wanting desperately for her to stay. However, his mind kept reminding him that she was complicit, if not guilty as sin, in a heinous plot to assassinate a presidential candidate.

As Manny escorted her to the driveway, where Carlos' driver was holding the door of the limousine, he gently held her arm and could feel her rapid pulse. Fatima made no attempt to remove his hand, which surprised herself most of all. When they arrived at the car, he summoned all of his strength not to try to kiss her. He simply said, "I hope you feel better. May I call you?"

Fatima had never given her phone number to anyone other than Mr. Hayes, at his direction, but she gave it to Manny. She smiled to herself. Maybe it was the birds and the bees.

After she departed, Manny encountered both Buck and Carlos waiting for him. Buck seemed pleased by the success of his plan and sought the icing on the cake. "Did you get her phone number?"

Manny handed it to him. "I need a shower now and some good tequila."

He was surprised later when Buck joined him on the patio for a night cap. Buck patted him on the back. "I know—check that—I don't know how you feel, but there's more about her you don't know, than you know. I'll make you a promise. If you can turn her around, so be it. I now have the name of her puppetmaster and I have a history with him. The question is, what's her role and can they carry this out without the Al Qaeda bomber? My guess is, they have a plan B."

"It's just— it's just that I've never felt like this before and not just one, but all of the alarms are going off. If this is love, it sucks."

"I'm no expert on the subject, but what you're experiencing is infatuation, not love. Infatuation acts like a drug. It's an intense and overwhelming sensation, but like a drug, it will wear off. Just hang in there."

"I never knew my father so I missed the so-called talk."

Buck laughed.

"Why is that funny?"

"It's funny because my father is eighty-five and we've never had the talk. You know why? Because he never had it with his father."

They clinked glasses.

"Here's what I don't understand. We are so different. I get the thing about opposites attracting, but I feel connected to her somehow."

"Want my unprofessional opinion? Actually, it's more of a guess."

Manny nodded.

"It's like this. For a woman to get in a position of power in that religious culture, where women are second class citizens, she had to have something besides feminine wiles. My guess is, something happened to her at an early age that has shaped her and set her on this course—whatever it is. You can relate to that pain because of your troubled childhood. Problem is, it's doubtful that she'll ever let you get close enough to help, and the clock is ticking."

"I needed that. Like I said, I never had a father to talk to, although Max has been great. I don't know where I'd be without him."

"I never had a son to counsel and console."

"Didn't you ever marry?"

"The answer is yes. I was actually married twice. I was married to my wife and to my career with the Company. My wife didn't know the details of my job, but knew that when I left on an assignment, there was no guarantee that I'd be coming back. Until I could assure her otherwise, she refused to have a family. I guess I was an adrenaline junkie. I kept promising myself and her that the next job was the last, but I couldn't fathom a nine-to-five life. We loved each other, but our marriage probably lasted because we each had our own life. She died of cancer two years ago. That's why this situation is so important to me. Fatima's government contact is named Hayes. We started around the same time and have worked together on assignments, though not for several years. This is the life I chose and it all seems so wrong now, yet Hayes is running this game."

"That's some heavy shit. I thought I was gonna have a pity party alone tonight. Looks like I've got company."

They refilled their glasses. There would be a sunrise tomorrow, but not for that bottle of tequila.

"So Buck, what's next?"

"We need to monitor her movements. Hopefully she'll lead us to Hayes."

CHAPTER THIRTY-FOUR

The Return of Geronimo

Apache Dunes

T he *Geronimo II* was a Beneteau Oceanis 55 foot sailboat. They had just returned to their slip in Estepona, on the Spanish Costa del Sol, from a shake-down cruise when Dylan got the call from Tom. His sixth sense had told him that something was amiss, so he wasn't totally caught off guard. In addition to Dusty, her friend Andre, Jake, and Ashley, they had been joined on the boat by Dylan's roommate from Yale, Brewster, "Brew," Simington the fourth or fifth—or was it the sixth or seventh? Even Brew couldn't be sure.

Brew was an apt sobriquet as, like Hemingway, life was a movable feast for him and he happened to be bumming around Europe when Dylan had arrived. As a point of clarification, roughing it for him meant five-star hotels and champagne with his breakfast. He had been the proverbial trust-fund baby and had grown into a trust-fund adult. Had he been born a couple of generations prior, he likely would have been the subject of an F. Scott Fitzgerald novel.

To his credit, he was the "hail fellow, well met" perfect companion for Dylan who was welcomed into Brew's family. As the quintessential scholar-athlete, star quarterback of the football team, Dylan was the son Brew's father dreamed of. Brew and his father were gun enthusiasts and Dylan enjoyed several hunting trips with them and hours spent practicing at the range. They were impressed with Dylan's marksmanship, but knew little of his past experiences, or life in the desert.

After dinner on the boardwalk in Estepona, they had a night cap on the boat to discuss the news from Apache Dunes. Dylan spoke first. "I have to go. When I needed Michael, he was there for me."

Jake jumped in. "Make that we and us. Dusty and I were there too."

"Sorry, I didn't mean it like that. I was the one who asked for his help and now he needs mine."

"Then count me in, too." Jake replied.

"Jake, someone has to stay here and watch over things. You know that. I'll catch a flight out of Malaga to Madrid and get a direct flight to the US where I can charter a plane to the Dunes."

Suddenly, Brew chimed in. "Dylan, I'll call Dad and have the corporate jet meet us in Madrid. We can fly direct to Apache Dunes."

Dylan appeared to digest Brew's offer before he turned to him. "Brew, that sounds great, but what do you mean, we? You've got no business getting involved in this. I love you, but this is way out of your league."

Brew smiled, partly fueled by the alcohol. "Dylan, you think I'm afraid of a little rough stuff? How many times have we been hunting together? And, I'm almost as good as you at the range."

"Brew, this is way different. Have you ever killed anyone?"

Brew laughed. "No and neither have any of you."

When awkward silence ensued, the smile evaporated from Brew's face. "Are you shitting me? You've killed someone?"

Dylan replied. "It was self-defense, as this will be."

Brew turned to Jake. "What about you?"

Jake's silence and shoulder shrug was answer enough.

As stunned as he could be, Brew turned to Dusty, Ashley, and Andre.

Andre and Ashley both shook their heads no, but Dusty replied that she couldn't be sure—it had been hectic.

Brew poured himself a large glass of wine and sat down. No one spoke for a while.

Brew stood back up. "Dylan, I'm coming with you. Our jet is the fastest way to get there. I promise I won't get in the way."

After appearing to be lost in his thoughts, which he was, Dylan turned to Brew. "Brew, if I let you come, you have to do exactly as I say. You hear me?"

"Loud and clear."

"You have no idea what you're getting yourself into and I want you to sleep on it. Actually, I hope you'll change your mind."

Brew climbed the steps to the cockpit where they could hear him call for the jet.

CHAPTER THIRTY-FIVE

Legerdemain

Las Vegas

Christopher had called ahead and told Sonny he had some news, but he hung up before he told him what the news was about. When Sonny answered the door Christopher was animated.

"Sonny, he did it. He fucking did it!"

Sonny motioned for Christopher to calm down and guided him into the den where Bobbie was waiting.

"Bobbie, he did it."

Sonny sat down and motioned for Christopher to do the same. When Christopher started to speak, Sonny interrupted him, "Take a deep breath. You calmed down?"

Christopher nodded, but was clearly still jacked up.

"Good. Now who did it and what did he do?"

Christopher leaned forward. "My friend Alex. I told you he was a genius."

"We're making some progress. Now, what was it that he did?"

"I— I don't always understand things so well, so I'm gonna let him tell you. It's about the Indian Treaty, but Sonny, before I get him on the phone, I gotta tell you that he's a little … different."

Sonny glanced at Bobbie. "Imagine that. One of your friends being different."

Bobbie frowned at Sonny.

Sonny handed the phone to Christopher.

Alex picked up on the third ring.

"Alex, I told you about Sonny. I'm gonna let you tell him, okay?"

Christopher handed Sonny the phone.

"Alex, this is Sonny. How ya doin?"

"Wait— how's that commercial go? Well, I'm doin just fine, thank you."

Sonny rolled his eyes while Christopher motioned for him to be cool.

"That's great to hear. Christopher, er, Petey told me you found out something about the Indian Treaty."

"I'm looking at it, as we speak. The 1872 Chiricahua Reservation Treaty and the amendment that cancelled it."

"You have a copy of it?"

"I have the original."

Sonny raised his eyebrows as Christopher beamed.

"How does that happen?"

"You mean, how did it happen? It's what I do. You see, in one of my incarnations, I am a highly respected researcher and have clearance and access to the National Archives where all of the Indian treaties are stored. I was able to, shall we say, borrow it and it will be returned sans the amendment that cancelled it."

"Whatta ya mean sans the amendment?"

Now Bobbie rolled her eyes.

"I take it you don't speak French."

"In case you didn't notice, I don't speak English that good."

Alex laughed. "That's good. Humility is a rare trait these days. In French, sans means without."

"You can detach it?"

"Already have."

"And no one will know?"

"According to the records, the last time it was viewed was over twenty years ago."

"That's great news. What can I do for you?"

"You don't need to do anything for me. Petey doesn't know this, but I have some Shoshone blood in me and enjoyed doing this. Having said that, I promised five thousand dollars worth of Bitcoins to one of the archivists. She was the one responsible for the legerdemain."

"There you go again. Legerdemain sounds like a horse I bet on at Santa Anita."

Alex laughed again. "Close. It means sleight of hand."

"Closer than you think. I had money in my hand when I placed the bet and then—poof—it was gone."

"I like you, Sonny. Petey, I mean Christopher, can tell you how to handle the Bitcoins. I'll give him the information."

After Christopher departed, Sonny turned to Bobbie.

"This is good news for the Indians and I know the sheriff is close to them. Maybe we can parlay this information for access to the dead agent's house."

Sonny's mood suddenly changed to somber.

"What is it? I think that's a fair trade."

Sonny shook his head. "It's got nothing to do with that. I still gotta figure out how to get to Vito and the clock is ticking."

Bobbie seemed pensive for a moment before speaking, "Oh, Sonny—I forgot to tell you. One of my prospective clients wants me to see her home in Beverly Hills. I'd only be gone a couple of days. Is that okay with you?"

Lost in his own thoughts, Sonny replied, "Sure, do you need anything?"

"Any ideas on where I should stay?"

"The Beverly Wilshire. We've got, whatta ya callit? A reciprocal arrangement. Just mention my name and they'll take care of you. When are you goin?"

"If it's okay with you, I'll go tomorrow."

Bobbie poured Sonny a glass of scotch to ensure he remained in the den while she went to the kitchen and searched for the note pad with Vito Rotelli's cell phone number on it.

She had no plan, but one thing she was certain of was the way to a man's heart was not through his stomach. It was true that she had never killed a man before, but it wasn't for lack of trying. She was still mystified how Del had survived. Regardless, she had crossed her personal Rubicon in that regard and this time she had everything at stake. Without Sonny, it would be Groundhog Day all over again, relying upon her looks and guile to just barely survive, knowing that time was not her friend.

Vito's death would require finesse. She understood that much. The old standard of a .22 in the back of the head might create more problems than it solved. Sonny would need a rock solid alibi. That he would have if Vito was killed in L.A., while Sonny was in Vegas. Suddenly a thought came into her mind. She had to laugh, she liked it so much.

Sonny called out from the den, "What's so funny?"

"I was just thinking of something. It's a girl thing."

Bobbie poked her head into the den. "Hey, I may not have to stay over in L.A. if things go right. Do you think that Christopher would drive me?"

Sonny seemed to digest the idea before responding. "That might be a good idea. Get him outta my hair while I have to think about things."

"Baby, relax. I have a feeling that things are gonna work out just fine."

"That's easy for you to say. You take care of your business and I'll take care of mine."

"Sonny, your business is my business. Or did you forget? I'll call Christopher."

CHAPTER THIRTY-SIX

A Shopping Trip

Hollywood

C hristopher was eager to do anything that either Sonny or Bobby requested and, truth is, regardless of how nice the suite at Pompeii was, he felt like he was cooped up and jumped at the chance to get away, if only for a day. For the first hour or so of the drive to L.A. only idle chit chat was exchanged as Bobbie mulled over how to broach her plan to Christopher. In the end, she decided that total transparency was best as Christopher would be a vital cog in her plan.

She turned to Christopher. "Christopher, you know that Sonny has a serious, and I mean serious, problem with Vito Rotelli."

Christopher banged his hands on the steering wheel. "I know and it's all my fault. Sonny should have whacked me when he had the chance."

"Don't ever say that again. Under that gruff exterior, Sonny has a heart of gold. He wants to pretend otherwise. He's the reason that both of us are alive. You know that right?"

"I would do anything for him. I just don't know what to do and I tend to fuck up everything I get involved with."

Bobbie let a minute or so pass before she responded. "Christopher, can I trust you?"

Christopher looked over at her. "Whatta you mean?"

"Just what I said. I have a plan to help Sonny and need to know if you will help me."

"I told you. I'll do anything I can to help Sonny. What's your plan?"

"I'm not going to L.A. to look at a house. I'm going to kill Vito Rotelli."

The car veered off the highway onto the shoulder before Christopher regained control. "How— how can you do that? Do you know who he is?"

"I do. Are you in?"

"Bobbie, I'm the wrong guy if any rough stuff is involved. I'm a cook, not a gangster."

"But you know how to drive, or at least I thought you did."

"Sorry, you just shocked me. Bobbie, I'm a good driver."

"That's all I need, but you have to do exactly as I say."

Christopher shook his head. "That's how I got in trouble in the first place, doing exactly as Sonny said."

"This will be different. I'll explain it to you."

When they arrived at the Beverly Wilshire, Bobbie checked into her room. Christopher accompanied her and seemed very nervous.

"We're not both staying in this room are we?"

Bobbie laughed. "If things go as planned, no one will be spending the night. Now I have a call to make, so chill out or take a walk."

"I'll stretch my legs."

"Good, but be back here in an hour. And, Christopher, ask the concierge for directions of how to get to the Beverly Hills Hotel from here. That's very important. You hear me?"

"I hear you. The Beverly Hills Hotel."

As soon as Christopher departed, Bobbie took the note pad with Vito's number on it and, after a few deep breaths, sat down and dialed the number. It was showtime. It dawned on her, however, that it was all for naught if Vito was out of town. That fear disappeared when he answered on the second ring.

Vito answered. "Who's this?"

"Vito, this is Bobbie. You met me with Sonny in Las Vegas."

Vito perked up. "Yeah, I remember you. Aren't you Sonny's girl?"

"Let's say I'm attracted to powerful men and Sonny takes good care of me—at least as good as he can."

"Are you sayin you're a hooker?"

"You know any women in Vegas who aren't?"

Vito laughed, "No. As a matter of fact I don't. So, Bobbie, tell me what can I do for you?"

"Well, I happen to be in town to do a little shopping."

"What're you shopping for?"

"Something I can't get in Las Vegas."

Vito laughed. "Something you can't get from Sonny, huh?"

"Let's just say I've got an itch that he can't scratch."

"And you think I can?"

"I thought so the moment I met you. I'm surprised you didn't notice."

Try as he may, Vito could barely recall their introduction, other than the fact that Bobbie was a knockout, but that was true of most of the broads in Vegas.

"Yeah, I did notice, but couldn't do nothin because of Sonny."

"Yeah, well Sonny's in Las Vegas and I'm out here. Is it true that you that you're a big player in Hollywood?"

"You wanna make a movie, you deal with me."

"That's so cool. Those little starlets are cute, but there's no substitute for experience."

"Maybe we should have dinner."

"I was hoping you'd say that. Hey, any chance we can go to the Polo Lounge at the Beverly Hills Hotel?"

"We can go anywhere. This is my town. You ever been to the Polo Lounge?"

"No, but I'm a film buff and I just finished a book about the golden age of Hollywood. It said that Errol Flynn got laid in every cabana at the Beverly Hills Hotel. Know what my dream is?"

"I can't wait."

"I want to get fucked in one of the cabanas."

"Bobbie, I'm gonna make your dream come true."

"I was hoping you'd say that."

"Where are you staying?"

"The Beverly Wilshire."

"I'll make reservations at the Polo Lounge and reserve a cabana. I'll pick you up in front of the hotel at seven. And, Bobbie, none of this gets back to Sonny."

"Sonny, who?"

When Vito hung up, he was smiling like the Cheshire cat. Sonny fucked with the wrong person. He was working for Vito now and the boss was fucking his girl. He couldn't wait to rub Sonny's nose in that. After the Indian deal was settled, he'd rat out both Sonny and Joey C. and take over the entire west. What a wonderful life it is, he thought.

Bobbie reached in her purse and withdrew a small metal pill box which contained two small pills. At first glance they appeared to be identical. On closer scrutiny, one had a tiny blue dot on one side. The pill with the blue dot was a placebo. The pill without the dot was ecstasy, MDMA, but laced with enough fentanyl to kill a mature water buffalo. They were part of Bobbie's arsenal that she had yet to have occasion to use. If her instincts were right, Vito would rush, not walk, into her trap. If not, she would have to re-enter that zone that would allow her to escape the pain of reality for a few minutes and try Plan B, which, at present, didn't exist.

After final review of instructions with Christopher, Bobbie left for the front entrance to be picked up by Vito. She wore a scarf and over-sized black sunglasses, which made her indistinguishable from the myriad of starlets and wannabes. That was the point.

Vito looked at her as she got in. "You sure you ain't a movie star?"

"I am tonight. In fact, I'm so excited I wouldn't mind skipping dinner and going right to the cabana."

Vito smiled. "How about if we do the cabana first, have dinner and then return to the cabana?"

"My mission tonight is going to be to wear your dick out and I have something that will help."

Vito shifted in his seat and it was clear that the head without a brain was taking charge. "And what would that be?"

"Just a little secret potion that one of the Vegas showgirls turned me on to. It's amazing. Your dick will be harder than Chinese arithmetic."

As Vito pulled up to the valet stand, a quick glance from Bobbie told her he was already there. She smiled. So far, so good.

They headed straight for the cabana and, once inside, Bobbie slid out of her short dress, sans panties or bra. Vito wrestled with his clothes, not believing his good fortune. Bobbie put most starlets to shame.

Vito may have been an egotistical asshole with limited social graces, but Italian stallion would be an apt sobriquet. It gave Bobbie pause. What a pity.

Now everything depended on timing. If she appeared too anxious with the pills, he might demur. It was certain he didn't need any artificial stimulation.

Bobbie knelt down and proceeded to provide her own stimulation of the oral kind. A battle royale was taking place in her mind. She was trying to pretend she didn't enjoy it, but had to do it as part of the plan. Her alter-ego told her she knew exactly what she was doing and it was the only thing she was good at. The truth was probably somewhere in between.

Vito was in seventh heaven and, try as she may, Bobbie couldn't stop herself before he exploded. She was now out of her mind with excitement. Truth is, she did have an itch and it did need to be scratched. She was trying to think. The ecstasy would make his dick hard again, but how long would it take for the fentanyl to deliver the coup de grace?

After having the best blow job of his life and seeing Bobbie consumed with lust, Vito pulled her up. "Baby, baby, that was incredible, but slow down. We've got all night. In fact, I might just keep you here. I'm married, but you're a whore so you don't mind, right? "

"I don't mind."

"Fuck Sonny, right?"

"Sonny who?"

Vito laughed, but then brought Bobbie back to reality. "Where's that magic potion you were talking about? This might be a good time for it."

At that moment of truth, Bobbie realized that her alter-ego had ruled her life by providing justification for everything she had done. It was now telling her that Vito was right. She was a whore and she did have an itch that Sonny couldn't scratch. Her heart, however, reminded her that Sonny had saved her life and she owed him this. She walked over to her purse and opened the box, but almost froze with fear when it was hard to make out the spot on the pill in the dim light of the cabana. She moved her purse over to the light coming through a crack, and found the placebo. She turned to Vito and made a dramatic scene of swallowing her pill.

She playfully dangled the other pill in front of him. "You sure you want to fuck all night?"

He grabbed the pill and swallowed it. The clock was ticking, but it wasn't long before the ecstasy did its part and Bobbie mounted him. At least for a few minutes they both appeared to be in heaven as Bobbie rode her stallion until she exploded, too. When she dismounted, his eyes were closed and he had a smile on his face. She believed he was still alive as she put her dress back on.

She took out her cell and called Christopher. After waiting five minutes, during which time Vito didn't move a muscle, Bobbie re-donned her scarf and sunglasses and went to the pick-up spot.

Christopher could tell she was in turmoil, but didn't appear to have been harmed although the odor of sex was heavy. "Are you okay?"

"Just drive. You got my bag from the hotel?"

"It's in the trunk."

"Good, then let's head home. I don't feel like talking."

"That's okay. Is Vito dead?"

"If he isn't, he will be."

CHAPTER THIRTY-SEVEN

What's Love Got to Do with It

Las Vegas

After a drive thru at In-N-Out Burger and a stop for gas, Christopher and Bobbie arrived back in Vegas at almost two a.m. Very few words were exchanged on the trip.

Sonny had fallen asleep in his recliner in the den and heard Bobbie come in, but by the time he cleared his cob webs she was in the guest bedroom with the door closed. He started to knock on the door, but heard her sobbing. He called through the door.

"Bobbie, are you okay?"

When she didn't answer he turned the knob, but she had locked the door. Now he was totally at sea.

"Bobbie, open up or I'll break the door down."

Bobbie opened the door a crack and it was obvious that she'd been crying.

"Bobbie, what the fuck did I do now?"

"Sonny, you didn't do anything. It's me that has the problem. I need to be alone tonight. We'll talk in the morning."

She closed the door and locked it.

Sonny just shook his head and spoke to himself. "Fucking broads. Go figure."

The headline of the *Los Angeles Times* in the morning read, "Mobster OD's in Cabana after Tryst with Mystery Actress". It went on to say that three supposed witnesses claimed to have seen three separate, well known actresses enter and emerge from the cabana. The only thing they could agree on was that it was definitely a movie star.

When Bobbie entered the kitchen with eyes still red and swollen from crying, Sonny pushed the paper over to her. "I don't suppose you know anything about this."

"Sonny, I had to do it."

Sonny threw an English muffin at her. "I told you I'd handle it. You coulda got killed."

"Sonny, you didn't have a plan and you know it. No one can trace it to me."

She paused when she remembered the call from the hotel to his cell phone.

He sat back down. "Well they're callin it an overdose and there's plenty of them these days, besides he could be connected to a hundred actresses—maybe more."

"He's dead and that's the important thing. You saved my life and now I returned the favor."

"What the fuck is that supposed to mean? And why were you so upset last night?"

Just then the phone rang. Sonny answered. It was Joey C.

"Sonny, we just got the news. You may be the luckiest motherfucker in the universe. Some actress just bailed you out. At first I thought you might have something to do with it, but, and no offense, I couldn't connect you to one of them movie stars."

Sonny tried to play dumb. "Yeah, I saw the paper this morning. Go figure. His dick got him in trouble."

Sonny didn't notice, but Bobbie winced at the comment.

"Well, like I was tellin you. Some people here aren't unhappy with the news."

"So what happens now with L.A. and the unions?"

"The old man said that was your call. He said L.A. might be more important than Vegas, now. He just wants to avoid a war."

"Well, Paulie has been loyal, but my guess is he'll be challenged and what about this biker gang that Vito was mixed up with?"

"The old man said that maybe you should take over L.A. and let Paulie have Vegas."

"The old man said that?"

"What'd I just say? If you think about it, it makes some sense."

"I'll talk to Paulie."

"By the way, just because you lucked out of this don't mean I'm not still pissed at you."

After they hung up, Sonny turned again to Bobbie. "What the fuck do you mean, you returned the favor?"

"Sonny, I don't deserve you. I'm seriously fucked up and you'll be better off without me."

Sonny was stunned. "What was all that stuff about love? Was that just bullshit?"

"Love's got nothing to do with it. Remember when I told you the story about the Scorpion and the Frog? Well, that applies to me, too. I'm the Scorpion. I have a nature and it's a dark one."

"I have a hard enough time understanding plain English. I got no fucking idea what you're talking about."

Bobbie got up to leave and then sat down again and held her head in her hands. She looked up. "Sonny, I did something terrible last night. I couldn't stop myself."

"Yeah, I read the news."

"It's not that."

"You mean you did something worse than kill a guy?"

"I don't mean it was worse than that, but—"

Sonny interrupted her. "If it wasn't worse than that, I don't wanna hear about it. I got my own problems."

Bobbie stayed and had a cup of coffee after Sonny left. She thought about what he said. She killed a guy she barely knew and had no feeling of remorse, yet she was persecuting herself for having sex and enjoying it. The guy deserved to die. He had to die. The sex issue was more complex and involved her personal demons. There was no way that she was going to get Vito to take the pill without having sex with him. That wasn't rationalization. That was the truth. But, using her sex as a means to an end wasn't just second nature to her. It *was* her nature. This time, the end happened to justify the means.

A line from Bob Dylan's, "Tangled Up in Blue," came to mind. "All the while I was alone, the past was close behind." Maybe Sonny didn't want to know about her past, but she couldn't change the channel if she wanted to. She could wish that things were different, but she remembered what her cynical, and perverted, Psychology professor told her, "Wish in one hand and shit in the other. See which one fills up the fastest."

CHAPTER THIRTY-EIGHT

Probabilities

Los Angeles

When Manny awoke, he was severely hung over and had that All-American breakfast of orange juice and Tylenol. Heavy on the latter. He found Robertson in the gazebo staring at his laptop. Buck looked up from the screen as Manny approached.

"Did you get the number of the truck that ran over you?"

"Very funny. How come you look so good?"

"Practice."

Manny started to sit down, but Buck motioned for him to move his chair so they both could see the screen. The picture was a map of the Los Angeles area with three tiny, blinking dots massed together.

"What's up?"

"Each dot represents a chip that was inserted when your future ex-wife was in La La land. One in her phone, one in her shoe and one in her backpack."

Manny appeared puzzled. "Why did we need three to trace her?"

"We didn't. One would typically suffice. The other two are going to lead us to Hayes."

"I'm not hitting on all cylinders this morning. I don't follow."

Buck, reached in his duffel bag and pulled out a small package the size of the packet of salt you get in a restaurant. He opened it and two tiny chips spilled out.

"These are standard issue tracking chips. They come two to a package. This game we play is all about probabilities. The odds are that she is going to contact Hayes today and explain the troubling coincidences of running into you and passing out while in your company. Hayes won't believe that either is a coincidence and will inspect her phone. When he finds the chip, he will recognize it for what it is and search for its companion. He'll find it in her shoe, assuming she is wearing the same pair as last night."

"What about the one in her backpack?"

"Again, it's all about probabilities. He will search for the second knowing they come in pairs, but isn't likely to search for more which he would regard as redundant. If I'm right—ah look at the screen. She's on the move."

The three dots were moving together.

"If I'm right, she will meet him somewhere convenient for him. When she departs, we should see one dot go with her and the two he discovered will hopefully lead us to him."

"But— if he recognizes them as CIA standard issue, won't he know something is wrong?"

"Bet your lunch money that his next call will be to Langley, but they will appear as surprised as he is. He won't believe them."

"How's that help us?"

"It doesn't, necessarily. He'll think the chips were to track her, not him, but it will give him something else to think about and that gives us an edge."

They each had a cup of coffee as they watched the screen. The dots had turned toward the ocean and stopped at Venice Beach.

As predicted, an hour later one dot appeared to retrace its path while the other two moved only slightly and came to rest in Venice Beach.

Buck would have won his bet as Hayes went through the secure protocol to contact Barry Stanton at headquarters in Langley, Virginia. When Hayes started to disclose what had happened, Stanton stopped him. "Hold on. I think the deputy director needs to hear this. Stay with me. I'll have the call transferred to his office."

Stanton instructed his secretary to transfer the call and hustled down to Aaron Nolan's office where he knocked once and entered. Nolan looked up, "What's up?"

"Hayes called, and I'm having the call transferred. You need to hear this."

Nolan picked up the phone and put it on speaker. Stanton spoke first. "Hayes, are you there?"

"I'm here."

"Good, I've got Deputy Director Nolan here. Start again at the beginning."

Hayes cleared his throat before speaking, "I got a call from my student today. She said she needed to see me. Yesterday she ran into a young man she had met in the Arizona desert when she went to meet our guest."

"Hayes, this is Deputy Director Nolan. What do you mean she ran into him and how did she meet him in the desert?"

"She said that she stopped for gas and he was working at the station because the pumps were broken. Yesterday he showed up in the library on campus in the room where she regularly studies. Somehow, he convinced her to come for dinner at a mansion in Holmby Hills where she passed out. When she came to, they told her she had fainted."

Nolan and Stanton exchanged looks of concern.

"I took her phone apart and guess what I found? A standard issue tracking chip."

"You mean one of ours?"

"I mean two of ours. The other one was in her shoe."

Nolan looked at Stanton who just shook his head. "Look, neither of us know anything about this. Do you have the chips?"

"Of course."

"What's the status of the, er, project?"

"She's committed, but now concerned. She's convinced the guy is with the government."

"Hayes, this is Stanton. I can assure you he's not one of ours. I'll check with the Fibs, they could fuck up a wet dream. Keep me informed if there are any more developments."

"Roger that. You're certain there aren't any rogues out there?"

"There has been some, er, shrinkage in the ranks."

"So I've heard. What about Robertson?"

"He supposedly died in an explosion in Nevada. We found his plane in Arizona. The Cowboy is checking it out. Regardless, he isn't a young man."

"Have you heard from the Cowboy?"

Nolan looked at Stanton again. Once more Stanton shook his head.

"We'll get back to you if we learn anything."

After they hung up, Stanton told Nolan, "Cowboy has gone off the radar screen."

"Something tells me I wouldn't want to be Hayes."

"Should we tell him?"

"Negative. From now on its plausible deniability."

"What do you tell the director?"

"That I'm grateful to have had the opportunity to serve my country, but it's time for me to hang up my spurs. I suggest you think about doing the same."

"You don't need to suggest, it's all I think about."

CHAPTER THIRTY-NINE

I Heard the News Today, Oh Boy!

Los Angeles

Like everyone else in the L.A. area who either read the newspaper, watched T.V. or had a cell phone, Paulie got the news in the morning and his phone had been ringing ever since. He wasn't surprised at the circumstances, but totally discounted the A-list names the so-called witnesses claimed to were the mystery woman. Vito had a steady pipeline of young talent provided by studios who understood the power he wielded, but they were the small-town beauties, and farmer's daughters from the Midwest who, like Lloyd in *Dumb and Dumber*, believed that one in a billion meant that they had a chance.

He hadn't answered any calls as he desperately needed time to think. The union prize and all of its perks was going to be like chum in the water to sharks, and L.A. was infested with sharks. It wasn't just the other mobsters. There were plenty powerful gangs of all ethnicities who would also covet the prize, none the least the bikers from East L.A. who Vito had gotten in bed with.

He thanked his lucky stars, if he had any, for the fact that he had interacted with both Joey C. and Sonny. He would need all of the goodwill he could get, but it wasn't like the old days when the mob called the shots. He would have to reach out to Sonny, but needed some advice before he did anything. When Vito needed advice, he called Nelson Wood, and Paulie had no better idea.

Motorcycles are ubiquitous in L.A., but Paulie was unnerved by the large group of bikers who appeared to be following him, on his way to Wood's office in Beverly Hills. Paulie had called ahead and Wood was expecting him, having also seen the news.

Paulie was ushered right into Wood's office and was surprised to find him boxing up files and memorabilia. He wasn't aware that Wood was the beneficiary of two substantial life insurance policies on Vito Rotelli and literally couldn't wait to exit the zoo that L.A. had become. A brochure on luxury yachts was open on the desk.

Before any pleasantries could be exchanged, Paulie's premonition about being followed proved to be real when four, huge, tattooed-bikers barged in behind him. Wood took in the scene.

He said to Paulie, "You didn't say you were bringing friends."

The alpha-dog biker replied, "We ain't friends. We're business partners, in case you forgot, and we're here to talk business."

Wood gestured for them to find a seat. "Move those boxes out of the way."

"The biker looked around. "You goin somewhere?"

Wood ignored the question. "If you want to talk business, you have the floor."

The biker stood and tossed the Indian Reservation partnership agreement on Wood's desk. Wood glanced at it quickly and pushed it back toward the biker.

"In case you haven't heard the news, my client, Mr. Rotelli, passed away last night."

"That's why we're here. So what happens to our agreement?"

"I guess you could say it died with him."

The biker turned to Paulie. "You ain't lookin to take his place?"

"Not in that deal. It's all yours."

The biker smiled at his homeys. "Bueno. That's what I was hopin you'd say."

Wood stood and said, "Well, now that that's settled—as you can see

I'm busy."

The bikers had yet to move. The alpha-dog looked addressed Paulie, "What happens now with the unions?"

Paulie was visibly surprised by the question, but quickly recovered.

"If I need you, I'll be in touch."

The biker laughed and was soon joined by the others.

"Oh, you'll need us. Question is—do we need you?"

He held out a card, but when Paulie ignored it, he let it fall to the floor. The bikers rose and left as if they'd just won the lottery, which in their minds they had.

Wood then listened patiently as Paulie described his predicament. He then reached into one of the boxes that contained books and handed Paulie *The Art of War* by Sun Tzu. "Read this. As you can see, I'm leaving this shithole before it gets worse. I suggest you think about doing the same. If you stay, my guess is that friends are going to be hard to find. I doubt that whomever Vito answered to in the mob are shedding crocodile tears today, but they may have somebody else in mind to replace him. You said that you know both of his bosses. The best I can tell you is to reach out to them and reiterate your loyalty."

"What about the bikers?"

"That's a problem I can't help you with. I argued against the partnership, but Vito wouldn't listen. He needed the muscle, but he didn't understand the laws of the jungle. The guy who had the golden goose, the unions, was telling them he wasn't strong enough to deal with a bunch of Indians. What's that say about the union business?"

"So they'll be coming after it."

"I think he told you as much, but they're probably going to have to get in line."

Paulie seemed totally deflated.

"Listen, Paulie. I don't have any first-hand knowledge, but I hear things and from what I've heard, it's not a good idea to go into the desert looking for trouble. I told Vito the same thing, but he wouldn't listen."

Paulie perked up a bit. "So it's no slam dunk for the bikers versus the Indians?"

"In betting parlance it'd be called a pick 'em, at best. Me, I'd be inclined to take the Indians and the points. Here's something that might help. Vito said his associates were opposed to the Indian play. If you were to pick up that card and stroke Pancho's outsized ego a bit, he might alert you to when they plan to move on the Indians. That could be valuable information to Vito's bosses and make you look good. The truth is, the only reason that the bikers know of the mob's vulnerability is that Vito reached out to them. The bikers get their come-uppance and it would send a strong message to others."

Paulie digested that advice and liked the sound of it. He picked up the biker's card.

"What do I owe you for the advice?"

Wood was already back to packing. "Nothing. That's my pro bono obligation."

Paulie had no idea what that meant. "Thanks. Where you headed?"

Wood held up the yacht brochure. "Two thirds of the world is water. Somewhere I can't be easily found."

As Paulie left Wood's office, another idea popped into his head. He and Vito had met with Carlos Garcia, and wasn't Garcia from the Arizona/Mexico border area? Nothing had come from their meeting, but Carlos seemed like a reasonable guy. Regardless, if he was an investor in the movie business he had a dog in this fight, as the unions could be a very good friend or a very bad enemy.

Paulie would try to contact Carlos before he reached out to the bikers. He wanted to have something for Sonny before he made that call.

CHAPTER FORTY

The Jihadis

Los Angeles

Fatima's brief flirtation with romance had only served to make her double down on her private war against men. Manny had proven to be duplicitous—pretending to care for her while he sought to destroy her. Hayes treated her like a child. His elitist airs were offensive. The ease with which he found the tracking devices was just more confirmation, in his mind, of male superiority. If that wasn't bad enough, Saleh had left three profane messages on her answering machine after being stood up last night.

Her alter ego told her that they were all right and she was pretending to be something she was incapable of being. She had the resources to tell them all to fuck off and return to a life of privilege and ease. However, it was the same hatred that had got her into this predicament that would impel her to try to finish her task.

The American candidate was the personification of everything she hated in men and, if Saleh succeeded, it would eliminate both of them. The thought made her smile. That would leave Manny and Hayes, but neither required her immediate attention. She actually feared Hayes. He was too good at what he did. Manny, she sensed, had the inherent vulnerability that most men possessed. She was confident that she could exploit that weakness, but first things first. She had to return Saleh's call, calls actually, and suffer his intolerable misogynistic bullshit and abuse. The only reason she would do so is knowing that he was digging his own grave.

She thought Saleh was incredibly naïve to believe that his jihad was against the infidels and that his martyrdom would be rewarded in Paradise. She considered all men to be infidels and the reward for her jihad was simply their destruction. The difference was, she didn't have to wait until the afterlife for her satisfaction.

She knew exactly how to prepare her web for Saleh's arrival. She would dress as seductively as possible, without being obvious. Her workout outfit was perfect. It left little to the imagination. She would even work up a sweat for the icing on the cake when she apologized for thinking he was coming later. He would rant and rave for her insolence, but his eyes would betray him, as would another part of his anatomy.

The meeting went as if scripted. Saleh railed at her and she feigned subservience. She explained that she had been having trouble sleeping, so excited about the coming event, that she had taken an over-the-counter sleep aid and didn't hear the phone. She was less convincing about why she hadn't returned his call after she awoke, but choreographed her explanation with toweling off the perspiration that had now permeated her outfit. Now, even less was left to the imagination. When she suggested she could take a quick shower and change, he replied, "No, no that won't be necessary."

She showed Saleh the explosive jacket that Hayes had provided. That information was strictly need-to-know and Saleh wasn't privy to it. The jacket fit, but she sensed some unease when Saleh donned it.

"Saleh, are you sure you can do this?"

He sneered at her. "It is my jihad. I will complete it, inshallah."

"We need to videotape your last statement."

Fatima thought she detected some hesitation in his reply.

"Yes, I— I'm working on it."

"Good. I've confirmed that the campaign rally is Thursday in Las

Vegas. I'll accompany you. We'll leave the night before. Are you ready?"

"Allahu Akbar!!"

Fatima replied, but with less passion, "Allahu Akbar."

CHAPTER FORTY-ONE

Homecoming

Apache Dunes

The Simington family corporate jet was a Gulfstream 650ER. Equipped with three separate living areas, it could sleep up to ten and accommodate up to nineteen passengers. With a maximum range of 7,500 nautical miles it could easily fly direct from Madrid to Tucson. Anyone with a spare 70 million dollars could have one. It was fueled up and waiting at Madrid-Barajas International Airport when Dylan and Brewster Simington arrived on their flight from Malaga. The jet could have met them in Malaga, but they saved a few hours by meeting it in Madrid. There would only be the two passengers plus crew on the flight to Tucson.

Dylan had flown first class on a commercial flight to Spain, but this was a totally new experience. Think a luxury suite at the Peninsula Hotel with wings. Brew's father had made his money the real old-fashioned way. He inherited it. It's a proverb that the way to make a small fortune is to take a large fortune and speculate, but, and to his credit, Brew's dad seemed to have the Midas touch and not only grew the fortune he inherited, but married into another. Who said that life was fair? Proof, though, that God has a sense of humor and equity, is that it was all destined for Brew and this apple fell way far away from the tree. It wasn't even in the same orchard.

There wasn't a lot of meaningful conversation on the flight. Dylan battled with his apprehension about Brew's involvement, while Brew focused on one of the hostesses and the booze, of course. One thing was certain, Dylan couldn't let Brew be in any jeopardy and that was a problem. He laughed to himself when he thought of sending him flying with Snoopy. That might be a marriage made in heaven as their room at college reeked of pot most of the time. You had to hand it to Brew, he was very flexible about from where he got his buzz.

The sheriff and Sandowski met Dylan and Brew at the Tucson Airport and drove them back to Apache Dunes. Unbeknownst to Dylan, Brew had one of his father's minions shop for an appropriate outfit for Brew's destination. When Brew emerged, after changing into his new duds, he looked like Roy Rogers, replete with bandana and Stetson hat. An inebriated Roy Rogers. The store must have been out of chaps and spurs in Brew's size.

Dylan had no idea what the outfit had cost, but knew that the looks on Tom's and Sandowski's faces would be priceless. He wasn't disappointed. With Brew in the infantry and Snoopy the air corps, what possibly could go wrong?

They stopped at the reservation on the way to the Dunes. It was clear to Dylan that a dark cloud was hanging overhead, but Michael's spirits picked up when he saw Dylan. "Geronimo, I'm sorry I had to reach out to you, but I didn't know where else to turn."

"Michael, my brother, I'm glad you did and I haven't forgotten that I owe you."

Michael grimaced, "It seems like trouble follows the Apaches, even when we try to get as far away as we can."

He kicked at the hard sand as a piece of tumbleweed drifted by. "We have nothing but this godforsaken land. Why won't they leave us alone?"

Dylan just shook his head. "I don't know, but I do know we can make sure it doesn't become a habit. Do you have any idea when this party gets started?"

That elicited a smile from Michael. "The party is for forty bad-to-the bone Hispanic bikers plus some mobsters from L.A. and they have high tech weapons and body armor. Geronimo, you don't know how much I've missed you."

Michael looked over at Brew. "Looks like you brought reinforcements."

It was Dylan's turn to laugh. "It's a long story."

It was decided that Dylan's entourage would head back to the Dunes and work on a battle plan. Michael was to move the women, children, and older men into the hills for the time being.

In the car, on the way to the Dunes, Tom was able to fill in more blanks, particularly in regards to the status of the treaty.

Dylan whistled and said, "So that rules out any state or federal help."

Brewster couldn't contain himself any longer. "Wait a minute. Are you telling me that we're going to fight a biker gang and some mobsters without help?"

Dylan replied, "WE aren't going to fight. You're not part of this and we'll get all the help we need from the Apaches."

"Dylan, you know I can shoot. If you're in this, I'm in it, too."

Dylan looked at Tom and then Sandowski, but each averted his gaze.

There wasn't a lot of talk the rest of the way as each man appeared consumed with their own thoughts. When they arrived at the jail, Dylan saw the prisoner in his cell.

"You didn't tell me you had a guest."

Tom smiled. "That's a whole separate can of worms, but no less deadly."

He pointed at the prisoner whose mouth was still taped. "This here is The Cowboy. He's one of the CIA's top assassin's."

"Doesn't look very deadly to me. The tape is a nice touch, though. I'm guessing it wasn't a minor traffic violation."

Brew had to sit down. His excellent adventure had taken a seriously wrong turn.

Tom laughed. "No, Cowboy here came to kill another CIA operative, Buck Robertson, who served in Nam with your daddy and me."

"And where is he?"

"He's in L.A. with Manny. They're staying with Carlos Garcia."

Dylan held up his hands. "Let's go to your office. I need a drink before I hear any more."

Brew jumped up. "Count me in."

Tom looked at Dylan. "Hold on a minute. We need to keep Cowboy from prying eyes until Buck returns. I was hoping you'd have a place in mind."

Dylan smiled. "You know I do. Can it wait until morning?"

"Morning's fine."

They went next door to Tom's office. Fortunately, he had replenished his supply of Bourbon and Tequila because this was going to be a long story.

CHAPTER FORTY-TWO

Fear and Greed

Los Angeles

Paulie knew that he needed some help if he was going to survive in these shark-infested waters. Reaching out to Carlos Garcia was a shot in the dark, but Paulie had nothing more to lose. Carlos was more than willing to meet for lunch, himself curious as to the status of the unions after the news of Vito Rotelli's death. He was surprised, however, that Paulie was more interested in quizzing him about the Mexican/Arizona desert and, in particular, the Apaches who called it home.

He explained to Carlos that the same East L.A. biker gang that was trying to muscle in on the union business, was also planning an assault on the Apache Reservation, after being rebuffed in their attempt to build a meth lab on the Indians' territory.

Carlos smiled at the news. "Do you have any idea how big the biker gang is?"

"I know how many they're sending. Forty, heavily-armed bikers, with body armor."

Carlos was pensive for a moment. "I assume they'll arrive by motorcycle?"

"As far as I know, that's the only way they travel."

"Well, unless there's something I'm missing, that won't be enough."

"But, but how can some Indians defend themselves being so outgunned?"

"If the battle was to take place in L.A., they couldn't. But the Apache's own the desert and they invented guerilla warfare. I'm speaking from personal experience. The Garcia cartel was once the most feared cartel in Mexico. Now they're just a footnote in history and all because they chose the wrong enemy, in the wrong place."

"You say they. Weren't you the leader?"

Carlos smiled. "I was the leader after the battle. Had I been involved then, we wouldn't be having this conversation."

"So, I shouldn't try to stop them?"

"If you consider them a threat to your business, I'd encourage them to go through with their plan. In fact, maybe I can help. Do you have a blank piece of paper?"

"Not with me."

He gave Paulie his card with his Holmby Hills address. "Give me a couple of hours and then stop by. I'll have something for you."

"Something what?"

"It's a map of the desert near the reservation that will be marked to show where the Apache's treasure is stored."

"What treasure?"

"Have you heard the story about El Dorado and the seven cities of gold?"

Paulie's eyes got big. "Is that true?"

Carlos smiled. "Maybe."

"If you know where it is, why don't you go after it?"

"You weren't listening. Number one, I don't need the money and, number two, it would be suicide for one man to go after it. Forty well-armed bikers? Who knows?"

"What are their chances of success?"

"Less than getting struck by lightning ten successive times."

Paulie smiled. "I'll stop by around three."

"Stay and have a drink. We'll talk about the union business."

After lunch, Paulie dialed the number on the biker's card. "Who's this?"

Paulie cleared his throat. "This is Paulie. We met in the lawyer's office."

"I thought you wasn't interested in talkin?"

"I needed to think things through."

"So, now you want to get on the winning team?"

"I don't see that I have a choice."

The biker laughed. "Maybe you ain't as dumb as you look. But, maybe we don't need you."

"You need me if you want a piece of the union business. Plus, I have a gift for you that makes the union business look like small potatoes."

"I'm listenin."

"You know the story of the seven cities of gold?"

"All Mexican's do, but that's a fairy tale."

"Is it?"

"You got somethin to say, you better say it."

"You thought that Vito wanted your help to take over a fucking Indian reservation? He would have given you the reservation. He wanted your muscle to help take the treasure that the Apaches have hidden in the hills nearby."

The biker was quiet.

"You there?"

"And you know where this treasure is?"

"Vito had the map and now I have it."

"And how'd he get it?"

"A blowtorch and a power drill are very persuasive instruments."

"Don't you forget it. When do I get the map?"

"We have to discuss my commission and I give it to you when you're ready to leave, not before. It's too valuable to be floating around."

"You get ten percent and that ain't negotiable. We leave here on Thursday, that's three days from now. Call me Wednesday night at this number."

When he hung up, Paulie couldn't help but smile. Maybe he was better at this business than he thought. He would meet Carlos and then call Sonny later.

Paulie understood what Carlos meant when he said he didn't need the money. The Holmby Hills mansion and grounds were incredible. His wheels were turning as he looked at Carlos in a new light. Money is power and Hollywood is all about power. Perhaps Carlos could be an ally in Paulie's quest to hang onto the unions.

Carlos handed Paulie a crudely drawn map marking the spot of the secret caves.

"Carlos, no offense, but this looks like you just drew it."

"That's because I did. The original map is falling apart from age."

"And, how do you know there is treasure there?"

"The seven cities are really seven caves where they stored gold from the mines nearby. When they translated the language, caves became cities."

"But you just have one x."

"That's because I only know where two of the caves are located—near that mark. I personally saw over thirty million dollars worth of gold removed from one of the caves."

Fear had now yielded to greed. Paulie was hooked.

"I still don't get how only a few Indians can protect it."

"They've done it for over three hundred years. Think about it. You'd need an army, literally, and that brings publicity. If the government finds out, they take it all."

"And, how did you witness the thirty million of gold?"

"That's a need to know situation and you, my new friend, don't need to know."

Paulie gazed around at the surroundings and smiled. "I think I have a good guess."

Carlos laughed. "Maybe you do and maybe you don't."

If Paulie was hooked the egotistical leader of the biker gang would be as well. Who wouldn't be?

After Paulie left, Carlos gave a copy of the map to Buck and Manny.

"Share this with the Sheriff. Tell them I gave it to the mob guy and told him that was where the treasure is stored."

Buck studied it. "What treasure is that?"

"Some call it El Dorado and some call it the seven cities of gold. Trust me, the bad guys will go looking for it and the Apaches will know what to do."

"Is it real?"

"Maybe yes, maybe no. No one who has gone looking for it has lived to say."

Buck understood. "I'll fax it to him right away."

CHAPTER FORTY-THREE

The Art of the Deal

Las Vegas

Bobbie answered the phone and told Sonny it was Paulie. Sonny had been expecting the call. "I was wonderin when you were gonna call."

"I was waiting to clear some things up before I called."

"What things?"

"Mainly Vito's Indian deal with the biker gang, but I got some other things to tell you."

"I was hopin that deal died with Vito."

"Me too, but I met with the bikers. Actually, they met with me, and they intend to go ahead with it. I told them that we were out."

"That's good. I mean the part about us not bein involved. What are the other things?"

"Well, the bikers brought up the union business."

"Shit. I was afraid of that."

"I hear rumors that others are snoopin around. Including some of our guys."

"That's what happens when they smell blood. What'd you tell the bikers?"

Paulie put some spin on his reply, as if he figured it out, rather than the attorney.

"Well, I was thinkin. The reason the bikers brought it up is that Vito admitted his weakness by seeking their muscle for the Indian deal.

They're the only outsiders, so to speak, that know that."

Sonny was impressed. Surprised by Paulie's intuition, but impressed. "I gotta say, that was good thinkin. Which of our guys are makin noise?"

"It'd be easier to tell you which ones aren't."

"Capiche. I'll deal with them. You got any ideas what to do with the bikers?"

"Not really, but I got some valuable information."

"You want me to guess what it is?"

"Sorry, Sonny, that's not what I meant. They told me when they're makin their move. It's Thursday."

"That's good to know. Anything else?"

"Just that I'd like to know where things stand after Vito's gone."

Sonny paused before replying, "Paulie, I'm gonna level with you. Nothin has been decided yet, but it was smart on your part to reach out. A lot's gonna depend on what happens with the bikers. If they can be dealt with, it will make the situation with the unions a lot easier. The best thing you can do right now is to keep me informed of any potential problems."

"Sonny, do I need to talk to Joey C., as well?"

"When you talk to me, you talk to Chicago. Capiche?"

"Yeah, capiche."

After hanging up with Paulie, Sonny rehashed the call with Bobbie. He had been planning on using the news of the treaty as leverage to gain access to Del's house. Now he had even more to offer and it was of more immediate concern. He dialed the Sheriff's number.

The sheriff's secretary answered and transferred the call. The sheriff smiled as he picked up the phone.

"Is this about the four hundred bucks I owe you for the taillights?"

"Sheriff, I got more important things to talk to you about."

"From now on, it's Tom. I'm all ears, but first, and again, I owe you for what you did for Buck Robertson and Manny."

"I'm glad you feel that way, because I need a favor from you, and I have two more bits of news that you're gonna be interested in."

"Why don't we start with the two bits of news?"

"Fair enough. Number one, our guy in L.A. got mixed up in the deal with the Apaches."

Tom cut in, "Your guy in L.A. was the deal."

"It was his play, which I opposed by the way, but he got in bed with some bad hombres, a biker gang from East L.A. for the muscle."

"That's old news."

"Understood. You gotta let me finish. I don't know if you got the news, but our guy died the other day. In the saddle, by the way."

"We should all be so lucky."

"Luck didn't have anything to do with it, but that's another story. Anyway, I got to wonderin why the Indians hadn't alerted the state or federal authorities."

Tom tensed.

"So I had someone look into it. Someone very skilled."

"And what did they find out?"

"They found out that the treaty that created the reservation had been cancelled by an amendment."

"Sonny, how many people know about this?"

"Only a trusted few."

"And you want to trade this information for a favor?"

"Far from it. I called to tell you that the only copy of the amendment, that cancelled the treaty, no longer exists. It disappeared from the National Archives."

"How'd that happen?"

"Shit happens."

"So, you're saying the treaty isn't cancelled?"

"I ain't sayin that. I'm sayin the National Archives doesn't have proof that it was."

"Sonny, you don't know how valuable that information is. You said you had something else."

"I do. I was hopin the Indian deal died with Vito, our guy in L.A., but I just learned that the bikers aren't giving it up."

"We figured as much. Was that the news?"

"No, the news is that they're coming on Thursday."

"Sonny, are you sure of that?"

"Unless something changes between now and then and that ain't likely. By the way, I'm sending you a surprise tomorrow."

"What kind of surprise?"

"If I tell you it won't be a surprise. Trust me, you'll like it."

"Do I need to sit back down for your favor?"

"Why are you always tryin to bust my balls? I'm tryin to be a friend."

"Sorry, it's just things are pretty fucked up around here right now."

"I got news for you. Things are pretty fucked up all over the world."

"Capiche."

"You ever think you secretly want to be Italian?"

Tom laughed. "Okay, I'm braced. What can I do for you?"

"You can relax. All I want is access to the dead agent's house, the one where the shootout was. I just need a day or two?"

"That's all?"

"That's all and then we're even."

Tom was perplexed. "You looking for those guns that disappeared?"

"What guns?"

Tom laughed. "Is this need to know?"

"I talked it over with Bobbie and we decided we'd be straight up with you if we find what we're looking for, but that's not guaranteed. Until then, yeah—it's need to know."

"Fair enough, but I gotta warn you. The feds scrubbed the house from top to bottom. They didn't find anything."

"From my experience with the FBI, they couldn't find their asses with a GPS. We'll take our chances."

CHAPTER FORTY-FOUR

The Trap

Apache Dunes

So far, it had been a good day for Tom, the sheriff. He had received the map from Buck Robertson via fax in the morning and Sonny's call shortly after noon. Both messages conveyed valuable intel and they needed all of the help they could muster. The clock was ticking and it was time to convene a meeting to formulate a plan of battle. It was decided to meet in Tom's office as Chief Michael Taza was concerned about prying eyes and ears on the reservation.

Tom and Michael were joined by Geronimo Dylan, Max, Homer, Snoop, and Dylan's friend Brew. Tom opened the meeting by sharing the information he received from Buck and Sonny and then decided to pass the gavel.

"It seems to me that this might be like deja vu and, God willing, might be a replay of the battle with El Diablo and the Garcia cartel. That being the case, and unless somebody objects, I'm going to turn things over to Geronimo who, with Michael, was the architect of that battle plan. Michael, you okay with that? This is your fight."

"I just did what Geronimo told me to do. He planned the battle."

"How about you, Max?"

"If it ain't broke, don't fix it."

"Geronimo, you have the floor."

Dylan was pensive for a moment before he stood. "If we succeed, we owe Carlos and Sonny for the intel. Without that, I'm not sure what our strategy would be. Here's what might work: I don't see them not coming after the treasure; Carlos gave them the GPS coordinates. So, we'll be fighting them on our turf and the high ground. Our positions, in the rocks, will check their weapons and body armor. Napoleon conquered the most brilliant generals and most powerful armies in Europe using a similar strategy. He would launch a half-hearted attack and then retreat, drawing the opposing forces into an ambush, made possible by favorable terrain. It's simple, but effective.

"The fact that they'll be coming by motorcycle exposes them, but they will have the body armor. If we can destroy or even disable the bikes, they will be on foot in the desert and the body armor will be stifling. Time will be all on our side. Michael, how many braves can you count on?"

Michael grimaced. "Twenty—maybe a few more. The rest will be needed to get the women, children, and old men to the high country. That is, if we want the reservation to be deserted."

Dylan turned to Tom, "How are we fixed for weapons?"

"Plenty of rifles and ammo, plus all the water, rations and blankets we'll need if this turns into a siege."

"Michael, go ahead with the evacuation plan. The deserted reservation should turn their attention to the map. I have an idea."

Dylan turned to Snoopy. "Snoopy, I need you to do aerial recon. Let us know where they are at all times."

Snoopy replied, "Roger that, but I can do you one better. The original, calibrated machine guns came with the Sopwith. I detached them, but have kept them greased and the ammo dry."

A visible buzz was developing among the team. Brew was nothing less than awestruck.

Dylan paced a bit before issuing the orders.

"Okay, here's the plan. Tom, you and Max organize the equipment and I'll take you to the cave. We'll take the prisoner, too. Snoopy, Homer can help you with the machine guns. Michael, get a couple of your best marksmen and set up an ambush to pick off the bikers who are bringing up the rear. If we stage it where the sand is soft, they won't be able to pursue the shooters on their motorcycles. Maybe two teams, five or so miles apart. Get into their heads. We'll erect a flimsy barricade on the road from the reservation to the hills. We'll fire a couple of volleys and appear to make a hasty retreat toward the hills. That will be the bait."

"Then, I clean up." Snoopy jumped in.

"Not yet. All we need to do is lure them into our trap."

Privately, the idea of a stoned Snoopy with twin machine guns scared the crap out of Dylan. He was sure that Tom, Max and Homer shared his concern.

"If any of them survive and try to escape, they're all yours and you'll have all the time in the world."

Brew looked at Dylan. "What do I do?"

"You stay with me and keep your head down."

Brew frowned. He had no intention of being left out of the action.

CHAPTER FORTY-FIVE

Failure to Plan

Los Angeles/Las Vegas

M anny had tried to reach Fatima by phone, but to no avail. He realized it was probably a futile quest, as she was now aware that she had been deceived by him. Deceived and bugged. Buck and Manny took turns tracking her movements via the tracking device in her backpack. After meeting Hayes in Venice Beach, her travels had been limited to her neighborhood. She had not returned to the USC campus.

Hayes' movements were more problematical. It was doubtful that he would be carrying around the two devices he had taken from Fatima. However, as long as he didn't discard them, they would be useful in locating his residence. First things first, however, as all eyes were focused on the target's campaign rally in Las Vegas on Thursday.

If Fatima hadn't abandoned her plans, her dot should be moving toward a connection to I-15 North and Las Vegas. That is, provided she took her backpack with her. Buck said the odds were heavy that Hayes had his own tracking device on Fatima and, if she headed to Vegas, he would likely be close behind.

On Wednesday morning Manny saw the dot begin to move rapidly in a northerly direction. He called out for Buck, "It's show time!"

Buck looked at the screen. "She's on the move and she'll connect with I-15 just west of San Bernardino. Let's rock."

They had been packed and prepped for the past two days. Carlos insisted that they take his Bentley. Buck's initial reaction was that the Bentley was too conspicuous, but his fears were soon allayed after they passed at least three others before even hitting I-15. He had to laugh to himself. A Ford or Chevy were more conspicuous in Las Vegas.

Manny drove while Buck watched his iPad and the tracking app. Hayes' dots hadn't moved. No surprise there, but he was looking forward to paying a visit to Venice Beach upon their return from Vegas.

Buck was on the horns of a real dilemma. If they failed to stop Fatima's plan, and why else would she be headed toward Las Vegas, an assassination attempt, via a bomb, would have considerable collateral damage. However, who could he alert if the government was complicit in the plot? He would try to stop her, but if he failed, he would notify the state and local authorities.

Manny and Buck continued on I-15 North at Primm just across the California/Nevada border. This was the main route from L.A. to Vegas and his hunch was right as Fatima's dot was also on I-15 North approximately five to ten miles ahead of them. They would have ample time to close the gap, but wanted to stay at least a mile behind. Unless she tossed the backpack, they would find out where she was headed. Plus, it was Wednesday and the event wasn't until tomorrow afternoon. They had plenty of time to locate her. The biggest unknown variable was the size of her team, if she had one. Buck was convinced that she had issues, but couldn't see her as a martyr, at least, not by plan.

Therein was the rub for Fatima. Her team consisted of Saleh and her plan was entirely dependent on him. She had failed to develop a Plan B. and, "Failure to plan is to plan for failure."

She was glad to be out of L.A. and to actually see the sky on her way to Las Vegas. She smiled to herself believing that Manny had no clue where she was and what she was about to orchestrate. She was wrong on both counts. The hunter was the prey. Hayes, on the other hand, was likely nearby. The difference was that Manny's mission was to stop her, while Hayes was there merely to observe.

When she snapped out of her reverie, she became concerned that Saleh hadn't spoken for the last hour or so. She could tell that he was nervous, but wasn't that natural for such a situation? How would she know? What if he got cold feet and refused to complete his task? She had to "change the channel" and think about something else. The consequences of a mission abort by Saleh were obvious, but too overwhelming to even think about. Hopefully, that wouldn't happen, inshallah!

As they neared Las Vegas, Buck had Manny edge closer to the signal, closing the gap to approximately a quarter mile. He doubted that she would have an entourage. The vast majority of assassination plots, particularly by bombing, were carried out by individuals. The bomber typically had a puppetmaster, but it wasn't a good idea to have too many others around when the suicide vest was donned. The bomber just may wonder why the other fervent disciples weren't interested in martyrdom themselves. Seventy-two virgins were enough to share. As expected, when they identified Fatima's vehicle, it appeared to be travelling alone.

Fatima, however, wasn't travelling alone. She was driving and there was a male passenger riding shotgun.

Manny had become a believer in Buck's intuition, understanding it came from experience. Buck had predicted that Fatima's destination would be Caesars Palace. That was where the campaign rally was scheduled for the following day. There would be security monitoring the attendees, but guests of the hotel would be otherwise free to come and go. Also, it was not uncommon to see Arab dress in Las Vegas as it was a popular destination for disposing of excess oil dollars while sampling the forbidden fruits of the infidels.

When Fatima pulled up to the valet, Buck instructed Manny to keep going. There was someone he wanted to see at the Pompeii.

CHAPTER FORTY-SIX

What Happens in Vegas Stays in Vegas

Las Vegas

Buck retrieved Sonny's card from his wallet and dialed his cell phone. Sonny answered immediately.

"Sonny here."

"Sonny, this is Buck Robertson. Buck and Manny. You remember?"

"My memory ain't that bad. What can I do for you?"

"We're in town. In Vegas, and I was hoping we could meet. I need a couple of favors."

Sonny sighed. "Doesn't everybody? I can't remember the last time somebody called just to say hello."

"I understand, but this involves Vegas. Can you meet us for a late lunch or a drink?"

"I was just headin down to Carlucci. Where are you?"

"No more than a couple of blocks away. We'll meet you there."

They dropped the Bentley off with the valet at Pompeii, noting there were two others in the queue. Sonny was seated in his booth, his office. He rose to greet them.

"I got bad news for you. Your suite is already booked."

Buck and Manny laughed. "No problem. We do need a room tonight, but at Caesars, not here. Can you help? We'll pay of course."

"Ask me something hard. Consider it done and your money isn't any good in this town. What else do you need?"

"A shovel."

Manny was as puzzled as Sonny at the request.

Sonny furrowed his brow. "You wanna tell me what's up?"

"It's kind of a long story."

"This ain't Mickey D's. You've got time, plus we haven't even ordered yet."

After ordering lunch and telling the waiter not to rush, Sonny motioned for Buck to continue.

"Are you aware there's a campaign rally for Donald Trump tomorrow at Caesars?"

"Yeah. Bobbie and I were talkin about goin. Just out of curiosity"

"Well, we're tailing a suicide bomber and his accomplice and they just checked into Caesars."

Sonny appeared pensive. "So that's it?"

Buck and Manny looked at each other. "What do you mean? You don't appear to be surprised."

"I heard a rumor from a pretty good source. I never asked you about your business after the explosion and you needin to disappear for a few days, but I kinda put two and two together. You got a plan?"

"It's a couple. A man and woman, but they're not married. We have a little history with her so he's got to be the bomber. Typically, they use explosive vests. The rally is tomorrow afternoon. There's no reason for him to be walking around with the vest until then, but chances are they want to case the premises. If we can isolate him, I recently learned of a good interrogation tool."

"That's where the shovel comes in?"

"Bingo."

"Well, you're in luck. I've got a shovel in my trunk that's never been used—which I still regret. And, there's no shortage of sand. The only danger is diggin a hole that's already occupied."

After lunch, Sonny drove them over to Caesars and arranged for the room while they stayed in the shadows, just in case. It turned out that Sonny had some experience in these types of things. Shortly after they went up to inspect their room, Sonny answered the knock on the door and two burly Caesars maintenance men delivered a large laundry cart. Apparently, the mob still controlled the union.

"This is Butch and Chip, two friends of ours."

Butch handed Sonny a card and the keys to a truck. Buck and Manny seemed puzzled.

"If the laundry cart gets full, just call Butch and they'll take it down to the loading dock where a green laundry truck is parked. They'll load it for you and you can drive it to the laundry."

Sonny gave Butch and Chip each ten black chips from Pompeii. They were more than happy. Buck smiled at the brilliance of Sonny's generosity. They would do the needful and odds were the chips would be back in Pompeii's coffers within twenty-four hours.

Now it was a waiting game. They took positions near the elevators, assuming that their prey would want to scout out the premises at some time. Buck and Manny were as disguised as possible: baseball hats, dark shades and newspapers as both had interacted with Fatima. The bomber wasn't a problem.

A little more than an hour later, Fatima and Saleh emerged from the elevator in the lobby. Just another couple of tourists blinded by the lights. As expected, they appeared particularly interested in the Colosseum where special events were held. Events like tomorrow's political rally.

The break came when Fatima and the bomber decided to split up. They appeared to have a disagreement. Fatima remained cool, but the bomber seemed anything but. Fatima headed toward the Forum shops while the bomber headed in the direction of the lobby elevators. Buck and Manny had to walk quickly to catch up with him. When they arrived at the elevator the bomber followed another couple onto the elevator. That posed a potential problem, but Buck and Manny had to run with it.

They knew that Fatima's room was on the forty-fourth floor, seven floors above theirs, and were relieved when the couple pressed twenty. As it turned out, if the couple had to travel a couple of more floors, they likely would have had sex in the elevator. The bomber was disgusted. Buck and Manny were amused.

As soon as the amorous couple exited and the elevator door closed, Buck struck with lightning-fast reflexes. Buck stabbed the bomber in the neck with the tranquilizer needle and he collapsed almost immediately. Manny was amazed and impressed, but realized this wasn't Buck's first rodeo. They propped the bomber between them—just a pal who couldn't hold his liquor. A scene that was probably played out several times a night in tinsel town and would arouse little suspicion, if they encountered anyone in the hallway. They didn't.

Butch and Chip arrived within thirty minutes, picked up the laundry cart and loaded it into the truck near the loading docks. Buck and Manny followed them down. Manny was the designated driver and Buck rode shotgun.

The drive into the desert took approximately forty-five minutes. They were well into the drive and not a word had been spoken. Finally, Buck turned to Manny. "You gonna tell me what's on your mind?"

Manny sighed. "I was just thinking, is all."

"And?"

"I was just thinking about the ride out to the desert with the Al Qaeda bomber. With the possible exception of Homer, you guys all have more experience in these types of things than me. And … it was interesting to me that no one spoke during the drive, knowing what was about to happen. Just like now."

"I can only speak for myself, Buck replied, but I believe this applies to the others, as well. Regardless of how many people you kill, it's not something you want to get used to. I think those periods of introspection, as brief as they may be, are to convince yourself that it hasn't become a second nature. If and when it does, and you become immune to doubt and emotion, you have a serious problem. Until that day arrives, we're dispensers of justice. Justice as we see it. It's what we do. You're still a young man. Me, I'm getting too old for this."

"I get that and understand why the Al Qaeda guy had to be interrogated and die, but what purpose does it serve to interrogate this guy?"

"None. I was thinking the same thing. Our job is to eliminate him before he kills countless innocent people. I don't get my jollies from torture unless it's a means to an end. I did hear a rumor, though, about a guy who was fed alive to some starving hogs. That was personal."

"Remind me to never piss you off. This looks good. Let's get this over with."

They dug a shallow grave and did a double tap at the base of Saleh's skull. He'd never regained consciousness.

It was a different kind of quiet on the drive back into town. It was now all about Fatima and Manny's inner turmoil in that regard was obvious. Buck struggled for words of solace, but none came to mind.

It was close to midnight when they hit the Strip again, however Sonny had insisted they call when they had completed their task. The first part of their task, regardless of the time. Buck had an idea and asked Sonny if there was a chance of getting a keycard for Fatima's room. Sonny said he would check and call them right back.

"When you get back to the hotel, stop by the front desk and ask for Carl. Tell him your Sonny's friends. The keycard will be waiting for you."

Neither Buck, nor Manny knew what to expect when they would encounter Fatima. They were confident that they had buried the real bomber, but had no clue as to what Fatima's reaction would be. They were hoping that she might be asleep, but that was doubtful with the bomber's disappearance.

They entered the room with guns drawn and as quietly as possible. No lights were on, but the odor of hashish permeated the room. That didn't surprise Buck as it was long suspected that suicide bombers were infused with false courage. A video camera was on a tripod. Probably for the bomber's final statement.

They found Fatima wrapped in a hotel robe and curled up in the fetal position in a corner of the room. She was aware of their presence, but made no effort to move. Manny spoke first. "Fatima, I'm going to turn the light on. Don't be startled."

She shielded her eyes from the light as she sat up, still clutching her robe. "I was expecting you. I knew it was you when Saleh didn't return. Is he dead?"

Manny just nodded.

Her gaze shifted to Buck. "I see you brought the Doctor with you."

Manny knelt to be at eye level with her. "Fatima, it's over. I don't know how you got mixed up in this, but maybe we can get you some help."

Fatima laughed. "You were the only man I ever wanted to believe and you lied to me. Why would I believe you now?"

"Fatima, you're involved up to your neck in a plot to assassinate a candidate for president and who knows how many innocent people would die in the process. You aren't a victim. Now get dressed and come with us. We'll try to get you some help. It's over."

She struggled to her feet. She faced them and let the robe fall open. She was wearing the explosive belt underneath. "You're right. It's over."

Buck and Manny were both startled. Buck started to back away, but Manny, now standing, didn't move. He motioned for Buck to get out, but Buck hesitated as Manny held both hands out to Fatima.

"If you want to die, fine. I'll go with you, but let him go. I'm the one who deceived you."

Manny again motioned for Buck to leave and this time he backed toward the door, opened it and fled.

Fatima wasn't just confused, again, by this strange young man. She was stoned and confused. Good riddance for Saleh, she thought. He was never going to go through with it. He was a coward, but who was this man who wasn't afraid of death?

Ironically, if Manny had shown fear, she might have reacted differently, but the bane of her existence had always been her need to be equal to any man. She toyed with the cord that would trigger the device. Tears started to stream down her face. The tears of sadness were mixed with tears of joy as she realized she now could face death without fear. No man could do more. Her life, as fucked up as it could be, was now complete. She gazed at Manny.

"I know you won't understand, but I have to die. You don't. I forgive you, but if you don't kill me we're both going to die."

Now, Manny was crying too and he couldn't remember the last time he cried. Probably when Davey was killed. He reached out for her. "Please don't. You don't have to die and I don't want to die. I'll get you help. I'll wait for you."

"Maybe in the next life it will be different. I have just one request."

"I'll do whatever you ask."

"Please kiss me and then kill me. It has to be. It is written."

Manny didn't want the kiss to ever end. He knew she was going to die, one way or another. He also knew the fate she faced if she lived.

Buck had gradually re-approached the room when there had been no explosion. He heard the gunshot through the door. He still had the keycard and entered to find Manny kneeling while he cradled Fatima's lifeless body and rocked it back and forth. He knelt beside him and tried to wipe away the tears that were flowing from Manny's eyes. There was nothing that could be said. Neither would remember how long they stayed in their positions. Eventually, Manny gently laid Fatima down and turned in silence to Buck.

Buck stood and helped Manny up. "I'll call Sonny."

Sonny must have been expecting the call as he arrived within thirty minutes with two other men he didn't introduce. In the meantime, Buck had removed the suicide vest from her body and disabled it.

It was apparent to Sonny that Manny was distressed. He walked over to him. "How do you want me to handle this?"

"I don't want her buried in the desert like an animal."

"How's this? We have friends with a crematorium. We'll take her there and nobody will know nothin. I'll have the ashes saved in a nice urn and kept for you. Someday, you can come back and decide what to do with them."

Manny looked up. "Thanks, Sonny. I'd like that."

Sonny gave his men their marching orders. "Go get a laundry cart. The truck is still by the loading docks. Take the body to the crematorium. I'll call ahead, but I want her cremated immediately. If anybody gives you any shit, you call me. Take the carpet cleaner and clean up before you leave and get rid of the clothes and stuff."

He then turned to Buck and Manny. "Let's get your stuff. I got a suite waitin for you and Bobbie's gonna make us some breakfast."

After Sonny's guys went to fetch the laundry cart, Manny asked if he could be alone with Fatima for a minute before they left. He knelt and kissed her again. "In the next life it will be different. I promise you that."

In the days that followed, Buck and Manny would share a symbiotic relationship. Buck provided consolation and moral support. He would be the father that Manny never knew and, in turn, Manny would be the son Buck's career had deprived him of.

It was clear to Buck that Manny had a void in his life. One that was improbable, if not impossible, for Fatima to fill. Holmby Hills was the perfect place for both to rest and recuperate.

Manny found Buck in the gazebo with his coffee, gazing at his laptop. "Morning."

"Good morning. How'd you sleep?"

"Like a log. I needed that."

"You know, I've been thinking. I haven't heard you mention Marta, wasn't that her name?"

Manny sat down. "I may not have mentioned her, but I've been thinking about her a lot. Her and little Max."

Buck sipped at his coffee to help collect his thoughts. "Manny, they say that 'God works in strange ways' and, whatever happens from now on out, the time we've spent together has been very special to me."

Manny started to speak, but Buck cut him off.

"I need to finish. This is important to both of us." He paused, then continued. "It's become clear to me that we both have voids in our lives. If only for a short period of time, you've been like a son to me. The son I never had. So, forgive me, but I'm going to give you some more fatherly advice. I think you were trying to make Fatima fill your void, knowing in your heart that it wasn't meant to be."

He held up his hands to stop Manny from interrupting. "I think you need to spend some time with Marta and the baby. They need you and I think that you need them."

Manny wiped at his eyes and took a deep breath before replying. "I can never tell you what you've meant to me. I didn't allow myself to think about Marta because, well … I didn't expect to survive this trip." He finally smiled. "And what a trip it's been!"

"Again, I'm not trying to intrude, but have you thought about having Marta and the baby come for a visit? Your house in Apache Dunes is certainly big enough for three."

Manny smiled again. "For four. You're forgetting about Max. Big Max. He'd be like the grandfather. I never thought about it, but I went from no father to two. God does work in strange ways."

Buck raised his coffee cup as if to toast. "I went for years, if not decades, wondering about what I was doing in life. I didn't question my orders. I just assumed the end justified the means. Well, this mission, which was off the books, has clearly been a righteous one."

"Is it over, now?"

Buck turned the laptop so that Manny could see the two beeping dots in Venice Beach. "Almost. We have one final task."

"Hayes?"

"How does a late lunch in Venice Beach sound?"
"Just what the doctor ordered."

CHAPTER FORTY-SEVEN

Matthew 26:52

The Desert

It was a bitter irony of history that so much blood had been spilled over such a godforsaken place as the Arizona/Northern Mexico desert. The ground was anything but fertile and the climate was as hostile as the desert denizens. As far as natural resources, the rumors of cities of gold had morphed into myth over the ages and were likely only sustained by the fact that no one, who had ever pursued that elusive treasure, had returned to talk about it.

For the Apaches, however, it was home and they had nowhere else to go. If the gold did exist, it was less valuable to them than maize or the fruit of the agave plant. Their sole desire was to be left alone to live as they had for centuries.

They always seemed to be at a strategic disadvantage to the so-called more advanced cultures. The Conquistadors had guns and germs, neither of which the Apaches could effectively counter, but their legacy included guns and horses left behind. Both would be of use to the Apaches.

Centuries later it was the doctrine of manifest destiny that would be used to try to evict the Apaches from their ancestral home. Indian leaders took part in many pow wows to determine why the whites and the Mexicans coveted such a place, when they had almost unlimited space—and better space—elsewhere. It made no sense. The conclusion was that the real goal was to destroy the Apaches and their culture.

The desert, itself, would be the Apache's only advantage, but a formidable one —schizophrenic in nature—possessing two polar opposite personalities. Daytime the temperatures frequently reached triple digits as the sand reflected, rather than absorbed the sun's intense rays. At night, however, with the sand bereft of any of the day's heat, the temperature plummets. The daytime hunter became the nighttime prey.

The hills that surrounded the desert contained a series of secret caves which the Apaches used to maximum advantage. They were always outnumbered and outgunned, but amazingly they could narrow the odds. Perhaps most notably, the legendary Apache Chief Geronimo, and a band of just thirty or so Apaches evaded capture by a combined force of ten thousand U.S. and Mexican army troops and bounty hunters for almost a year—disappearing into the hills each time they appeared to be surrounded.

It was the same knowledge of the caves and mastery of the hostile environment that allowed Dylan, Jake, Chief Taza and a handful of Apaches to kill El Diablo, the ruthless leader of the Garcia cartel, and the majority of his soldiers barely a year ago. Call it what you like, déjà vu or Groundhog Day, it was happening again.

What was different this time was the invaders were a violent motorcycle gang from East L.A. armed with even more sophisticated weapons and body armor. What hadn't changed were the Apache defenders and the desert itself. That, and the fact that the motorcycle gang had no historical perspective. Arrogance and ignorance is a deadly cocktail.

Snoopy got airborne as per plan and the original equipment twin machine guns had been re-installed on the Sopwith. Unfortunately, they hadn't had time for a meaningful test, but after a couple of quick bursts, the propellers were still intact. Dylan's biggest fear was that Snoopy was too anxious to use them.

Dylan was a disciple of Sun Tzu and understood the danger of leaving defeated survivors, who would harbor their hatred and live to fight another day. This had to end, now. Key to that plan was for Snoopy not to spook the bikers before they were lured into the trap. He would have an open road for at least a hundred miles for cleanup duty, if any survived the battle.

It wasn't that Snoopy was blood thirsty, quite to the contrary. Rather, the only conflict he had ever participated in turned out to be anything but righteous. In a strange way, he looked forward to balancing the books a bit.

Snoopy had radioed in that the bikers numbered forty by his count and were approximately eighty miles from the reservation. Dylan communicated as much to his troops. The Apaches invented, and then perfected, guerilla warfare. Constantly outnumbered and outgunned, they needed every trick in the book. The first part of the plan involved having two teams, each composed of a sniper and a spotter, distanced five miles apart, twenty and twenty-five miles from the reservation. Each of the markers were selected for the slight bend in the road and the soft, adjacent sand. Their jobs would be to pick off the last two riders at each stage.

With any luck, the gunshots would be masked by the roar of the bikes and the bikers might not know immediately that they were thirty-eight and then thirty-six before they reached the reservation. The logic in not trying to kill more at that time, was the fear of them panicking and turning back. If they were successful in eliminating four bad guys, it would spook them psychologically. Particularly the ones now bringing up the rear.

After agonizing over the safest haven for Brew, who insisted on participating, Dylan placed him on the first sniper team. Brew was a skilled marksman, at least on a range, but initially the targets shouldn't be firing back before Brew and his spotter could escape. Reality proved even better than hoped for. The bikers had made the five hundred mile trip a two-day ride and, even after more than two hundred miles on the second day, the pairs of riders were spaced yards apart. Brew followed Dylan's instructions and started breathing deeply after the first bikers passed the marker. He was as relaxed as possible when the trailing pair approached. On cue from the spotter, Brew fired off four head shots in rapid succession. At least two found their marks and the riders and their bikes skidded out of control into the desert. Most importantly, it didn't appear that they had been immediately missed by the others. Two ATVs would take Brew and his Apache spotter on a short cut across the desert to the rendezvous with Dylan and the team.

Before Brew could check in, Snoopy had witnessed the hits from high above the desert and radioed the news. As the bikers approached the second marker, they had yet to appear to notice that there had been attrition in their ranks.

Things didn't go as smoothly with the second team. The first bullet found its target, but the second was a whiff. Even then, however, it took valuable time for the other targeted biker to alert the line in front. It was then that they noticed that not just one biker had been killed, but three. In the confusion, helmets were donned for the first time, but the hiatus gave the sniper team ample time to make their getaway. Once they got off the road, the hogs wouldn't be able to compete with the ATVs on the terrain. The bikers learned this quickly after two of the bikes got bogged down in the soft sand. The spots had been chosen specifically for that reason. Dylan was hoping that the bikers might assume that all of the desert sand was soft. Truth is, some, if not most, was as hard as pavement.

Snoopy reported in that one more biker was down and the gang now appeared to be spooked with weapons drawn and necks craning in all directions. They even noticed the plane above and fired off a series of shots that came too close for comfort and Snoopy maneuvered the plane out of harm's way. It took all of his self-control not to circle back with machine guns blazing, but he would stick to the script and took another hit on his doobie and played "Brothers in Arms" by Mark Knopfler and Dire Straits. Every man has to die.

Snoopy observed animated discussion among the bikers, and when they took off again, they stayed in a more compact formation as they proceeded toward the reservation. It was clear, that Dylan had gotten into their heads. Thank you Sun Tzu.

When they arrived at the reservation they noticed what appeared to be a barricade approximately half a mile up the road. The leader signaled for them to turn onto the reservation. They could check out the barricade later. The leader relaxed a bit with that decision. He fashioned himself back in control of the situation. However, and as per design, all of the residents had been moved to higher ground, days before. Save for a couple of stray dogs, the reservation was totally deserted. The bikers worked off some nervous energy by firing indiscriminately at the structures and vehicles that remained.

The bikers gathered near the new schoolhouse, sans windows from their most recent visit. They would extract their revenge on a building, as they had previously threatened. The gang watched as two of the bikers wired the school with the plastique supplied by Uncle Sam. They put plenty of distance between themselves and the building before detonating the explosives. The tremor and the boom traveled miles in all directions. With the plume of smoke reaching to the heavens, it was confirmation that the bikers had done what Dylan et al hoped to avoid, by vacating the reservation. The message was sent and received. It was game on and only one side would survive.

Thirty-seven strong with AK-47s and clad in helmets and body armor, the leader was confident to the point of smugness. They had planned for victory. Apparently, he was not familiar with the Yiddish proverb, "Man plans and God laughs."

The purpose of the flimsy barricade, which should have been a tip-off, was simply to create the illusion of a retreat that would draw the enemy into the ambush. Napoleon would have been proud. As the bikers approached, re-invigorated by laying waste to an unoccupied building, two Apaches fired off a few rounds of regular ammo with no expectation of doing any damage. Their random volley was met with withering fire from the AK-47s, but the Apaches had already taken flight. The time it took the bikers to disassemble the barricade bought them some valuable time.

The adrenaline rush apparently made them forget about their three fallen comrades. The leader consulted the treasure map and smiled. He knew exactly where the Apaches were headed and barricades might slow them down, but nothing would stop them now. Particularly now that they had the Indians on the run.

When they arrived at the designated coordinates, they saw no evidence of any resistance. The hills were as depicted on the map. The cave had to be up among the rocks. The only thing that was unusual was a large cardboard box on the desert floor below the rocks. They knew that the Apaches had to be hiding in the rocks, but the bikers were emboldened by their body armor. They would spread out and comb through the rocks, overwhelming any opposition.

What they didn't know, one of the many things they didn't know, was that "The Wolf" had actually delivered the more lethal Colt AR-15 rifles with 5.56 x 45 rounds of armor-piercing ammunition for his East L.A. partners. Vito may have been naïve to get into bed with them, but, and to his credit, there was no way that they were getting lethal weaponry that could be/would have been used against him. He simply substituted the popular Kalashnikov AK-47s and kept the Armalite designed AR-15s. When Paulie disclosed that to Sonny, he was instructed to rent a truck immediately and have a couple of his soldiers drive the AR-15s and the ammo down to Apache Dunes where they were to be delivered to the sheriff.

First thing the bikers did was inspect the curious box, wary that it could be some type of booby trap. They found no wires and it appeared to be empty—although they could swear they heard some type of sound. The leader kept his distance while he ordered one of his minions to remove it. When he did so, he was so shocked that he fell down as he backpedaled. Hardened bikers suddenly shivered in fear despite the intense desert heat.

What unnerved them so was the head of a man who was alive, barely, but buried up to his neck in the desert sand. It was the Cowboy. Their shock and fear was palpable which is what the unexpected will do. The leader tried to regain control of the situation as they saw a scorpion emerge from the victim's hair and strike at his face. "He didn't have no weapon or no body armor. We do."

With that pronouncement the Apaches opened fire and the protective vests might as well have been terrycloth. A minimum of half of the bikers were killed immediately, including their leader. Several others were killed as they tried to flee, but at least ten made it to their bikes and headed pell-mell back to the road.

Dylan radioed Snoopy, "It's show time."

Snoopy was ready. He had toked up and selected "Twilight Zone" by Golden Earrings for accompaniment as he transformed the desert highway into a killing floor. His victims never saw it coming. Snoopy swooped in from behind and unleashed the twin machine guns on his prey. Then he circled around and made one more pass for good measure. Even Snoopy might not have known whom his wrath was directed at. The military industrial complex? The establishment? The Red Baron? One thing was certain, the bikers were just proxies in the wrong place at the wrong time. He had carried the yoke of guilt for dropping bombs on innocent civilians for years. It was like the great Muhammad Ali said, "The North Vietnamese never did anything to me." But, this was righteous—of that much he was sure. He switched to Bob Dylan's "Knocking on Heaven's Door" for the flight back to the Dunes.

Dylan, Tom, Max, Brew, Chief Taza and the Apaches emerged from the rocks. Some of the younger braves made war whoops, but most were somber. One more time, the desert was littered with dead bodies, but the spectacle of the Cowboy, though a victim of his own devices, gave no one joy.

Like with the Al Qaeda bomber, Max would deliver the coup de gras. The Cowboy was no different than the bikers. He came to the desert as a merchant of death. Matthew 26:52, "Live by the sword, die by the sword."

The intent had been for Buck Robertson, the Cowboy's intended victim, to render justice after an interrogation, but the verdict was a foregone conclusion and it wasn't likely that the Cowboy could tell Buck anything he didn't already know. They had received Buck's approval beforehand.

Chief Michael Taza turned to Dylan. "Geronimo, we have to stop meeting like this."

Dylan smiled finally. "Do you still have the pit on the reservation?"

"They're waiting for my call. This one's gonna take a little time. What about the motorcycles?"

"Any that will still run, you're welcome to."

That elicited a few smiles from the young Apaches.

Michael then kicked at the sand. "You know the explosion was the school."

Dylan replied, "We didn't lose anybody, which is a miracle. What man destroys, man can rebuild."

Dylan walked over to Brew, sitting on a rock, seemingly lost in his thoughts. "You okay?"

Brew snapped out of his reverie. "Me? Yeah … I guess, but if I wake up and this was all a dream, I won't be unhappy."

Dylan patted him on the back. "Reality is a bit different in the desert."

"Yeah, no shit."

"I'm proud of you. You did well today."

Brew looked up. "I'm ready to go back to Spain if you'll have me."

Dylan smiled, "Me too, and you've paid your dues. We've got a boat to break in. Give me a couple of days to catch my breath."

Tom had wandered over. He and Dylan embraced. "Well, Dad, you were right again. You said I'd return."

"I didn't think it would be so soon, and I would have preferred different circumstances, but since you're here, let's slay the fatted calf."

"You saying I'm the prodigal son?"

Tom laughed. "No, that would be Jake."

They both laughed and walked away with their arms around each other's shoulders.

CHAPTER FORTY-EIGHT

If You Can't Feed the Entire World...

Venice Beach, California

Buck Robertson and Manny had scouted the villa in Venice Beach for the past two days, but saw no sign of its inhabitant, the CIA black ops operative who was known simply as Hayes. He had chosen the location well. The views from the three mile stretch of beach were among California's best as were the bars and dining options, but what Venice Beach was really famous for was its unparalleled location for people watching. Venice Beach was a haven for artists and those who identified with a Bohemian life-style. It was the perfect place to blend in, as there was no norm, per se. On any given day, visitors would see things they had never seen before. The only thing better than outrageous was more outrageous.

Actually, Buck would have been surprised if Hayes had been home, suspecting that he'd been in or around Las Vegas to monitor his operation—his failed operation. They had traced him first, through his phone calls with Fatima. Hayes had been careful to have both his phone and title to his villa registered in the name of an offshore LLC, which wasn't uncommon for an area where people valued their privacy. It turned out that his particular LLC was one of the Company's numerous fronts. He had no reason to suspect that anyone from the CIA would be seeking him. The people he answered to knew how to contact him.

On day two, Hayes returned. Buck knew that Manny blamed Hayes for Fatima's death in which he, at minimum, was complicit. For that reason, Buck's original instinct was to proceed without Manny, but he relented after being assured that Manny could control his emotions. That and the fact that Hayes was a consummate professional. He would be no piece of cake even for the two of them. The ultimate rendering of justice was never in question. As in the finest Judge Roy Bean fashion, Hayes' execution was a fait accompli, but Buck needed to fill in some blanks beforehand.

Buck was aware that Hayes was an avid runner and was likely to avail himself of the perfect day. Particularly, after being away. When Hayes emerged on his balcony to perform some martial arts katas in his running shorts, Buck's intuition proved correct. Buck was impressed with how fit Hayes was, since they were close to the same age. The difference was Hayes was still in the game, and needed every edge, while Buck was looking for the exit ramp. He had no intention of having any more hand to hand combat. He would shoot first and ask questions later. The older one gets, the less of a deterrent life in prison becomes.

Buck and Manny nursed their cappuccinos at a nearby café when Hayes jogged by, zoned into his iTunes. After watching him make the turn toward the beach, they paid their check and headed toward Hayes' villa, as if out for a mid-day stroll. Being the quintessential live and let live kind of place, Buck was betting that Hayes' Venice Beach neighbors wouldn't think it unusual for two strangers to approach the villa. It was highly doubtful that they knew anything about the secretive Hayes and Buck and Manny were dressed for the beach.

As they arrived at the villa, they pretended to be engaged in conversation and strode purposefully past the front door and around the side of the building, where they were blocked from view. Manny started to reach for the side door, but Buck grabbed his arm.

"What? Aren't we going in?"

Buck reached in the shopping bag he was carrying and retrieved a small magnifying glass. He carefully scanned the door, but found nothing.

Manny was puzzled. "What were you looking for?"

"A piece of scotch tape. A strand of hair. Anything that might let him know someone had entered."

"You think he's coming in the side door?"

"No I don't, but lesson number one in my business is you don't assume anything." Buck handed Manny his small burglar kit. "You know how to use these?"

Manny smirked. "What do you think?"

Once inside, they were careful to avoid any booby traps, but found none. It was dark inside with the shades drawn to protect from the sun. Buck settled into a deep leather recliner in the corner of the living room, while Manny found a space on the other side of the room. The only sound was the slow tick-tock of a grandfather clock magnified by the silent space of the room.

Slightly more than an hour later, they heard the front door open. To get to his bedroom and shower, Hayes had to pass through the living room. He didn't turn on any lights, thus was startled by Buck's voice.

"Put your hands on your head and don't move."

Hayes did as he was told as he pivoted around to make out not one, but two shapes in the room.

"I recognize that voice, but I can't see you."

Buck switched on the reading lamp adjacent to his chair.

Hayes blinked his eyes as he acclimated them to the light and saw Buck sitting in the chair, pointing a silenced pistol at him.

"Ah, there you are, or are you a ghost? Rumor has it that you died in an unfortunate explosion."

"You know what Mark Twain said."

Hayes smiled. "The reports of his demise were greatly exaggerated. It's been a long time Buck. Are you going to introduce me to your friend?"

"His name is Manny. I would be on my best behavior if I were you. He was a friend of Fatima's and the last person who pissed him off was fed to the pigs."

Hayes was now clearly off-guard. "Hey, wait a minute. I didn't kill Fatima."

"You may not have killed her, but you recruited her and put her on the path that led to her death."

"Buck, we had her on the radar screen for over two years. She was here to wreak havoc."

"So you decided to help her."

"Duh, it's my job. Neither you, nor I ever decided anything. You know that. We just did what we were told."

"So, let me get this straight. You arranged for a terrorist bomber to be smuggled across the border and armed a dangerous biker gang in exchange for their help. All with the goal of assassinating an American candidate for president! You don't think that's wrong?"

"Whoa. When did you get religion? It's okay to assassinate someone in South America, Central America or Africa, but not in America? And what about JFK? First of all, look around and wake up. America is no more. It's gone and it's not coming back. They control the schools, the press, and soon the economy. You don't think Obamacare was about healthcare do you? It was about controlling your healthcare, which is a substantial portion of the GDP. It was the last piece of the puzzle. Wake the fuck up. Wait till they tear up the Constitution—and it's coming. Free speech—gone. The right to bear arms—gone. They indoctrinate our children, who don't dare mention God in school. They're rewriting history. Try to protest and their goons will attack you. Everything is going to be electric, even cars, and the government will control the switch. It's too late. There are going to be only two classes. The elite rulers and the masses, who will be reliant upon the rulers for everything. You and I are on the team. Go with it."

"You're talking about communism and it's never worked—anywhere."

"If you put the gun down we can have an intellectual debate. I don't disagree with you in principle. I'm just saying that you and I, and your friend, can't make a difference. It's too late. You want religion, try the Serenity Prayer. You need to accept what you can't change. I get that you may have some bad dreams at night over things you've done in the past. I do, too, but we can't change the past. So bully for you if you want to reinvent yourself as a male Mother Teresa, but I'm going with the flow, thank you. I strongly suggest that you do the same."

There was a pregnant pause before Buck replied. "It's interesting that you brought up Mother Teresa. I read a quote attributed to her, "If you can't feed the entire world, feed a single person.""

"What, what the fuck is that supposed to mean?"

"To paraphrase, it says, 'If you can't kill them all, kill one of them'."

Buck and Manny had agreed beforehand that Manny would have first dibs on the kill shot if the situation allowed. Buck motioned to him and Manny stepped out of the shadows. "This is for Fatima."

Hayes was dead before his body hit the floor.

They were silent for a moment before either spoke. Manny turned to Buck. "What do we do with the body?"

"I told Carlos to find us a van. We'll come back after dark. I made contact with one of my old assets out here. He's got a junkyard with a compactor. He's expecting me. Hayes is more of a threat to the Company if they think he disappeared. Truth is, they wouldn't be unhappy to know he's dead."

"Buck—those things he said. Some of them are happening. Do you think he was right?"

"I don't know. I know this. The guy they targeted is still alive. At least one of their plans didn't work."

"Hey Buck, what happens to us, now?"

"I have some unfinished business to take care of. If all goes well, I'll be officially retired and have my life back. If you want my advice, you'll send Marta a couple of airplane tickets and see how things work out here in La La land. You've got two good options, stay here, or go back to Apache Dunes. I know that Carlos isn't anxious to see you go and it's not like there isn't enough room or money. Speaking about money, if we snoop around a bit, chances are we'll find a stash here. I'd be surprised if Hayes ever had a credit card or an on-shore bank account."

CHAPTER FORTY-NINE

After the Storm

Apache Dunes and Las Vegas

The news traveled fast. Tom's first call was to Sonny to thank him for the AR-15s and the armor piercing bullets without which the outcome of the battle would have been dramatically different. It was inconceivable to believe that casualties could have been avoided otherwise.

"In fact, Sonny, I understand from speaking to Buck that you did a major favor for him and Manny, too."

"It's what I do. They're stand-up guys."

"They are indeed. So, you still interested in getting into Del's house?"

"The sooner, the better."

"You call it. I've got the keys. As far as I'm concerned, you can stay as long as you like."

"We just need a couple of days."

"Will it be just you and Bobbie?"

"And Christopher, you know—Petey."

"I heard something happened at the restaurant. People are complaining about the food since he's been gone."

"It's a long story. I'll tell you about it, sometime."

"You need anything else from me?"

"Just access to the house. I have some issues I have to deal with, so Bobbie and Christopher may come down tomorrow and I'll follow as soon as I can."

"It'll be like old home week. Geronimo's home.

"I never thought I'd say this, but I'm looking forward to comin back."

"It's an acquired taste."

"Must be."

After they hung up, Sonny told Bobbie to get packed and let Christopher know that they were leaving in the morning. He explained that he needed to deal with some issues in L.A. Just the mention of L.A. served to wake up her demons. Sonny noticed the change in her demeanor.

"You okay?"

"Yeah, I just got a little chill, is all."

"You sure you're okay to go tomorrow? Maybe you should wait until I get things settled in L.A. and I can go with you."

There it was again. What she told Vito was true. She had an itch that Sonny couldn't scratch.

"No, Sonny. This is perfect. We don't know how long it's going to take Petey."

"Christopher."

"I don't know about you, but I'm a little tired of that game. I don't care what he wants others to call him, but to me, he's Petey."

Sonny raised his eyebrows. "Wow, listen to you. Actually, I agree with you. Petey it is."

"We'll leave tomorrow and how about I call you and tell you how he's doing?"

"That works for me. I might have to go to L.A. for a couple of days."

Bobbie went to her bedroom to pack. She had an absolute war going on in her mind, but the most puzzling thing is that she wasn't even putting up a fight. Maybe it's true. Maybe you can't change the spots on a leopard. One thing is certain, you can't change if you don't try. She thought she had it all with Kelsey as her slave and thirty million dollars, but Kelsey was dead and the money was long gone. Initially, she thought it was fate that Sonny rescued her and offered her a chance at a new beginning. There was a vacuum, however, that Sonny couldn't fill. Now, fate had offered a possible second chance at millions of dollars that could allow her to become whomever she wanted to be. The only thing standing in her way was an idiot. It would be no contest.

She had a couple of errands to run. She would stop by Barclays and then do a little shopping for some designer cruise wear.

Clueless to Bobbie's inner turmoil, Sonny dialed Paulie's number in L.A. Paulie recognized the number and answered immediately.

"Hey, Sonny. You hear anything?"

"That's why I'm callin. Things went off without a hitch. The guns made a difference."

"So, like— the bikers got the message?"

"The last message they ever got."

"You mean … all of them?"

"I told Vito it was a bad idea. I heard too many stories about Apaches and the desert."

"That's— that's good news, isn't it? It was on the street that we had issues with the bikers. When word gets out that they disappeared, all of them, we won't have anybody sniffin around the union business. Particularly our so called friends. They didn't have nothin to do with this. Maybe I'll get some respect now."

"Look Paulie, I don't know what happens now, but I'll make sure the right people know. I got some ideas, but I need to think 'em over first. Don't tell nobody what happened. If anybody asks, just say that you had a problem and you took care of it."

"Okay, Sonny. I'll look after things here until I hear differently from you. And, Sonny, I just told you about the guns. You're the one who knew what to do with 'em."

"We'll keep that between us for now. Like I said. I got some ideas. I'll run 'em by Joey and then I may come to L.A for a couple of days. Capiche?

"Capiche."

CHAPTER FIFTY

The Tango

Las Vegas and Apache Dunes

Bobbie had allowed her demons to take complete control and was actually titillated by the prospect of using, more appropriately, abusing, a man to achieve her goal. She would never be able to even the score for the sexual and physical abuse that she had been subjected to since childhood. Truth be told, Petey wasn't much of a challenge. She smiled to herself, truth be told, Petey wasn't much of a man.

They had driven the first hour or so in silence, reminiscent of their trip to L.A.. Now it was time for Petey's education to begin and class was in session.

"Petey, it's time for us to level with each other."

"It's Christopher, remember?"

"That's a good place to start. I'm tired of your stupid name game. You're Petey, period. You got that?"

Petey couldn't have been more shocked. "Are you mad at me?"

"I'm mad at you pretending to be someone you're not. You are who you are. Why can't you accept that?"

"I— I don't understand what you mean."

"That's another thing that has to change—that stupid act. If anything, you're a little autistic, because you understand computers. Just like your friend Alex. In fact, I want to ask you about him."

"What do you want to know?"

"How close are you two?"

"I— I don't know what you mean."

"Oh yes you do. You said you two were the only ones in your class. You must have spent a lot of time alone together."

"They didn't let us play with the other kids."

"So you played with each other."

"What do you mean?"

"You know exactly what I mean. I heard you tell us about him. I could tell that you were more than friends."

"I really don't want to talk about it."

"That's not an option. We need to be honest with each other, but more importantly, we need to be honest with ourselves. You and I are going on an adventure and we need each other. It's like a dance and you know what they say about the Tango? 'It takes two to Tango.' You understand that, right?"

"Yeah. It takes two to dance."

"Exactly, but one has to lead and one has to follow. You understand?"

"You lead and I follow."

"If you do as I say, we're going to split a fortune. Fuck you money. You know why they call it fuck you money?"

"If you've got enough money you can say fuck you to the world, but what about Sonny?"

"Petey, I've got some news for you. When Sonny didn't kill you in the desert, he signed his own death warrant. As long as you're alive, you're a threat to him."

"But Vito is dead."

"I know. I killed him, but not until after I gave him a blow job and fucked his brains out."

Petey was shocked and the car veered onto the shoulder and back.

"It's who I am, and I thought I could change, but I can't. Neither can you and, sooner or later, we both could wind up in holes in the desert. Now, I have a little surprise for you—something I think Alex will like."

Bobbie took a small Tiffany's box out of her purse. "You're driving, I'll open it for you."

The box contained two small diamond earrings. Petey's eyes got big.

"I noticed you have both ears pierced, but wear only one stud. After we get the money, you can wear these for Alex.

"How are we so sure the money's there?"

"The cartels smuggled hundreds of millions of dollars of drugs across the border and the dead agent was the gatekeeper for this section of the border. Wait till you see his house. He has to have millions stashed offshore."

"But, what happens after we locate it? How do we get it?"

"Do you have an offshore bank account?"

"I'm not even sure what that means."

"Most people don't. Fortunately for us, I happen to have an account with Barclays in the Cayman Islands. When we find out where the funds are and the account information, we simply give instructions for them to transfer the money to my account. Once it's in my account, we split the money. I'll bet that Alex has an offshore account."

"I gotta ask again, what about Sonny? Is he just going to forget about us?"

"I'll leave him a Dear John letter and tell him we couldn't hack into the computer. Truthfully, he'll probably be glad to be rid of us."

CHAPTER FIFTY-ONE

The Safe Room

Apache Dunes

When they arrived in Apache Dunes they went directly to the sheriff's office to pick up the keys to Del's house. Bobbie had reverted to character and wore a tiny slip dress that left nothing to the imagination. The original purpose was to see if it elicited a response from Petey. It didn't, which confirmed her suspicions. However, it definitely elicited a response from the crew gathered in Tom's office—particularly Brew.

"Holy shit! Who was that?"

Tom laughed. "Brew, you need a cold shower. That was Bobbie and she's about as harmless as a Diamondback with a bad attitude."

"I don't care. Fucking bite me!"

Tom, Max and Dylan all laughed.

Dylan turned to Tom. "What's she up to?"

"I don't have a clue. Sonny asked for access to the house. He said he would let us know if they found what they're looking for."

"That's a wee bit mysterious."

"Yeah, but Sonny not only got us the AR-15s and the armor-piercing ammo, but also alerted us to when the bikers were coming."

"Sounds like more than a fair trade, to me."

"My sentiments, indeed."

Del's Mansion

Petey was completely blown away by the house and grounds, which someone had been maintaining. Bobbie was also impressed, even though she had been there before—even lived there with Kelsey for a few days.

That thought hit her hard, as it was also the place where Kelsey had committed suicide. Petey noticed her sudden change.

"Are you okay?"

Bobbie wiped the tears from her eyes. "Yeah, I'll be okay. This place just brings back some bad memories."

Whoever had done the housecleaning had done a great job. Either the carpet in the den had been thoroughly cleaned, or replaced. Bobbie showed Petey around including the pool and patio area. The pool had also been maintained and looked inviting, but Bobbie told Petey that nothing he'd seen so far would prepare him for what he was about to see.

The massive library was situated at the end of the hall on the second floor. The secret was that it had been even more massive at one time. Bobbie found the secreted button and an entire section of the book case opened to reveal a safe room that looked like something out of a James Bond movie. It was smokeproof, soundproof, fireproof and bombproof. It contained every modern convenience and supplies necessary for a family of six to disappear off the radar screen for at least thirty days. It also included a state-of-the-art surveillance system that provided audio and video coverage of every room of the house and area of the property.

Del had been totally paranoid of the psychotic and schizophrenic El Diablo, leader of the ruthless Garcia drug cartel, and money was no object. He hired a team of unrelated experts in the field of electronic surveillance and offered to pay them handsomely to construct the safe room. While they were on site, they had to relinquish all electronic devices and each was required to sign a non-disclosure agreement.

His ultimate guarantee of secrecy was a remote controlled explosive device that guaranteed that their departing flight would never reach its destination. The plane exploded in a fireball over the desert, whose sand

and predators would complete the cycle of life.

The first thing Bobbie did was pick up the two pistols that were laying on the floor. She pre-empted any question from Petey, "It's a long story."

Petey was amazed and couldn't believe that such a place existed.

"Alex has to see this."

"Let's get situated first and then you can Facetime him. Before you call, explain how this is going to work?"

Petey replied, "It's like this. Like I told you and Sonny, users are always warned to make their passwords as unique as possible, but, in truth, they almost always make them something that they won't forget. That means, they generally have something to do with the user. The more we know about him, the easier our task will be. Alex has access to a super computer that can run thousands of variations per minute. What do you know about Del—wasn't that his name?"

"It was. All I know is that he was a former Marine, he worked for the DEA and here are his birth date and social security number."

"That's a great start. Why don't you hang out by the pool while Alex and I play with this information? It's pretty boring stuff, actually. I'll call you over the intercom if we find something."

"Okay. I'll be at the pool."

Petey followed Bobbie on the security cam as she went down to the pool area. He then Facetimed Alex.

Bobbie had slipped out of her skimpy dress and was sunbathing when Petey called her barely an hour later. She didn't even bother to dress. She was so excited. She found Petey in front of the computer. He had a huge smile on his face and betrayed no emotion to her being sans clothes.

"Did you do it?"

"Actually it was Alex who deserves the credit. It turns out that this was not the first Marine he had hacked. It seems like all of them have something about the Corps in their password. Jarhead, Leatherneck or Devil Dog. This guy was Devil Dog. Then we played with his birthdate and social security number and, bingo! Devildog4798. Are you ready to see his bank statement?"

Bobbie could hardly contain herself. "I can't wait."

Petey did his magic with the keyboard and accessed the most recent monthly statement for an account with Royal Canadian National Bank in the Cayman Islands. Bobbie had to steady herself when she saw the bottom line: $27,856,423. 50.

Petey smiled. "It's possible that there's more. I'll keep playing around. I'll print out this statement for you."

Bobbie's mind was now in overdrive. She had secretly been hoping for at least ten million. Almost twenty-eight million divided by two was fourteen million, but divided by one it was still twenty-eight million dollars. Bobbie had always been good at math.

She had already done her research. She could catch a plane from Tucson to Miami and connect to Grand Cayman Island from there. She would lose at least four hours traveling, but she could arrive on Grand Cayman tomorrow and be well rested for her fateful visit to Barclays the following day.

She was almost trembling with excitement. "I'll get my account information. Do you know how to make the transfer?"

"Piece of cake. Alex showed me. All I need is your bank and account information. Then it's just a matter of following the instructions."

Bobbie ran downstairs and returned with her purse, still not bothering to dress. She fumbled with the purse before she found the card from Barclays.

"Here's my account number and bank information."

Petey turned to her. "You know, this requires a celebration. You don't suppose there's any champagne around here do you?"

Bobbie pointed to the video monitor of the wine cellar which, amazingly, appeared untouched. Del had a vast wine cellar full of wine and champagne.

"I know where the champagne is. I'll be right back."

When she returned with a chilled bottle of Bollinger RD, Petey was smiling. "Congratulations! The transfer went through."

What a sight they made. She, totally nude and him, with his new diamond earrings. They took turns drinking from the bottle.

Petey said, "I've got some primo weed downstairs, but before we get completely fucked up, what's the next step?"

"Here's what I suggest. We need to get out of Dodge before Sonny arrives. Tomorrow morning we'll hit the road. You drop me off at the airport in Tucson. Are you going to Alex's?"

"He wants me to."

"Perfect. I'll fly to the Caymans and call your cell when I get there. If you give me Alex's instructions, I'll wire your half to his account."

Bobbie smiled to herself. The simpleton actually believed she was going to share the money with him.

CHAPTER FIFTY-TWO

Dear Sonny

Apache Dunes

When Sonny decided that he didn't have to make a special trip to L.A., he called Bobbie's cell phone to tell her that he'd be leaving for Apache Dunes in the morning. When he failed to get an answer the fourth time he called, he wrote it off to poor cell reception in the desert. No problem, he'd surprise her.

It was Sonny, however, who was surprised when he arrived and found Del's house locked and Petey's car missing. He drove into town and parked in front of the sheriff's office. He found Tom in his office holding court with Max, Dylan and Brew.

Tom and Sonny were genuinely happy to see each other and shared a man hug before Tom made the introductions.

"Sonny, you've met Max and Dylan/Geronimo before. This is Dylan's friend Brew."

After exchanging handshakes, Sonny turned to Tom. "Have you seen Bobbie and Petey?"

Tom looked surprised at the question. "They stopped by to get the keys two days ago. I assume they're at the house."

Sonny shook his head. "I stopped there first. The door was locked and Petey's car wasn't there."

"Did you try calling her?"

"No answer."

Tom reached in his drawer and produced another set of keys. "I've got a second set of keys. Do you mind if we tag along? I've been telling them about the house."

"Not at all. A couple of you can ride with me."

When they arrived at the house there was still no sign of Bobbie and Petey. After they entered it was clear that the house was vacant. The only sign that someone had been there were a couple of empty champagne bottles on the patio.

Brew was taking it all in and couldn't fathom that such a place existed in the desert. Sonny said, "If you're impressed so far, you're not going to believe what I'm about to show you, if I can remember where the button is."

They followed him upstairs and down the hall to the library. Sonny didn't need the button. The book case had been left open. When they followed Sonny into the safe room, they were literally speechless. Neither Tom, nor Dylan had a clue as to the safe room's existence. Brew was blown away.

Tom smiled when he saw the two pistols that Bobbie had thrown on one of the beds and forgotten about. He pointed them out to Max.

Dylan noticed an envelope near the computer. It was addressed to Sonny. "Hey Sonny, this is for you."

Tom guessed what it might be and herded the others out of the room. "Let's give Sonny some privacy. I'll show you the rest of the house. Brew, wait till you see the wine cellar and observatory."

Sonny sat down and opened the letter.

Dear Sonny, and you are my dear Sonny, by the time you read this letter I will be long gone. Trust me—you will be better off without me. I was foolish to think that I could re-invent myself. Do you remember when I told you the story of the Scorpion and the Frog. I told you that Vito was like the Scorpion. He couldn't change his nature. Some recent events made me realize that the same applies to me. I tried to tell you, but you wouldn't listen. I'm not even sure

who I am anymore. Don't blame Petey, he's clueless, as you know,
and just one more of my victims. You saved my life and I may
have saved yours. I hope so. In the meantime, I don't know where
I'm going or what I'm going to do. The only difference is, now I'm
financially independent for the first time in my life. I know you'll
be okay and, Sonny, I do love you, but you deserve better than I can
offer, Bobbie

Sonny saw a paper shredder under the desk and shredded the letter. In his heart he knew that they had been an odd couple from Jump Street. He vowed to protect her and he did—at least from everything but herself. He wasn't sure what to make about her comments about Petey, but that was another burden he could do without. He saw the video of the pool area. The sun was shining and his new friends were enjoying themselves. It was time for him to get his life back. Maybe he'd hang around for a couple of days.

When he rejoined the group Tom asked if everything was okay. Sonny smiled, "It's a beautiful day."

Tom said, "Sonny, we were talking about having a little celebration before Dylan goes back. We've got a pool here and grills and there are hundreds of bottles of good wine that need to be drunk. Will you stay and join us?"

Sonny replied. "I've got nothing but time."

It would be hard to describe the party. The word went out far and wide and everyone was invited. Eclectic doesn't do it justice. There were federal agents and smugglers; real cowboys and real Indians; Mexicans and Americans; the uber wealthy and peasants. They roasted steers and pigs, and drank rare vintage wines out of solo cups. Two Mariachi bands showed up to entertain and the party lasted throughout the night.

Dylan had not strayed far from Tom and they appeared to have been engaged in a serious conversation. He excused himself and went upstairs seeking the solitude of the safe room, now that he knew the secret. Once inside he called Dusty. It was early afternoon in Spain.

"Dusty, we need to talk."

"Dylan, are you drunk?"

"Not yet, but I'm working on it."

"What's so urgent that we need to talk?"

"I've been thinking. I love Estepona and know that you do, too, but I've got something to propose."

"Dylan, maybe you should wait until you're sober."

"Dusty, I know exactly what I want for the first time in my life."

"Which is?"

"Okay, here's the plan. We'll take the *Geronimo II* down the coast of Africa and catch the tradewinds to the Keys."

"We have a sailboat in Key West."

"We'll have two. Andre can run the gallery in Key West. He'll fit right in."

"And what will we do?"

"We'll live part of the year in Apache Dunes. We'll live in the dead agent's house. You won't believe it. I'm there right now. The rest of the time we'll divide up between Key West and Estepona."

"What are we going to do in Apache Dunes?"

"Have babies. Lots and lots of babies."

"Dylan, do you have any idea what you're saying? We aren't married, in case you forgot."

"I told you I had something to propose."

Dusty was now sobbing with joy. "Dylan, are you sure you know what you're saying?"

"I've never been more certain. Dusty, will you marry me?"

Dusty screamed through her tears, "Yes! Yes! Yes!"

"Brew and I will fly back in a couple of days. I'll make arrangements for the house. Start getting the boat provisioned for the trip. See if we can hire Christer to be Captain. We'll take our time. We'll have our honeymoon cruise before the wedding because I want to be married at the Shrine in Apache Dunes. Tell Jake and Ashley."

"Dylan—slow down. Slow down. Go back to the party and call me tomorrow. I love you, Dylan."

"I love you, too. And, Dusty …"

"Yes."

"Remember when Tom said if it was meant to be, it would be?"

"Dylan, I always knew it was meant to be. I just didn't know if you knew."

"I do now."

CHAPTER FIFTY-THREE

Say a Prayer for Lefty, Too

Langley, Virginia

The meeting had been arranged by Robertson's attorney from a prestigious D.C. law firm. It would just be Robertson, Deputy Director Aaron Nolan and Barrington Stanton. They would meet in Nolan's office and each signed an affidavit that the meeting would be off the record.

The terms had been previously negotiated. Robertson would be submitting his notice of retirement and would be entitled to full benefits and pension with no reprisals. In exchange, certain tape recordings of interrogations Robertson claimed to have with the Al Qaeda terrorist, Abdullah al Somali, and with the CIA contractor, known as The Cowboy, would remain concealed. If, however, Robertson was struck by lightning or befell other such fate, copies of the recordings would be distributed to media sources in the U.S. and the U.K.

The purpose of the meeting was a final debriefing of sorts between three career agents who had a long history with each other.

They took their seats in a small sitting area that was more comfortable, and less formal, than a conference table. Each was aware that Diogenes would come up empty handed in his quest with current company and circumstances. Robertson didn't come seeking the truth. He knew that dog wouldn't hunt. Rather, he hoped to be able to fill in some gaps that lingered in his mind.

Nolan cleared his throat and began, "Buck, I don't know how things got so bollixed up. I assure you that Barry and I were just following orders. This project, this clusterfuck, was strictly need to know and conceived at the highest level. Higher than deputy director, if you get my drift."

Stanton was eager to add, "Amen."

Robertson believed the part about the plan's conception, but would have been a fool to believe that Nolan and Stanton weren't in the loop. Even, if not by choice. "What happened to Morgan?"

Nolan motioned for Stanton to reply. It was obvious there had been some rehearsal. "John died of an overdose of fentanyl. Tragic."

Robertson was incredulous. "John Morgan doing drugs? Give me a break."

Nolan and Stanton exchanged glances before Stanton replied. "We were as shocked as you are. He was working on a Chinese opiod connection and was depressed about the events in Nevada. Apparently, he sampled some of the evidence seeking comfort, but took too much. Either that, or he knew what he was doing. He felt responsible for the innocent victims."

"Wasn't he?"

Both Nolan and Stanton feigned surprise at the question. These guys were good, but so was Robertson. Nolan replied, "Buck, I know you may find this hard to believe. In fact, Morgan couldn't be convinced, but it was the Fibs, our partners in the project, who were responsible for the explosion. Morgan didn't trigger it."

"You're right. I do find that hard to believe. So, let me ask you this. Who gave the order for Stone and Weathers to kill Matthews and Richards?"

Nolan pounded his arm rest, "No one. That was Weathers. He was a psycho. We just turned a blind eye when it suited our purposes. We should have dealt with him long ago." He then eyed Robertson with some suspicion. "Did the Cowboy tell you differently?"

"The Cowboy claimed he didn't know what happened. Only that he was dispatched by you, by the way, to take care of Stone and Weathers. Just as he was dispatched to take care of me."

"Now, wait a minute. You were missing and your motives were very much in doubt. He was sent to find you, not kill you. If he told you differently, he was lying."

Robertson milked the silence, noting that Nolan and Stanton appeared uncomfortable.

"Someone is lying."

Nolan tried to turn the table. "Tell us something. What happened to the bomber? What happened to the Cowboy?"

"Just as I said. That's all I know. What do you think happened to them?"

"Did you kill them?"

Robertson leaned forward. "If, and I emphasize *if* they are dead, I didn't kill them."

Nolan glanced at Stanton and then back to Robertson. "Maybe this meeting wasn't a good idea, but for what it's worth, we've each drafted our letters of intent to retire. It's time—probably past time."

Robertson pondered that bit of news and then sighed. "Are you guys familiar with the Willie Nelson classic 'Pancho and Lefty'?"

Nolan and Stanton looked confused, but nodded.

"There's a poignant line in the song that I can't get out of my mind. 'Say a prayer for Lefty, too. He only did what he had to do, and now he's growing old.' Maybe we all did what we felt we had to do. We're certainly growing old. You keep your end of the bargain and I'll keep mine."

As Robertson turned to leave, Nolan called out to him. "One more thing, Hayes seems to have dropped off the radar screen. You wouldn't know anything about that would you?"

Robertson smiled. "It's been years since I worked with Hayes."

"That wasn't my question."

"I know, but that's my answer."

CHAPTER FIFTY-FOUR

A Nice Day for a Cruise

Grand Cayman Island

Rationalization is a key component of our mental tool boxes. We have all used it, but some more often than others. To most, it is just another tool to be used when needed. To others, it's like a pacemaker—a device needed for survival. Buck Robertson was in the former group. Bobbie was in the latter.

Regardless, Willie Nelson's lyrics could have applied to Bobbie, as well as Lefty. Maybe she, also, only did what she had to do.

It was curious that the ride to the Tucson airport was mostly cloaked in silence. Bobbie and Petey both devoid of any emotion, which seemed an anomaly for what should have been a time for celebration. Bobbie wrote it off to the fact that Petey was clueless, while she on the other hand, was trying to rationalize her actions.

She was at peace about Sonny. He saved her life and she had returned the favor. Vito was arguably more powerful than Sonny, with his L.A. and Hollywood franchise. Not to mention that he could definitely scratch whatever itch she had, and he accepted her for what she was. If she was only out for herself, she could have jettisoned Sonny in favor of Vito, but she didn't—she had a debt to repay and she paid it. Give her credit for that. She was actually doing Sonny a favor by leaving as, sooner or later, their make-believe relationship was doomed to fail. As to the money, it had been her idea, not Sonny's, and Sonny could survive quite well without it, while she couldn't.

Petey was a bit more problematical, as she wouldn't have the money without his help, but she could rationalize that as well. It would be wasted on someone without guile or ambition and, secondly, even if he wasn't gay, as she suspected, Alex could take care of him.

As most of her dilemmas did, it eventually came down to the concept of social Darwinism—survival of the fittest. She could easily justify giving him his promised share of half of the bounty. But, in nature, where there were two animals but only one piece of meat, did the animals say, "Hey, why don't we split it?" Never to her knowledge.

For a brief moment, she felt sorry for him as he pulled up for the skycap to get her bags. Petey actually smiled as he wished her a good flight. "You have my cell number, right?"

"I do and I'll call you to get Alex's banking coordinates. Sorry if I've been so quiet."

"No problem. You've got a lot on your mind. Well, good luck."

"You too, Petey."

She had used the ten thousand she had left, to open the Cayman account, but with the transfer of more than $27,000,000, she could afford to fly first class—forever. She Googled hotels on Grand Cayman and selected the Ritz-Carlton as being the most appropriate for a person of her wealth and taste. After she unpacked her new, designer wardrobe and locked, what had been, Kelsey's jewelry in her safe, she decided she would order a masseuse and then have a relaxing dinner at the hotel. She would book the spa for the full treatment in the morning. She wanted to look like a million, make that twenty-seven million, dollars when she met her new banker at Barclays, the next day at one p.m.

It was a balmy, moonlit evening, with a gentle ocean breeze so she decided to have dinner on the patio. Bobbie could turn heads wearing a potato sack, but with couture evening wear and designer jewelry, with real, precious gems, forget about it! All eyes were on her as she was escorted to her table. She had really enjoyed the Bollinger RD champagne she had shared with Petey and ordered a bottle, even though she was dining alone. She was undaunted by the more than $800 price. She would leave what was left for the waiters. For her entrée, she chose the Lobster salad—with extra lobster.

It wasn't long before a handsome late fifty/sixtyish gentleman approached. "Forgive me for intruding, but I noticed you are dining alone. May I invite you to join me? My treat, of course."

Bobbie smiled, but replied, "I appreciate the offer, but I'm afraid I wouldn't be very good company tonight. I have to get ready for a meeting tomorrow."

The gentleman frowned, "A pity, but bon appetit and I hope your meeting goes well. Very good choice of champagne, by the way."

No sooner had he excused himself, but her waitress stopped to refill her glass and muttered, "Well, that's a first."

Bobbie looked up. "I'm sorry, what did you say?"

"Oh, forgive me. I was just saying that that was the first time I've ever seen a woman turn down an invitation from the Count."

"Who is the Count?"

"That's his title. I'm not sure I've ever heard his last name. Around here, everyone refers to him as the Count. He's Swiss, I think. That's his 150-foot yacht in the harbor, and he keeps a master suite here at the hotel year round. They say he's a billionaire. So, bully for you. You're the first woman, I know of, who turned down his invitation."

When the waitress departed, Bobbie smiled to herself. *When it rains it pours. Just when I don't need anyone, a billionaire tries to hit on me. If only he knew how lucky he was that I refused his offer.* She savored her champagne as her entrée was served. *Life was good and it was about to get even better!*

Barclays Grand Cayman

The Ritz arranged for a car and driver to take Bobbie to Barclays House on Shedden Road. After a massage, delightful dinner, great night's sleep, and a morning at the spa, Bobbie positively glowed as she entered Barclays House. Her designer linen pantsuit was highlighted by its tasteful décolletage.

She was escorted into the office of Jeremy Hines-Falworth, senior Vice-President of the bank. He rose while she took a seat facing his desk.

"Welcome to Barclays Miss … Smith. I'm Jeremy Hines-Falworth and feel free to call me Jeremy. I see you are a new client of ours. How may I be of service to you, today?"

"Thank you, Jeremy and please call me Bobbie, if you like. I recently had some money wired into my account and I'd just like to confirm my balance."

"Of course, no problem. As a matter of security, do you have some identification with you and can you confirm the security questions attached to your account?"

Bobbie handed over her Arizona driver's license and answered that her favorite pet's name had been Kelsey.

Jeremy excused himself to retrieve a print out of her account.

He returned with the statement and glanced at it briefly before passing it across his desk. "The wire proceeds were credited to your account. Here's your statement."

Bobbie could barely contain herself as she took the statement from him, but experienced a bout of vertigo when she saw the balance, $9,750.00 after deduction of fees. Jeremy noticed the color drain from her face and reacted quickly.

"Dear me. Are you okay?"

He poured her a glass of water and placed it in front of her. Bobbie took a generous drink and tried to catch her breath.

"I— I think there has been some mistake. I was expecting more than twenty-seven million dollars. It was wired two days ago."

Jeremy was wide-eyed. "Oh dear. Are you certain it was wired to this account?"

All of a sudden Bobbie flashed on Petey sitting behind the computer.

No, no, he couldn't have. She looked at Jeremy, "I have the account information for the bank it was wired from. It's the Royal Canadian Bank here on Grand Cayman."

"If you give me the information, I can check with them. We're all friends here."

Bobbie handed him a copy of Del's most recent statement. Jeremy dialed a number from memory.

"Ken Evans, here."

"Oh hello Ken, this is Jeremy. Yes, all is well. Ken, I need a favor. I have a new client who was expecting a rather substantial wire transfer from one of your accounts. She says that the wire transfer was made two days ago, but it hasn't shown up in her account yet. Yes, strange indeed. Here's the account information."

Jeremy motioned to Bobbie that it would just be a minute.

"Yes, yes, that's right. Almost twenty-eight million dollars. It was wired two days ago. I see, I see."

Her spirits rose as she listened to the conversation, but were quickly deflated by the frown on Jeremy's face when he hung up.

"I'm afraid there has been a misunderstanding. The money was wired two days ago, more than twenty-seven million dollars, but not to this account."

Bobbie felt faint again when it sank in. "Can you— can you tell me where the money was wired to?"

"Oh, I'm afraid not. That is completely against our policy and regulations. I'm afraid I can't help you anymore."

He rose and walked to the door to see her out.

As she waited by the elevator, she realized that she had barely enough money to pay her hotel bill and get a flight to Miami. Had she not written the Dear John letter to Sonny, she might be able to return to Vegas, but she'd burned that bridge. Just when she thought she was on the top of her game, she had lost her edge. She had lost everything. She was supposed to be the ultimate survivor, but she had made the most fundamental of mistakes—underestimating her opponent.

Petey may look like a dope and act like a dope, but he had convinced Sonny to disobey a contract that came from the head of the Chicago mob simply by wearing a St. Christopher medal, and had just taken Bobbie for over twenty-seven million fucking dollars by acting stupid. How the fuck could he be an expert with computers and stupid at the same time? It's not that she didn't see. It's that she saw what she wanted to see.

Just then, the elevator door opened and, to her amazement, the Count was inside. He noticed her obvious distress.

"What a pleasant surprise. What's the sad look? Did your trust fund take a beating?"

"Something like that."

"Well, I have the perfect solution. It's a nice day for a cruise and I have a little boat out in the harbor."

"Unfortunately, I need more than a day cruise."

"A day, a week, a month—come for as long as you like."

Bobbie was getting her mojo back. "I have another problem. I didn't pack a swimsuit. Do I need one on your little boat?"

The Count was now hooked. "On my boat, clothing is optional."

"But you don't know me."

"I know that you stay at the Ritz, are wearing a fortune in jewelry, have an account at Barclays and have excellent taste in Champagne."

Bobbie smiled, "You are very perceptive."

"Does your boat have a name?"

"*The Scorpion.*"

G. D. Flashman's life experience took him from a small farm in Central Illinois literally around the world via an international business career.

His first published novel, *Apache Dunes*, was a 2020 CIPA EVVY Award Winner for Thrillers/Suspense. *Every Man Must Die* is the sequel to that book.

He followed up with *Justice Is Pronounced: Just Us*, a work of fiction based upon one of the true exploits of the legendary DEA agent Tommy O'Brien. He is currently working on a sequel that will take the reader into the heart of the Medellin Cartel and the narco wars.

Two of his greatest literary influences are Elmore Leonard and Mark Twain. Leonard taught Flashman to view the world and humanity through an unfiltered lens and look for humor, grace, evil and virtue in unexpected places.

Referring to one of his tales, Mark Twain stated, "If that's not the way the story happened—it's the way it should have happened."

Flashman resides in Chicago with his wife Susanna.